ROBBER'S ROOST

ROBBER'S ROOST

A WESTERN DUO

WILLIAM MACLEOD RAINE

FIVE STAR

A part of Gale, Cengage Learning

Detroit • New York • San Francisco • New Haven, Conn • Waterville, Maine • London

GALE
CENGAGE Learning®

LIBRARY OF CONGRESS CATALOGING-IN-PUBLICATION DATA

Raine, William MacLeod, 1871-1954.
  Robber's roost : a western duo / by William MacLeod Raine.
  — 1st ed.
    p. cm.
  "Five Star western."
  ISBN 978-1-4328-2614-7 (hardcover) — ISBN 1-4328-2614-X (hardcover)
  I. Raine, William MacLeod, 1871-1954. Troubled waters. II. Title.
PS3535.A385R63 2012
813'.52—dc23   2012003816

First Edition. First Printing: July, 2012.
Published in conjunction with Golden West Literary Agency.
Find us on Facebook– https://www.facebook.com/FiveStarCengage
Visit our Web site– http://www.gale.cengage.com/fivestar/
Contact Five Star™ Publishing at FiveStar@cengage.com

Printed in Mexico
1 2 3 4 5 6 7 16 15 14 13 12

ADDITIONAL COPYRIGHT INFORMATION

CONTENTS

FOREWORD BY
VICKI PIEKARSKI

Hailed in his later years by reviewers and contemporaries alike to be the "greatest living practitioner" of the genre and the "dean of Westerns", William MacLeod Raine was born in London, England, on June 22, 1871. Although raised in London, where his father, William, Sr., was a merchant, William, Jr., spent his summers, along with his three brothers, James, Forrester, and Edgar, in the cattle country of Ayrshire with his grandparents. Following the death of his wife in 1881, William, Sr. decided to take his sons to the United States. The Raines settled on a fruit farm on the Arkansas/Texas border that had been purchased sight unseen, where William, Sr. also began raising cattle. Years later, his brand, the Circle WR, would become a hallmark on the spine or title page of the majority of William, Jr.'s Western novels. Always delicate and unable to engage in strenuous activities, the young Raine experienced a frontier existence mostly through observation, but he could write that it was his luck to be in the West "when the Man on Horseback was still king of that vast domain."

Raine attended Sarcey College in Arkansas briefly and then Oberlin College in Ohio, receiving a Bachelor of Arts degree from the latter in 1894. He got his first taste of journalism while at Oberlin when, to help defray the costs of his education, he persuaded both the *Chicago Tribune* and the *Cincinnati Enquirer* to use him as a local correspondent. Following graduation, Raine made his way west to Seattle, where his father had relocated after a series of catastrophes in Arkansas, including the death of his son Forrester. Failing in an attempt to work as a ranch hand, William, Jr. found a job as a teacher for $36 a month in rural Seattle and then, later, as principal—for which his salary was increased to $70 a month provided he also supplied janitorial services. Years afterward he admitted to being "a rotten teacher." Craving a more adventurous profession, he finally landed a job as a reporter for the *Seattle Times,* receiving $3 a column. He tried to enlist with the First Washington Volunteers for the Philippine campaign in the Spanish-American War, but he was deemed ineligible by medical examiners who diagnosed his lingering illness as tuberculosis. The hope of improving his health was behind his decision to head for the drier air of Colorado.

Raine arrived in Denver in 1898 with $14 in his pocket. Due to his health problems, he worked intermittently for the *Denver Republican* and *The News* (the former eventually merged with the latter) and spent those times, when his condition flared up and his funds were not yet exhausted, absorbing the sun outside the north Denver boarding house that he now called home. He loved reporting but was convinced that he would have to find "some way to make a living sitting on my front porch." He began writing short stories, mostly romantic, swashbuckling tales. Although he would receive his share of rejection slips, the first story he sent out in 1899 was accepted. Titled "The Luck of Eustace Blount," it was bought by *Argosy* for $25. He soon began selling stories regularly to *McClure's, Ladies' Home Journal,* and *Harper's,* generating a total income his first full year of creative writing of $225. As his success as a writer improved, apparently so did his health.

His first novel, *A Daughter of Raasay: A Tale of the '45* (Stokes, 1902), first serialized in *The American Magazine* in 1901, had as its background the Jacobite rebellion. It sold four hundred copies. That same year *The American Magazine* hired Raine as a correspondent, and he traveled to Arizona Territory and rode with the Arizona Rangers. He penned articles on the Montana copper war and the Tonto Basin feud as well as of meetings with Pat Garrett and Billy Breckenridge. This was the type of life about which Raine had dreamed, and he decided to make use of the West in his fiction.

Wyoming (Dillingham, 1908) was his first Western novel. Years later he reflected that it was "really a terrible story . . . melodramatic . . . a hash of two novelettes joined together." Notwithstanding, with the appearance of *Wyoming,* his output shifted almost exclusively to the Western genre. Ultimately it was Raine's ability to depict ranch life accurately through character detail, dialect, and topography that quickly established his reputation as a Western writer who was intimately familiar with his subject. His work appeared regularly in a number of pulp publications, and beginning with *Steve Yeager* (Houghton Mifflin, 1915), a story using Western filmmaking as a background, Raine began a forty year relationship with Houghton Mifflin that would continue through his final Western novel, *High Grass Valley* (Houghton Mifflin, 1955), which, left unfinished at the time of his death, was completed by Wayne D. Overholser. He wrote over eighty novels during the span of his career that sold over twenty million copies during his lifetime.

From the very beginning, Raine considered himself a conscientious writer, part professional and part craftsman, rather than an artist. He approached writing fiction as a business, rising early so that he could produce his requisite one thousand words per day. Once his income was sufficient, he worked in a downtown office, hammering out stories on a typewriter with two fingers and minimal revision. He rewarded himself by playing bridge in the afternoons, and was known as a notorious under-bidder. He was astute at marketing his work, implementing a practice of selling first serial rights, then book rights in the States and abroad, then reprint rights, then second serial rights to newspapers, and finally movie rights. It proved a lucrative strategy. While his income prior to 1915 had been under $5,000, that year it topped $7,500. Between 1919 and 1940, his income from magazines and book editions averaged between $20,000 and $30,000 annually.

Despite this success, Raine persisted in thinking of himself as primarily a newspaperman and throughout his writing career he was wont to set aside his Westerns to take a journalistic assignment. He was one of the few to have contributed to all five of Denver's turn-of-the-century newspapers, including contributing editorials for *The Rocky Mountain News.* His reputation led to his involvement in 1932 in setting up the first journalism course at the University of Colorado in Boulder where he also taught for five years.

Wyoming first appeared as a novelette in *The Popular Magazine,* a Street and Smith publication. As his second novel, *Ridgway of Montana* (Dillingham, 1909) serialized in *Ainslee's* as "His Little Partner," it features a somewhat contemporary setting with modernisms such as automobiles, as would others among his Western novels, such as *Tangled Trails* (Houghton Mifflin, 1921), *Sons of the Saddle* (Houghton Mifflin, 1938), and *Justice Deferred* (Houghton Mifflin, 1941). While *Wyoming* is basically a traditional story concerned with sheepman Ned Bannister's reign of terror in the Bighorn country, and a plot hinging on a case of mistaken identity, it shows Raine's proclivity to experiment with the Western story and its characters, something that would win him a wide audience over the years as he perfected his own brand of Western storytelling. Another unique aspect of *Wyoming* is Raine's focus on the story's heroine, Helen Messiter, a gutsy, intelligent schoolteacher from the East who inherits a ranch and who is the antithesis of the majority of fictional Western schoolteachers. Raine continued to portray a wide variety of unique and sympathetic heroines, the majority of whom play active rôles in the conflicts as well as supplying the romantic interest.

If Raine's heroes are in possession of fine constitutions, they also possess a great many other admirable characteristics, even if they are not completely invincible as illustrated by frequent scenes in which the hero is wounded and must spend time recuperating. Above all, youth is the hallmark of a Raine hero. It is rare in his stories to find a hero over thirty years of age; most often, they are just barely one side or the other of their majority. In looks, they are often compared to the gods, but perhaps the best description of a Raine hero occurs in the laconic economy of words found in "Last Warning" in *Short Stories* (1/10/43): "He sat lightly in the saddle, a figure to draw the eyes of men as well as women."

Beyond the physical traits, a Raine hero stands out because of his extraordinary moral character. As the hero's friend says of him to the heroine in *On the Dodge* (Houghton Mifflin, 1938): " 'It isn't what he does for you. It's what he is.' " Raine's heroes never boast; indeed, they exhibit an extraordinary "capacity for silence," particularly when it comes to their own good deeds or courageous acts. His heroes are capable of tears at times of intense sorrow as in Gunsight Pass (Houghton Mifflin, 1921), or at times of extreme joy as in The Sheriff's Son (Houghton Mifflin, 1918), an unusual occurrence in Western novels written during the first half of the 20th Century.

The focus of a Raine Western is the destiny or character of a *settled* frontier that still lacks the safeguards of established and civilized life, in which very often prior to the emergence of the hero on the scene villains have maintained an unchallenged stranglehold on the community, owning the law and oftentimes terrorizing the citizenry. While the hero is not looking for trouble, once confronted by it he is guided by a code that tells him how he must play out his hand. It is this code of the West, a set of principles as encompassing as the feudal code of chivalry, that is the most striking characteristic of Raine's West. Over the years he articulated an ever-growing body of tenets that were set forth for the reader in story after story. In his novels from the early 1920s, a particularly strong period of writing for Raine in terms of plotting and characterization, these principles are scattered throughout the narratives. Thus we learn in *Gunsight Pass* that "it is written in their code that a man must take his punishment without whining," and that a man clenches his teeth against pain "because he had been brought up in the outdoor code of the West which demands of a man that he grin and stand the guff," and that "at a time of action speech, beyond the curtest of monosyllables, was surplussage." Loyalty and trust are central to this code and the testing of these virtues between friends and among family members through periods of severe adversity is a common thread in all of Raine's Westerns. In fact, in a Raine story the highest compliment one character can pay another is that a person will "do to ride the river with." With his interest in loyalty to a moral code, it was perhaps inevitable that Raine would occasionally include members of the Northwest Mounted Police among his heroes, as in *Man-Size* (Houghton Mifflin, 1922) and the short story, "Without Fear or Favor," in *Frontier Stories* (5/28).

In *The Fighting Edge* (Houghton Mifflin, 1922), Raine perhaps best summed up the qualities that make a hero: "Courage is the basis upon which other virtues are built, the fundamental upon which he is most searchingly judged. Let a man tell the truth, stick to his pal, and fight when trouble is forced on him, and he will do to ride the river with. . . ." While courage, sometimes to the point of recklessness (particularly among his outlaw heroes), is present in the majority of Raine's heroes, some of his most gripping stories are those in which the hero lacks such fundamental courage in the beginning of the story. This plot ingredient is probably nowhere better exemplified than in *The Sheriff's Son,* which remains one of Raine's most haunting and strongly imagistic stories, first serialized as "One Who Was Afraid" in *All-Story Weekly.* A poignant prologue to the story recounts the last night five-year-old Royal Beaudry spends with his father, John Beaudry, "one of the great sheriffs of the West," who is ambushed and killed in front of his son when they arrive in town the following morning. Raine shows the reader an interior view of John's troubled soul, torn by his duties as lawman and his love for his son, when Beaudry speaks his thoughts to his sleeping child that night. " 'Son, one of these here days they're sure a-goin' to get your dad. Maybe he'll ride out of town and after a while the hawss will come gallopin' back with an empty saddle. A man can be mighty unpopular and die of old age, but not if he keeps bustin' up the plans of rampageous two-gun men, not if he shoots them up when they're full of the devil and bad whiskey. It ain't on the cyards for me to beat them to the draw every time, let alone that they'll see to it all the breaks are with them. No, sir. I reckon one of these days you're goin' to be an orphan, little son.' " Raine skillfully and sympathetically portrays Royal's battles with his demon, cowardice. In contrast *Justice Deferred,* a reworking of the same plotline in which the hero, who also witnesses his father's murder twenty years earlier, is Royal's antithesis, only awaiting the death of his mother so that he can finally avenge that cold-blooded killing.

Raine's villains are a mixed group, from the visionary empire builders of *The Yukon Trail* (Houghton Mifflin, 1917), a story with a sub-theme about conservation in Alaska, to the greed-driven empire builders in *Ridgway of Montana.* Generally Raine's villains have such an insatiable appetite for land or power or money that even when they appear to be respectable and law-abiding, the laws are of their own making. Russell Mosely of *Trail's End* (Houghton Mifflin, 1940) epitomizes the breed: "He had no sense of moral values. He could see nothing except what was to his own advantage. When he thought of right and wrong, he twisted the meanings of the words to suit himself."

By his own admission, Raine concentrated on character in his Westerns. "I'm not very strong on plot. Some of my writing friends say you have to have the plot all laid out before you start. I don't see it that way. If you have it all laid out, your characters can't develop naturally as the story unfolds. Sometimes there's someone you start out as a minor character. By the time you're through, he's the major character of the book. I like to preside over it all, but to let the book do its own growing."

Although Raine's storylines may be amazingly various, if he liked an image or a turn of phrase he would frequently reuse it. In *Gunsight Pass* there is the image of the heroine "at home in the kitchen. She was making pies energetically. The sleeves of her dress are rolled up to her elbows and there is a dab of flour on her temple where she had brushed back a rebellious wisp of hair." Almost this exact description of a woman in the kitchen can be found elsewhere, including in *Rutledge Trails the Ace of Spades* (Doubleday, 1930). A description of men pouring out of a bar as "seeds are squirted out of a pressed lemon" can be found in at least four novels including *Bonanza* (Doubleday, Page, 1926) and *On the Dodge*. In *The Sheriff's Son*, a character comments " 'Guns are going out, . . . and little red school houses are coming in.' " Thirteen years later in his exceptional short story, "Doan Whispers" in *Short Stories* (10/25/31), this same remark is echoed nearly verbatim. Words to the effect of "I once knew a man who lived to be one hundred minding his own business" is a common adage used by at least one of Raine's characters in a number of novels.

Notwithstanding the impressive and consistent output of two books a year over a forty-year period, the progression of Raine's work as a writer showed continuous and inspired development. Perhaps his most skilled accomplishment was to have made the Western story seem infinitely adaptable and effortlessly versatile. "The best thing about a Western," he once said, "is that it can't become dated. Like Tennyson's brook it goes on forever." He might have added that they could be written anywhere. In the years after the First World War, Raine, who was head of the division in charge of syndicate features supplying longer articles to newspapers as part of the committee of public information, desired to see the world. He took time out to travel with his wife and typewriter, writing *Judge Colt* (Doubleday, 1927) in Antibes and Nice and *Moran Beats Back* (Hodder and Stoughton, 1928) in Africa.

It was his intimate knowledge of the American West that provides verisimilitude to all of his stories, whether in a large sense such as the booming industries of the West or the cruelties of Nature—a flood in *Ironheart* (Houghton Mifflin, 1923), blizzards in *Ridgway of Montana* and *The Yukon Trail*, a fire in *Gunsight Pass*—or in minor details. He raised any number of social issues and everyday human problems in the course of his storytelling. His weaknesses early in his career—a reliance on foreshadowing, multiple sets of lovers, and the cliché of the weak brother—disappeared for the most part as he gained mastery at his craft. There are, of course, novels that are off the mark, but this is not surprising considering his impressive output, and they are the exceptions.

Raine's interest in historical figures and history prompted him to write four Western histories—*Famous Sheriffs and Western Outlaws* (Doubleday, 1929), *Cattle* (Doubleday, 1930) in collaboration with Will C. Barnes, *Guns of the Frontier: The Story of How Law Came to the West* (Houghton Mifflin, 1940), and *.45-Caliber Law: The Way of Life of the Frontier Peace Officer* (Row Peterson 1941). Although they are not without factual errors, these books are considered indispensable works for researchers in the field. Historical figures were also used in some fictional pieces, including *The Bandit Trail* (Houghton Mifflin, 1949) which features Butch Cassidy, Harry Longabaugh, and Kid Curry as characters and "A Friend of Buck Hollister" in *Zane Grey's Western Magazine* (11/47) which includes Billy the Kid. Raine tended to interweave snatches of history in his fiction whenever he could, usually by way of footnotes that covered a wide variety of topics from pronunciations, Western phrases, or even the ingredients in White River country lard to the design of a Red River cart, as well as mining terminology.

Throughout his career, reviewers commented that Raine's writing just kept getting better and better. In 1945, one critic wrote: "It'll be a sad day for us Western fans when fate decides it ain't goin' to Raine no mo'." Although he preferred socializing outside his profession, Raine was active in writers' organizations such as the Colorado Author's League. In 1953, as a charter member of the newly-formed Western Writers of America, he wrote in the first issue of WWA's *The Round-Up:* "It is my opinion that there is no more honest or competent writing in the country than that done by our group. Our fiction is far less stylized and pattern-built than that of other types which receive more consideration from the pundits who review books." In June, 1954, he was made the first honorary president of the WWA. In spite of failing health, he appeared at the awards banquet where he addressed the group by saying: "There's only one reason why we are gathered here tonight: it is because we are all engaged in recreating and recording the most vital and fascinating era of our history since the creation of our nation. . . ." He died a month later, on July 25, 1954.

Notwithstanding his achievements as a Western author, including the support of his publishers, highly laudatory reviews, and a wide readership, Raine knew well the obstacles facing a writer of Westerns and he spoke out against those obstacles, simply yet strongly, with words that are as applicable today as they were forty years ago. "A story set in our terrain ought to be judged solely on its merits as other novels are without having a black mark against it before it is even read." For all who met him, he was a gentleman of the old school, while for writers like Wayne D. Overholser, he was "a legend". Although his popularity continued for some time after his death, by the 1980s he had virtually disappeared from book racks. Yet, it is perhaps Raine's love of the West of his youth, the place and the people where there existed the "fine free feeling of man as an individual," glimmering in the pages of his books that will warrant the attention of readers for a long time to come.

The two stories in this book, "Troubled Waters" (6/20/18) and "Robber's Roost" (3/07), both originally published in Street & Smith's *The Popular Magazine*, were written fairly early in Raine's career. In fact "Robber's Roost" was used, along with the novelette "Wyoming," also in *The Popular Magazine* (11/07), as the basis for Raine's first Western novel, *Wyoming* in 1908. "Troubled Waters" was expanded to novel length for Hodder and Stoughton in 1924. This is the first appearance in book form of both stories as originally published.

★ ★ ★ ★ ★

TROUBLED WATERS

★ ★ ★ ★ ★

I

The young man drew up his horse at the side of the dusty road and looked across the barbed-wire fence into the orchard beyond. Far distant against the horizon could be seen the blue mountain range of the Big Horns, sharp-toothed, with fields of snow lying in the gulches. But in the valley basin where he rode an untempered sun, too hot for May, beat upon his brown neck and through the gray flannel shirt stretched taut across his flat back.

The trees were clouds of soft blossoms and the green alfalfa beneath looked delightfully cool. Warm and dry from travel as he was, that shadowy paradise of pink and white bloom and lush deep grass called mightily to him. A reader of character might have guessed that handsome Larry Silcott followed the line of least resistance.

If his face betrayed no weakness, certainly it showed self-satisfaction, an assured smug acceptance of the fact that he was popular and knew it. Yet his friends, and he had many of them, would have protested that word smug. He was a good fellow, amiable, friendly, anxious to please. At dance and roundup he always had a smile or a laugh ready.

He caught a glimpse of the weathered roof of the ranch house where the rambling road dipped into a draw. Well, it would wait there for him. Why not climb the fence and steal a long luxurious nap in the orchard of the Elkhorn Lodge? He looked at his watch—and ten seconds later was trespassing with long strides through the grass.

Larry was Irish by descent. He was five-and-twenty. He had the digestion of an ostrich. For which good reasons and several others he whistled as his quirt whipped the alfalfa tops from the stems.

For the young range rider was in love with life. Take last night, now. He had flirted outrageously at the Circle OT Ranch dance with Jack Cole's girl, though he had known she was expecting to be married before winter. Jack was his friend, and he had annoyed him and made him jealous. Larry had excited Kate with the flattery of a new conquest, and he had made the ranchers and their wives smile tolerantly at the way he had rushed her.

Flinging himself down beneath a tree, he drew a deep breath of content. His blinking lids closed sleepily and opened again while he nestled closer to the ground and pillowed a dusky head on an arm. He had slept only two hours the night before.

From the foliage above came a faint rustle followed by what might pass as a discreet little cough. The range rider sat up as though he were hinged at the hips, rose to his feet, and lifted the pinched-in felt hat to a glimpse of blue in the shower of blossoms.

"Where did you come from?" he demanded, face lifted to the foliage.

"From Keokuk, Iowa," came the prompt answer.

He laughed at this literal response. "I'll never believe it, ma'am. You're one of these banshees my mother used to talk about, or else you're a fairy or one of these here nymphs that dwell in trees." Through the blossoms he made out a slim figure of grace, vaguely outlined in the mass of efflorescence.

Her laughter rippled down to him. "Sorry to disappoint you, sir. But I'm a mere woman."

"I ain't so sure you won't open up your wings an' fly away," he protested. "But if you're giving me the straight of it, all I've got to say is that I like women. I been waiting for one twenty-odd years. Last night I dreamed I was gonna find her before sunset today. That's straight."

She was seated on a branch, chin tilted in a little cupped fist, one heel caught on the bough below to steady her. "You'll have to hasten on your way, then. The sun sets in half an hour," she told him.

His grin was genial, insinuating, an unfriendly critic might have said impudent. "Room for argument, ma'am," he demurred. "Funny, ain't it, that of all the millions of apple trees in the world I sat down under this one . . . an' while you were in it? Here we are, the man, the tree, an' the girl, as you might say."

"Are you listing the items in the order of their importance?" she asked. "And anyhow we won't be here long, since I am leaving now."

"Why are you going?" he wanted to know.

"A little matter, a mere trifle. You seem to have forgotten it, but . . . we haven't been introduced."

"Now looky here, ma'am. What's in a name? Some guys say . . . 'Meet Mister Jones,' an' you claim you know me. Not a thing to that. I'm anything you want to call me, an' you're Miss Lady in the Apple Blossoms. An' now that's been fixed, I reckon I'll climb up."

The girl's eyes sparkled. There was something attractive about this young fellow's impudence. Woman-like, her mind ran to evasions. "You can't come up. You'd shake down all the blossoms."

"If I shook 'em all down but one, I'll bet the tree would bloom to beat any other in the orchard." He caught the lowest limb and was about to swing himself up. Her sharp—"No!"—

25

held him an instant while their eyes met. A smile crept into his eyes.

"Will you come down then?"

"At my convenience, sir."

An upward swing brought him to the fork of the tree. Yet a moment, and he was beside her among the blossoms. Her eyes swept him in one swift glance, curiously, a little shyly.

"With not even a by your leave. You are a claim-jumper," she said.

"No, ma'am. I'm locating the one adjoining yours."

"You may have mine, since I'm vacating it."

"Now don't you," he protested. "Let yourself go once an' be natural. Like a human being. Hear that meadowlark calling to his mate. He's telling his lady friend how strong he is for her. Why even the irrigation ditch is singing a right nice song about what a peach of a day it is."

The girl's eyes appraised him without seeming to do so. So far the cowpunchers she had met had been shy and awkward, red-faced and perspiring. But this youth was none of these. The sun and the wind of the Rockies had painted the tan on face and neck and hands, had chiseled tiny humorous wrinkles that radiated from the corners of his eyes. Every inch of the broad-brimmed felt hat, of the fancy silk kerchief, of the decorated chaps, certified him a rider of the range.

"He travels fast," the girl announced to the world at large. "Which reminds me that so must I."

Larry, too, made a confidant of his environment. "I wonder how she'll get past me . . . unless she really has wings."

"I've heard that all Westerners are gentlemen at heart," she mused aloud. "Of course he'll let me past."

"Now she's trying to flatter me. Nothing doing. We'll give it out right now that I'm no gentleman," he replied impersonally. Then, abandoning his communion with the apple blossoms, he put a question to the young woman: "Mind if I smoke?"

"Why should you ask me, since you confess . . . or do you boast? . . . that you are no gentleman?"

From the pocket of his shirt he drew tobacco and paper, then rolled a cigarette. "I'm one off an' on," he explained. "Whenever it don't cramp my style."

She took advantage of his preoccupation with the makings, stepped lightly to a neighboring branch, swung to a lower one, and dropped easily to earth. The eyes that looked up at him sparkled triumph. "I wish you luck in your search for that sweetheart you're to meet before sunset," she said.

"I'll be lucky. Don't you worry about that," he boasted coolly. "Only I don't have to find her now. I've found her."

Then, unexpectedly, they went down into the alfalfa together amid a shower of apple blossoms. For he, swinging from the branch upon which he sat, had dropped, turned his ankle on an outcropping root, and clutched at her as he fell.

The girl merely sat down abruptly, but he plunged cheek first into the soft loam of the plowed orchard. His nose and the side of his face were decorated with débris. Mopping his face with a handkerchief, he succeeded in scattering more widely the soil he had accumulated.

She looked at him, gave a little giggle, suppressed it decorously, then went off into a gale of laughter. He joined her mirth.

"Not that there's anything really to laugh at," he presently assured her with dignity.

The young woman made an honest attempt at gravity, but one look at his embellished face set her off again.

"We just sat down," he explained.

"Yes. On your bubble of romance. It's gone . . . punctured. . . ."

"No, no, Miss Lady in the Apple Blossoms. I'm sticking to my story."

"But it won't stick to you, as for instance the dirt does that you grubbed into."

"Sho!" He mopped his face again. "You know blame well we're gonna be friends. Starting from right now."

She started to rise, but he was before her. With both hands he drew her to her feet. She looked at him, warily, with a little alarm, for he had not released her hands.

"If you please," she suggested, a warning in her voice.

He laughed triumphantly, and swiftly drew her to him. His lips brushed her hot cheek before she could push him away.

She snatched her hands from him, glared indignantly for an instant at him, then turned on her heel in contemptuous silence.

Smilingly he watched her disappear.

Slowly, jubilation still dancing in his eyes, he waded through the alfalfa to the fence, crept between two strands, and mounted the patient cow pony.

As he rode by the ranch house the girl he had kissed heard his unabashed voice lifted gaily in song. The words drifted to her down the wind.

> *Foot in the stirrup and hand on the horn,*
> *Best damned cowboy that ever was born.*

It came to her as a boast, almost as a challenge. The blood burned in her cheeks. Fire sparkled in her eyes. If he ever gave her a chance, she would put him in his place, she vowed.

II

After dinner at the Elkhorn Lodge, Ruth Trovillion left her aunt reading a magazine and drifted across to the large log cabin that was used as a recreation hall by guests of the dude ranch.

Tim Flanders, owner of the ranch, was sitting on the porch smoking a pipe, his chair tilted back and his feet propped against one of the posts. At sight of Miss Trovillion, who was a favorite of his, the legs of his chair and his feet came to the floor simultaneously.

"Don't disturb yourself on my account, Mister Flanders," she told him.

"Might as well 'light an' stay for a while," he said, and dragged a chair forward.

Ruth stood for a moment, as though uncertain, before she sat down. "Well, I will, thank you, since you've taken so much trouble."

They sat in silence, the girl looking across at the dark blue-black line of mountains that made a jagged outline against a sky not quite so dark.

"It's been kinda hot today for this time o' year," her host said at last.

"Yes," she agreed. "But it will be June in a few days. Doesn't it begin to get warmer here then?"

"Not what you'd call real warm, ma'am. We're a mile high," he reminded her. Presently the subject of the weather having been exhausted, Flanders offered another gambit. "I hope, ma'am, you don't break any more cowboy hearts today."

She turned eyes of amiable scorn upon him. "Cowboys! Where are they, these cowboys you promised me?"

"They been kinda scarce down this way lately, sure enough," he admitted. "But you mighta seen one today if you'd happen' to have been looking when he passed. His name is Larry Silcott."

Tim's shrewd eyes rested on her. It happened that he had seen Silcott come out of the orchard only a few moments before Miss Trovillion had arrived at the house, evidently also from the orchard.

Indifferently Miss Trovillion answered, her eyes again on the distant blue-black silhouette. "Is he the one that was claiming so loudly to be the best cowboy in the world?"

"Yes, ma'am. Larry's liable to claim anything. He's that-a-way."

"Just what do you mean by that?"

"He's got his nerve, Larry has." He chuckled. "Last night, for instance, by what the boys say."

"Yes?"

"There was a dance at the Circle OT. I reckon Larry was pretty scand'lous the way he shined up to another fellow's girl."

"I suppose he's one of the kind that thinks he's irresistible," she said, an edge of contempt in her voice.

"Maybe he has got notions along that line. Probably he's got some basis for them, too. Larry is the sort women like, I judge."

"You seem to know all about women, Mister Flanders. Why don't you write a book about us?"

He refused to be daunted by her sarcasm. "I notice what I notice."

"And I suppose this Mister Silcott is really what they call a four-flusher?" she asked.

"Well, no, he ain't. In his way Larry is a top hand. He's mighty popular, an' he delivers the goods. None of the boys can ride a bucking bronco with him, unless it's Rowan McCoy."

"And who's he? Another poser?"

Flanders's answer came instantly and emphatically. "No, ma'am. He's a genuine dyed-in-the-wool he-man, Rowan is. If you want to see a real Westerner, one of the best of the breed, why Rowan McCoy is your man."

"Yes . . . and where is he on exhibit?" she asked lightly.

"He's a cattleman. Owns the Circle Diamond Ranch . . . not so gosh awful far from here. I'll ride over with you someday when I get time."

Ruth knew he would never find time. Tim was temperamentally indolent. He could work hard when he once got his big body into action. But it took a charge of dynamite to start him.

The girl referred again to her pretended grievance. "You're a false alarm, Mister Flanders, and I'm going to sue you for breach of contract. You promised me the second day we were here . . . you know you did . . . to round up a likely bunch of cowpunchers for me to study. We dudes don't come out here just for the scenery, you know. We want all the local color there is. It's your business to supply it. I suppose it isn't reasonable to ask for Indian raids any more, or hold-ups, or anything of that sort. But the least you can do is to supply us a few picturesque cowboys, even if you have to send to the moving-picture people to get them."

"Say, Miss Trovillion, I've been reading about these new moving pictures. Last time I was in Denver I went to see one. It's great. Of course, I reckon it's only a fad, but. . . ."

"You're dodging the issue, Mister Flanders. Are you going to make good on those cowboys or aren't you?"

The owner of the Elkhorn Lodge scratched his gray head. "Sure I am. Right now most of the boys are busy up in the hills, but they'll be drifting down soon. Say, I'm sure thick-haided. I'd ought to have taken you to that Circle OT dance last night. I expect Missus Flanders would have gone if I'd mentioned it. You would have seen plenty of the boys there. But one of these days there will be another dance. And say, ma'am, there's roundup week at Bad Axe pretty soon. They'll come riding in for a hundred miles for that, every last one of these lads that throw a rope. That's one real rodeo . . . roping, riding, bulldogging, pony races, Indian dances, anything you like."

"Will they let a tenderfoot attend?"

"That's what it's for, to grab off the tenderfoot's dough. But honest, it's a good show. You'll like it."

31

"I'll certainly be there, if my aunt is well enough," Ruth announced with decision.

III

The road meandered over and through brown Wyoming in the line of least resistance. It would no doubt reach the Fryingpan some time and ultimately Wagon Wheel, but the original surveyors of the trail were leisurely in their habits. They had chewed the bovine cud and circled hills with a saving instinct that wasted no effort. The ranchmen of the Hill Creek district had taken the wise hint of their cattle. They, too, were in no haste and preferred to detour rather than climb.

If Rowan McCoy was in any hurry, he gave no sign of it. He let his horse fall into a slow walk of its own choice. The problem of an overstocked range was worrying him. Sheep had come bleating across the badlands to steal the grass from the cattle, regardless of priority of occupancy. It was a question that touched McCoy and his neighbors nearby. They had seen their stock pushed back from one feeding ground after another by herds of woolly invaders. Rowan could name a dozen cattlemen within as many miles who were face to face with ruin. All of them had well-stocked ranches, were heavily in debt, yet stood to make a good thing if they could hold the range even for two years longer. The price of cattle had begun to go up and was due for a big rise. The point was whether they could hang on long enough to take advantage of this.

With a sweeping curve the road swung to the rim of a saucer-shaped valley and dipped abruptly over the brow—a white ribbon zigzagging across the tender spring green of the mountain park. Bovier's Camp the place was called. The camp was a trading center for thirty miles, though there was nothing to it but a blacksmith shop, a doctor's office, a stage station, a general store and post office, and the houses of the Pin and Feather Ranch.

A man was swinging from his saddle just as McCoy rode up to the store. He was a big, loose-jointed fellow, hook-nosed, sullen of eye and mouth. His hard gaze met the glance of the cattleman with jeering hostility, but he offered no greeting before he turned away.

Two or three cowpunchers and a ranch owner were in the store. The hook-nosed man exchanged curt nods with them and went directly to the post office cage.

"Any mail for J.C. Tait?" he asked.

The postmistress handed him a letter and two circulars from liquor houses. She was an angular woman, plain, middle-aged, severe of feature. "How's Norma?" she asked.

"Nothing the matter with her far as I know," answered Tait sulkily. His manner gave the impression that he resented her question.

A shout of welcome met McCoy as he appeared in the doorway. It was plain that he was in the good books of those present as much as Tait was the opposite. For Rowan McCoy, owner of the Circle Diamond Ranch, was the leader of the cattle interests in this neighborhood, and big Joe Tait was the most aggressive and most bitter of the sheepmen fighting for the range.

Bovier's Camp was in the heart of the cattle country, but Tait made no concession to the fact that he was unwelcome here. He leaned against the counter, a revolver in its holster lying along his thigh. There was something sinister and deadly in the sneer with which he returned the coldness of the men he was facing.

He glanced over the liquor circulars before he ripped open the envelope of the letter. His black eyes, set in deep sockets, began to blaze. The red-veined cheeks of his beefy face darkened to an apoplectic purple. Joe Tait enraged was not a pleasant object to see.

He flung a sudden profane defiance at them all. "You're a fine bunch of four-flushers. It's about your size to send a skull-and-crossbones threat through the mail, but I notice you haven't the guts to sign it. I'm not to cross the badlands, eh? I'm to keep on the other side of the deadline you've drawn. And if I don't, you warn me, I'll get into trouble. To hell with your warning!" Tait crumpled the letter in his sinewy fist, flung it down, spat tobacco juice on it, and ground it savagely under his heel. "That's what I think of your warning, McCoy. Trouble! Me, I eat trouble. If you or any of your bunch of false alarms want any, you can have it right now and here."

McCoy, sitting on a nail keg, had been talking with one of his friends. He did not move. There was a moment's chill silence. "I'm not looking for trouble," the cattleman said coldly.

"I thought you weren't," jeered Tait. "You never have been, far as I can make out."

The blood mounted to McCoy's face. Nobody in the room could miss the point of that last taunt. It was common knowledge in the Hill Creek country that years before Norma Davis had jilted him to run away with Joe Tait.

"I reckon you've said enough," suggested Falkner, the range rider to whom Rowan had been talking. "And enough is aplenty, Joe."

"Do I have to get your say-so before I can talk, Falkner? I'll say to you, too, what I'm saying to the man beside you. There can't any of you . . . no, nor all of you . . . run me out the way you did Pap Thomson. Try anything like that, and you'll find me lying right in the door of my sheep wagon with hell popping. Hear that, McCoy?"

"Yes, I hear you." McCoy looked at him hard. One could have gathered no impression of weakness from the lean, brown face of the cattleman. "I didn't write that letter to you, and I don't know who did. But I'll give you a piece of advice. Keep your sheep on the other side of the deadline. They'll maybe live longer."

The sheepman shook a fist at him furiously. "That's a threat, McCoy. Don't you back it. Don't you dare lift a finger to my sheep. I'll run them where I please. I'll bring 'em right up to the door of the Circle Diamond, too, if it suits me."

A young ranchman lounging in the doorway cut into the talk. "I reckon you can bring 'em there, Joe, but I ain't so sure you could take 'em away again."

"Who'd stop me?" demanded Tait, whirling on him. "Would it be you, Jack Cole?"

"I might be there, and I might not. You never can tell."

Tait took a step toward him. "Might as well settle this now . . . the sooner the quicker," he said thickly.

Sharply McCoy spoke: "We're none of us armed, Tait. Don't make a mistake."

The sheep owner threw his revolver on the counter. "I don't need any gun to settle any business I've got with Jack Cole."

"Don't you start anything here, Joe Tait," ordered the postmistress in a shrill voice. She ran out from her cage and confronted the big man indomitably. "You can't bully me. I'm the United States government when I'm in this room. Don't you forget it, either."

A shadow darkened the doorway, and a young woman came into the store. She stopped, surprised, aware that she had interrupted a scene.

There was an awkward silence. The sheepman turned with a half-suppressed oath, snatched up his weapon, thrust it into the holster, and strode from the room. Yet a moment, and the thudding of hoofs could be heard.

The postmistress turned in explanation to the girl. "It's Joe

Tait. He's always trying to raise a ruckus, that man is. But he can't bully me, no matter how bad an actor he is. I'm not his wife." She walked around the counter and resumed a dry manner of business. "Do you want all the mail for the Elkhorn Lodge or just your own?"

"I'll take it all, Missus Stovall."

The young woman handed through the cage opening a canvas bag, into which papers and letters were stuffed.

"Three letters for you, Miss Trovillion," the older woman said, sliding them across to her.

Ruth Trovillion buckled the mail bag and turned to go. As she walked out of the store, her glance flashed curiously over the men. It lingered for a scarcely perceptible instant on McCoy.

McCoy followed a road that led from Bovier's Camp into the hills. He was annoyed at the altercation with Tait that had flared up in the store. Between the sheep and cattle interests on the Fryingpan there had been a good deal of bickering and recrimination, some night raiding, an occasional interchange of shots. But for the most part, so far at least, there had been a decent pretense of respect for the law.

Except for Tait a compromise settlement might have been effected. But the big sheepman was not reasonable. Originally a cattleman himself, he had quarreled violently with all of his range neighbors, and at last gone into sheep out of spite. What he wanted, he intended to take with a high hand.

There were personal reasons why McCoy desired no trouble with him. Rowan had not seen Norma half a dozen times since she had run away with Tait in anger after a quarrel between the lovers. If she regretted her folly, no word to that effect had ever reached McCoy or any other outsider. On the few occasions when she came out into her little neighborhood world it was with a head still high. Without impertinence, one could do no more than guess at her unhappiness. Upon one thing her former lover was determined: there would be no trouble of his making between him and the man Norma had chosen for a husband.

The cattleman turned up a cañon, followed it to its head, cut across the hills, and descended into the valley of the Fryingpan. The river was high from the spring thaw of the mountain snows.

On the road in front of him a trap was moving toward the stream. He recognized the straight back of the slim driver as that of the girl he had seen at the post office. Evidently she was taking the cut-off back to the ranch, unaware that the bridge had been washed out by the freshet. Would she turn back or would she try the ford just below the bridge? He touched his horse with the spur and put it to a canter.

The girl drew up and viewed the remains of the bridge, then turned to the ford. Presently she drove slowly down to its edge. After a moment's apparent hesitation she forced the reluctant horse to take the water. As the wheels sank deeper, as the turbid current swept above the axles and into the bed of the trap, the heart of the young woman failed. She gave a little cry of alarm and tried to turn back.

The man galloping toward the ford shouted a warning: "Keep going! Swing to the right!"

It is likely the driver did not hear his call. She tried to cramp to the left. The horse, frightened, plunged forward into the deep pool below the ford. The force of the stream swept horse and rig down. The girl screamed and started to rise, appalled by the whirling torrent.

Miraculously a horse and rider appeared beside her. She was lifted bodily from the trap in to the arms of the rescuer. For a few moments the cow pony struggled with the waters. It fought hard for a footing, splashed into the shallows nearer shore, and emerged safely at the farther bank.

She found herself lifted to the ground and deserted. The

heaven-sent horseman unfastened the rope at his saddle, swung it round his head, and dropped a large loop over the back of the trap. The other end he tied to the pommel of the saddle. The cow pony obeyed orders, braced its legs, and began to pull. The owner of the animal did not wait for results, but waded deep into the river and seized the bridle of the exhausted buggy horse.

Even then it was a near thing. The Fryingpan fought with a heavy plunging suction to keep its prey. The man and the horses could barely hold their own, far less make headway against the current. As to the girl, she watched the battle with big, fascinated eyes, the blood driven from her heart by terror. Soon it flashed across her brain that these three creatures of flesh and blood could not win, for while they wore out their strength in vain the cruel river pounded down on them with undiminished energy.

She flew to the rope and pulled, digging her heels into the sand for a better purchase. After what seemed to her a long time, almost imperceptibly, at first by fitful starts, the rope moved. McCoy inched his way to the shallower water and a more secure footing. Man, horse, and trap came jerkily to land.

Almost exhausted, the cattleman staggered to his bronco and leaned against its heaving flanks. His eyes met those of the girl. Her tremulous lips were ashen. He guessed that she was keeping a tight rein on a hysterical urge to collapse into tears.

"It's all right," he said, and she liked the pleasant smile that went with the words. "We're all safe now. No harm done. None a-tall."

"I thought . . . I was afraid. . . ." She caught her lips between her white teeth.

"Sure. Anybody would be. You oughtn't to have tried the ford. There should be a sign up there."

Ruth knew he was talking to give her time to recover composure.

He went on, casually and cheerfully. "The Fryingpan is mighty deceiving. When she's in flood, she certainly tears along in a hurry. More than one cowpuncher has been drowned in her."

She managed a smile. "I've been complaining because I couldn't find an adventure. This was a little too serious. I thought, one time, that . . . that you might not get out."

"So you pulled me out. That was fine. I won't forget it."

The girl looked at the blisters on her soft palms, and again a faint little smile twitched at her face. "Neither shall I for a day or two. I have souvenirs."

He began to arrange the disordered harness. Dark eyes, under long, curved lashes observed him as he moved, lean-loined and broad of shoulder, the bronze of the eternal outdoors burned into his hands and neck and lean face.

"My name is Trovillion . . . Ruth Trovillion," she said shyly. "I'm staying at Elkhorn Lodge, or the dude ranch, as you people call it."

He shook hands without embarrassment. "My name is Rowan McCoy."

Level eyes, with the blue of Western skies in them, looked straight into hers. A little wave of emotion beat through her veins. She knew, warned by the sure instinct of her sex, that this man who had borne her from the hands of death was to be no stranger in her life.

"I think I saw you at the store today. And I've heard of you, from Mister Flanders."

"Yes."

She abandoned that avenue of approach, and came to a more personal one—came to it with a face of marble except for the naïve eyes. "But for you I would have drowned," she said, and shuddered.

"Maybe so . . . maybe not."

"Yes. I couldn't have got out alone," she insisted. "Of course, I can't thank you. There's no use trying. But I'll never forget . . . never as long as I live."

About her there was a proud, delicate beauty that charmed him. She was at once so slender and so vital. Her face was like a fine, exquisitely cut cameo.

"All right," he agreed cheerfully. "Honors are easy then, Miss Trovillion. I lifted you out and you pulled me out."

"Oh, you can say that. As if I did anything that counted." The fount of her feelings had been touched, and she was still tremulous. It was impossible for her to dismiss this adventure as casually as he seemed ready to do. After all, it had been the most tremendous hazard of her young, well-sheltered life.

When he had made sure the trap was fit for the road, McCoy turned to his companion and helped her in. She drove slowly. The cattleman rode slowly beside her. He was going out of his way, but he found for himself a sufficient excuse. She was a slim slip of a girl who had lived her nineteen or twenty years in cities far from the primitive dangers of the wild. Probably she was unstrung from her experience and might collapse. Anyhow, he was not going to take the chance of it.

IV

Still at the age when she was frankly the center of her own universe, Ruth Trovillion had an abundant sense of romance. Rowan McCoy had impressed himself upon her imagination. He had not come into her life with jingling spurs, garnished like Larry Silcott with all the picturesque trimmings of the frontier. Larry was too free, too fresh, she thought. But McCoy, quiet, competent son of the hard-riding West, depended on no aid of costume. He was as genuine as one of his own hill cattle. Ruth had admirers in plenty, but they dwindled to non-heroic proportions before his brown virility, his gentle, reticent strength.

Quietly she gathered information about him. The owner of the Circle Diamond was a leader in the community by grace of natural fitness. Tim Flanders, who kept the Elkhorn Lodge, summed him up for Ruth.

"He's a straight-up rider, Mac is. He'll do to take along. There's no yellow in Rowan McCoy."

She thought over that a good deal. Her judgment concurred. So far as it went, the verdict of Flanders was sound. But it did not go far enough. During the ride to the ranch she had discovered that the cattleman had a capacity for silence. Ruth found herself fascinated by the desire to push through to the personality behind the wall of reserve.

For some time she was given no chance. It was ten days after the rescue before she saw him again. Unexpectedly she met him on a hill trail.

"Why haven't you been to see me?" she asked with the directness that characterized her at times.

He thought a moment before he committed himself to words. He had wanted to come, but he had passed through an experience that made him very reserved with women. He never called on any, nor did he go to dances or merrymakings.

"I've been pretty busy, Miss Trovillion," he said.

"That's no excuse. I might have got pneumonia from wet feet or gone into a nervous breakdown from the shock. You've got no right to pull a girl out of the river and then ride away and forget she ever existed. It's not good form."

He laughed at the jaunty impudence of her tilted chin. He suspected shyness back of her audacity. Yet he was surprised at his own answer when he heard it; at least he was surprised at the impulse that had led him to make it.

"Oh, I haven't forgotten you. I'll be glad to come to see you, if I may."

"When?"

"Will this evening do?"

"I'll be looking for you, Mister McCoy."

The cattleman told the simple truth when he said that he had not forgotten her. The girl had been very much in his mind ever since he had left her at the gate of the lodge.

When McCoy reached Elkhorn Lodge after dinner, Ruth introduced him to her aunt, a thin, flat-bosomed spinster with the marks of ill health of her face. Miss Morgan and her niece had come to the Rockies for the health of the older woman, and were scheduled to make an indefinite stay. Before the cattleman had talked with her five minutes he knew that Miss Morgan viewed life from a narrow, Puritanic standpoint. He guessed that there was little real sympathy between her and the vivid girl by her side.

In her early years Ruth had been a lonely, repressed little soul. An orphaned child, she had been brought up by this maiden lady, who looked on the leggy, helter-skelter youngster with the tangled flying hair as a burden laid upon her by the Lord. Ruth had been a lawless, willful little thing.

Surprisingly she had blossomed from the ugly-duckling stage into a most attractive girl. Nobody had been more amazed at the transformation than her aunt. The change was not merely external. The manner of Ruth had become gentler, less willful. As a nurse she had developed patience toward the invalid.

"Do you mind if Mister McCoy and I ride out to Flat Top for the sunset?" she asked now.

"No, child. I'll be all right."

The riders passed a poster tacked to a tree just outside the gates of the ranch. It bore this:

RIDE 'EM COWBOYS!
ANNUAL ROUNDUP AT
BAD AXE

July 2, 3, and 4

Best Bronco Busters, Ropers,
and Bulldoggers
From a Dozen States Will Compete
FOR WORLD'S CHAMPIONSHIP

Pony Races, Indian Dances, Balls, and
Street Carnival

Also Fancy Roping and Riding

Don't Miss This Great
Roundup
It's a Big League Show

Ruth drew up to read it. She turned to her companion. "You'll ride, I suppose? Mister Flanders says you're a famous bronco buster."

"I don't reckon I will," he answered. "Some of the boys entered me, but I've decided not to go this year."

"Why not?"

"Getting too old to be jolted around so rough," he replied, smiling. "The younger lads can take their turn."

"Yes, you look as though you had one foot in the grave," she derided with a swift glance at the muscular shoulders above the long, lean body. "Of course you'll ride. You've got to. Aren't you champion of the world?"

"That's just a way of talking," he explained. "They have one of these shows each year at Cheyenne. Other places have 'em, too. The winners can't all be champions of the world."

"But I want to see you ride," she told him, as though he could not without discourtesy refuse so small a favor.

He dismissed this with a smile.

43

From Flat Top they watched the sun go down behind a sea of rounded hills. The flame of it was in her blood, the glow of it on her face. She was in love with Wyoming these days. Impulsively she turned to her companion a face luminous with joy.

"Don't you just love it all?"

He nodded. The picture struck a spark from his imagination. By some trick of light and shade she seemed the heart of the sunset, a golden, glowing creature of soft, warm flesh through which an ardent soul quivered and palpitated with vague yearnings and inarticulate desires.

Into the perfect peace of a harmonious world jarred a raucous shout. From a hill pocket back of Flat Top came a cloud of dust. In the falling light a dim, gray mass poured out upon the mesa. It moved with a soft rustle of small hoofs, of wool fleeces rubbing against each other.

A horseman cantered into view and caught sight of McCoy. With a jeering laugh he shouted a greeting: "Fine sheep weather these days, McCoy! How about cows?"

The eyes of the cattleman blazed. The girl noticed the swift flush under the tan of the cheeks, the lips that closed like a steel trap.

"I'm still waiting in the door of my sheep wagon for you and your friends," scoffed the drunken voice. "And my wagon is a whole lot nearer the Circle Diamond than it was. One of these days I'll drive up to your door like I promised."

Still McCoy said nothing, but the muscles stood out on his clamped jaws like ropes. The sheepman rode closer, turned insolent eyes on the girl. From his ribald, hateful mirth she shrank back with a sense of degradation.

Tait turned his horse and galloped away. The girl asked a question: "Has he crossed the deadline?"

"Yes." Then: "What do you know about the deadline?" asked her companion, surprised.

"Oh, I have eyes and ears." She put herself swiftly on his side. "I think you're right. He's bad . . . hateful. Your cattle were here first. He brought sheep in to spite you and his other neighbors. Isn't that true?"

"Yes."

McCoy wondered how much this uncannily shrewd young person knew about the relations between him and Tait. Did she know, for instance, the story of how Norma Davis had jilted him to marry the sheepman?

"What will you do? Will you fight for the range?"

"Yes." This was a subject the cattleman could not discuss. He dismissed it promptly. "Hadn't we better be moving toward the ranch, Miss Trovillion?"

They rode back together in the gathering dusk.

V

"Larry Silcott on Rocking Chair!" boomed a deep voice through a megaphone.

A girl in one of the front boxes of the grand stand saw a young cowpuncher move with jingling spurs across the wide racetrack toward the corral beyond. He looked up, easy and debonair as an actor, and raked with his eyes the big crowd watching him. Smile met smile, when his glance came to halt at the eager girl looking down.

Ruth Trovillion's smile went out like the flame of a blown candle. She had not caught the name announced through the megaphone, but now she recognized him. She turned away, flaming, chin in the air. "Is he a good rider?" she asked the man sitting beside her.

"Wyoming doesn't raise better riders than Larry Silcott," he answered promptly. "He's an A-One rider . . . the best of the lot."

"You beat him last year, didn't you?" she challenged.

McCoy did not quite understand her imperious resentment. "That was the luck of the day. I happened. . . ."

"Oh, yes, you happened!" scoffed Ruth. "You could go out and beat him now if you wanted to. Why don't you ride? Your name is entered. I should think you would defend your championship. Everybody wants to see last year's winner ride. I haven't any patience with you."

Rowan smiled. "I see you haven't, Miss Ruth. I've tried to explain. I like Larry. We're friends. Besides, I taught him his riding. Looks to me as if it is now the younger fellow's turn. Now is a good time for me to quit after I have won two years running."

The young woman was not convinced, but she dropped the argument. Her resentful eyes moved back to the arena, into which a meek-looking claybank had been driven. It stood with blinking eyes, drooping at the hip, palpably uninterested in the proceedings.

Of a sudden the ears of the bronco pricked, its eyes dilated. A man in chaps was moving toward it, a rope in his hands. The loop of the lariat circled, went whistling forward, fell true over the head of the outlaw horse. The claybank reared, tried to bolt, came strangling to a halt as the loop tightened. A second rope slid into place beside the first. The horse stood trembling while a third man coaxed a blanket over its eyes.

Warily and deftly Silcott saddled. "All ready," he told his assistants.

Ropes and blanket were whipped off as he swung to the seat. Rocking Chair stood motionless for a moment, bewildered at the things happening so fast. Then the outlaw realized that a human clothespin was straddling its back. It went whirling upward as if trying to tie itself into a knot. The rider clamped his knees against the sides of the bronco and swung his hat with a joyous whoop.

Rocking Chair had a reputation to live up to. It was a noted fence-rower, weaver, and sun-fisher. Savagely it whirled, went up in another buck, came down stiff-legged, with arched back. The jolt was like that of a pile driver, but Silcott met it with limp spine, his hat still fanning against the flank of the animal. The outlaw went around and around in a vicious circle. The incubus was still astride of its back. It bolted, jarred to a sudden, sideways halt. Spurs were roweling its sides cruelly.

Up again it went in a series of furious bucks, one after another, short, sharp, violent. Meanwhile, Silcott, who was a trick rider, went through his little performance. He drank a bottle of ginger ale and flung away the bottle. He took the rein between his teeth and slipped off coat and waistcoat. He rode with his feet out of the stirrups. The grandstand clamored with applause. The young cattleman from the Open ANC was easily the hero of the day.

The outlaw horse stopped bucking as suddenly as it had begun. Larry slipped from the saddle in front of the grandstand and stood bowing.

Abruptly Ruth turned to McCoy. "I want you to ride," she told him in a low voice.

The cattleman hesitated. He did not want to ride. Without saying so in words, he had let the other competitors understand that he did not mean to defend his title.

He turned to decline, but the words died on his lips. The eyes of the girl were stormy, her cheeks flushed. It was plain that for some reason she had set her heart on his winning. Why? His pulses crashed with the swift, tumultuous beating of the red blood in him. Rowan McCoy was not a vain man. It was hard for him to accept the conclusion for which his whole soul longed. But what other reason could there be for her insistence?

During the past few weeks he had been with Ruth Trovillion a great deal. He had ridden with her, climbed Old Baldy by her side, eaten picnic lunches as her companion far up in flower-strewn mountain parks. He had taught her to shoot, to fish, to make camp. They had been gay and wholesome comrades for long summer days. The new and secret thing that had come into his life he had hidden from her as if it had been a sin. How could it be otherwise? This fine, spirited young creature would go back to her own kind when the time came. Meanwhile, let him make the best of his little day of sunshine.

"I told the boys I wasn't expecting to ride," he parried. "It has been rather understood that I wouldn't."

"But if I ask you?" she demanded. There was no resisting that low, imperious appeal.

He looked straight into her eyes. "If you ask it, I'll ride."

"I do ask it."

He rose. "It's your say so, little partner. I'll let the committee know."

The eyes of the girl followed him, a brown, sun-baked man, quiet and strong and resolute. Her glance questioned shyly what manner of man this was, after all, who had imposed himself so greatly upon her thoughts. He was genuine. So much she knew. He did not need the gay trappings of Larry Silcott to brand him a rider of the hills, foursquare to every wind that blew. Behind the curtain of his reticence she had divined some vague hint of a woman in his life. Now a queer little thrill of jealousy, savage and primeval, claimed her for the first time.

A cowpuncher from Laramie, in yellow wool chaps and a shirt of robin's-egg blue, took the stage after Silcott. He drew a roan with a red-hot devil of malice in its eye. The bronco hunched itself over to the fence in a series of jarring bucks, and jammed the leg of the rider against a post. The Laramie youth, beside himself with pain, caught at the saddle horn to save his seat. The nearest judge fired a revolver to tell him he was out of the running. He had touched leather.

"Rowan McCoy on Tenderfoot!" announced the leather-lunged megaphone man.

A wave of interest swept through the grandstand. Everybody had wanted to see the champion ride. Now they were going to get the chance.

The owner of the Circle Diamond rode like a centaur. He tried no tricks, no fancy business to win the applause of the spectators. But he held his seat with such ease and mastery that his long, lithe body might have been a part of the horse. His riding was characteristic of him—straight and strong and genuine.

The outlaw tried its wicked best, and no bronco in the Rockies was better known than Tenderfoot for the fighting devil that slumbered in its heart. Neither side bucking nor pitching, sunfishing or weaving could shake the lean-loined, broad-shouldered figure from his seat. It was not merely that McCoy could not be unseated; there was never a moment when there was any doubt of whether man or beast was master. Even when the bronco flung itself backward, McCoy was in the saddle again before the animal was on its feet.

The eyes of Ruth never left the fighting pair. She leaned forward, fascinated, lost to everything in the world but the duel that was being fought out in front of her. Slowly Tenderfoot answered to its master, acknowledged the dominion of the man.

Its pitching became less violent, its bucking half-hearted. At a signal from one of the judges, McCoy slipped from the saddle. Without an instant's delay, without a single glance at the storm-tossed grandstand, the rider strode across the arena and disappeared. He did not know that Ruth Trovillion was beating her gloved hands excitedly along with five thousand other cheering spectators. He could not guess how her heart had stood still when the bronco toppled backward, nor how it had raced when his toes found again the stirrups as the horse struggled to its feet.

The judges conferred for a few minutes before the megaphone man announced that the championship belt went to McCoy, second prize to Silcott. Once more the grandstand gave itself to eager applause of the decision.

Just before the wild-horse race, which was the last event on the program, McCoy made his way to the box where Miss Trovillion was sitting with Tim Flanders, of the Elkhorn Lodge, and his wife.

The girl looked up, her eyes shining. "Congratulations, Mister Champion of the World." She felt after a fashion that she had helped to beat the conceited Silcott, the youth who had affronted her with his presumptuous kiss.

"I was lucky," he said simply.

"You were the best rider." Then, with a little touch of feminine ferocity: "I knew you would beat him."

"Silcott? I still think I was lucky."

Already the grandstand was beginning to empty. Roundup week was almost over.

"We'd better be getting back to town if we want any supper," proposed Flanders.

The same idea had suggested itself to several thousand more visitors to Bad Axe. A throng of automobiles was presently creeping toward the gates, every engine racing and every horn squawking. Once outside, the whole plain seemed alive with moving cars, buckboards, wagons, and horses all going swiftly townward in a mad race for hotels and restaurants.

In the crowded streets, after they had found something to eat, McCoy and Miss Trovillion became separated from their friends. Hours later they wandered from the crowd toward the suburb where the young woman and the Flanders family had found rooms.

Unaccountably their animation ebbed when they were alone under the stars. They had been full of laughter and small talk so long as the crowd jostled them. Now they could find neither. In every fiber of him Rowan was aware of the slight, dainty figure moving by his side so lightly. The delicate, penetrating fragrance of her personality came to him with poignant sweetness.

Once his hand crept out and touched her white gown in the darkness. If she knew, she gave no sign. Her eyes were on the hills that rose sheer back of the town high into the skyline. They seemed to press in closely and to lift her vision to the heavens to shut out all the little commonplace things of life.

They stood silently, and presently she turned reluctantly back toward the town. He fell into step beside her. Soon now, he knew, they would be caught again in the hubbub of the town. So he spoke, abruptly, to hold in his heart some permanent comfort from the hour when they had been alone with each other and the voices of the world had been very far and faint.

"Why did you want me to ride?"

It was a simple question, but one not so easily answered. She could have told him the truth, that she did not want Larry Silcott to win. But that would have been only part of the truth. She wanted Rowan McCoy to win, wanted it more than she had wished anything for a long time. Yet why? She was not ready to give a candid reason even to herself, far less to him.

Woman-like, she evaded. "Why shouldn't I want you to win? You're my friend. I thought. . . ."

He surprised himself almost as much as he did her by his answer. "I'm not your friend."

She looked at him, startled at his brusqueness.

"I'm a man that loves you," he said roughly.

A tremor passed through her. She was conscious of a strange sweet faintness. The soft eyes veiled themselves beneath dark lashes.

"Have I spoiled everything, little partner?" he asked gently.

"How can I tell . . . yet?" she whispered, and looked up at him shyly, tremulously.

He knew, as his arms went around her, that he had entered upon the greatest joy of his life.

VI

Rowan McCoy drove his new car—it was a flivver, although they did not call it that in those days—with a meticulous care of one who still distrusts the intentions of the brute and his own skill at circumventing them.

As he skidded to a halt in front of the store with brakes set hard, a woman came out on the porch and nodded to him. She waited until the noise of the engine had died before she spoke: "Going down to Wagon Wheel, Mac?"

"If I can stay with this gasoline bronc' that far. Anything I can do for you, Missus Stovall?"

The woman hesitated, her thin lips pressed tight in a habitual expression of dry irony. She moved closer. "That hound Joe Tait has been a-beating up Norma again. She phoned up, she wanted to get down to the train. I've a fool notion she's quitting him for good."

The cattleman waited in silence. It was not a habit of his to waste words.

"Wanted I should find someone to take her and her traps to Wagon Wheel. But seems like everybody's right busy all of a sudden." A light sarcasm filtered through the thin, cool voice of the postmistress. "Folks just hate to be unneighborly, but their team has done gone lame or the wife's sick or the wagon broke a wheel. O' course, it ain't that any of them's afraid to mad that crazy gunman, Tait. Nothing like that."

McCoy looked across at the blue-ribbed mountains. Mrs. Stovall noticed that the muscles stood out like ropes on the brown cheeks of his close-gripped jaw. She did not need to ask the reason. Everybody in the Hill Creek country knew the story of Norma Davis and Rowan.

"I'm not asking you to take her, Mac," the woman ran on sharply. "You got more right to have a flat tire than Pete Henderson has to have. . . ."

"Where is she?" interrupted the man.

"You'll find her the yon side of the creek."

Mrs. Stovall knew when she had said enough. Silently she watched him crank the car and drive away. As he disappeared at the rim of the park, a faint, grim smile of triumph touched her sunken mouth.

"I 'most knew he'd take her," she said aloud to herself. " 'Course, there'll be a ruckus between him and Joe Tait, but I reckon that's his business."

At intervals during the morning that sardonic smile lit the wrinkled face. It was an odd swing of the pendulum, she thought, that had reversed the situation. Years ago Norma had run away from her lover with good-for-nothing Joe Tait. Now she was escaping from Tait with McCoy at her side. How far would fate carry the ironic jest?

A woman came out from the cottonwoods beyond the ford to meet McCoy. She was dressed in a cheap gown hopelessly out of date, and she carried a telescope valise with two broken straps.

If any of the bitterness McCoy had felt toward her when his wound was fresh survived the years, it must have died now. Life had dealt harshly with her. There had been a time when she was the belle of all this ranch country, when she had bloomed with health and spirits, had been as full of fire as an unbroken bronco. Now her step dragged. The spark of frolicsome deviltry had long been quenched from her eye. Her pride had been dragged in the dust, her courage brutally derided. Even the good looks with which she had queened it were marred. She was on the way to become that unattractive creature, the household drudge. Yet on her latest birthday she had reached only the age of twenty-six.

At recognition of the man in the car she gave a startled little cry: "You . . . Rowan!"

It was the first time they had been alone together in seven years, the first time she had directly addressed him since the hour of their quarrel. At the unexpectedness of the meeting emotion welled up in her throat and registered there like the quicksilver in a thermometer.

He tossed her grip into the back of the car, along with his own, and turned to help her to the seat beside the driver. For just an instant she hesitated, then with a bitter, choking little laugh gave way. What else could she do? It was merely another ironic blow of fate that the lover she had discarded should be the man to help her fly from the destiny her willfulness had invited.

In silence they sat knee to knee while the car rolled the miles.

Neither of them welcomed the chance that had thrown them together again. It shocked the pride of the woman, put her under an obligation to the man against whom she had nursed resentment for years. His presence stressed the degradation into which she seemed to herself to have fallen. For him, too, the meeting was untimely. Today of all days he wanted to forget the past, to turn over a page that was to begin the story of a new record.

The heady willfulness of the girl had given place to the tight-lipped self-repression of a suffering woman. Not once in all the years had she complained to an outsider. But her flight was a confession. The stress of her feeling overflowed into words bitter and stinging.

"You've got your revenge, Rowan McCoy. If I treated you

shabbily, you can say . . . 'I told you so' . . . now. They used to say I was too proud. Maybe I was. Well, I've been paid for it a thousand times. I've got mighty little to be proud of today."

"Norma!" he pleaded in a low voice.

With the instinct of one who bites on an ulcerated tooth to accept the pain, she drew up a loose sleeve and showed him blue-and-yellow bruises. "Look!" she ordered in an ecstasy of self-contempt. "I've hidden this sort of thing for years . . . and worse . . . a hundred times worse."

"The hound." His strong, clenched teeth smothered the word.

Instantly the mood of the woman changed. She would have none of his sympathy. "I'm a fool," she snapped. "I've made my bed. I'll lie in it. Why should I complain?"

Never a talkative man, McCoy said nothing now.

They had reached the Fryingpan, and the road wound down beside the little river as it tumbled toward the plains over boulders and around them. The trout were feeding, and occasionally one leaped for a fly, a flash of silver in the sunlight. Both of them recalled vividly the time they had last gone fishing there. They had taken a picnic lunch, and it had been on the way home that a quarrel had flashed between them about the attentions of Joe Tait to her. That night she had eloped.

The woman noticed that McCoy was not wearing today the broad-rimmed white felt hat and the wrinkled corduroys that were so much an expression of his personality. He was in a new, dark suit, new shoes, and an up-to-date straw hat. The suitcase that jostled her shabby telescope valise would have done credit to a Chicago traveling salesman.

"You're going to take the train," she suggested.

"To Cheyenne," he answered.

"Why I'm going to Laramie, if. . . ."

She cut her sentence short. It was not to be presumed that he cared where she was going. Moreover, she could not finish without telling more than she wanted to. But McCoy guessed the condition. She would go if she could borrow at Wagon Wheel the money for a ticket.

They drove into the county seat long before train time.

"Where shall I take you?" he asked.

"To Moody's, if you will."

He helped her from the car and carried the valise into the store. Moody was in the cubbyhole that had been cut off from the store for an office. Rowan hailed him cheerfully.

"Look here, Trent. What's the best price you can give me for those hides?" He walked toward the storekeeper and bargained with him audibly, but he found time to slip in an undertone: "If Missus Tait wants any money, give it to her. I'll be responsible. But don't tell her I said so."

Moody grinned dubiously. He was a little embarrassed and not a little curious. "All right, Mac. Whatever you say."

As Rowan went out of the office, Norma timidly entered. Moody was a tight, hard little man, and she did not expect him to let her have the money. If he refused, she did not know what she would do.

McCoy strolled down to the station to inquire about the lower he had reserved in the Pullman.

"You're in luck, Mac," the station agent told him. "Travel is heavy. There isn't another berth left . . . not even an upper. You got the last."

"Then I'm out of luck, Tim." The cattleman smiled. "A lady from our part of the country is going to Laramie. Give her my berth, but don't let her know I had reserved it. The lady is Missus Tait."

A quarter of an hour later Norma Tait, not yet fully recovered from her surprise at the ease with which she had acquired the small roll of bills now in her pocketbook, learned from the station agent that there was one sleeper berth left. She exchanged

$3 for the ticket, and sat down to wait until the Limited arrived. It was a nervous hour she spent before her train drew in, for at any moment her husband might arrive to make trouble. At the first chance she vanished into the Pullman.

Just as the conductor shouted his—"All aboard!"—a big, raw-boned man galloped up to the station and flung himself from the saddle. He caught sight of McCoy standing by the last sleeper.

"What have you done with my wife?" he roared.

The train began to move. McCoy climbed to the step and looked down contemptuously at the furious man. "Try not to be a fool, Tait," he advised.

The man running beside the train answered the spirit of the words rather than the letter. "You're a liar. She's in that car. You're running away with her. You sneak, I'm going in to see." He caught at the railing to swing himself up.

The cattleman wasted no words. His left fist doubled, shot forward a scant six inches, collided with the heavy chin of Tait. The big sheepman's head snapped back, and he went down heavily like a sack of meal.

The white-rimmed eyes of the porter rolled admiringly toward McCoy as the cattleman disappeared into the sleeper. "Some kick, b'lieve me!" he murmured to the world at large.

Rowan stopped at the section where Norma Tait sat. "I'm going forward to the day coach," he explained. "If there's anything I can do for you, Norma, now or at any time, I want you to call on me."

The woman looked at him, a man from his soles up, coffee-brown, lean, steady as a ground-sunk rock. It came to her with a surge of emotion that here a woman's love could find safe anchorage. What a fool she had been to throw him aside in the pride of her youth!

"Why should I ask favors of you? What have I ever done but

bring trouble and unhappiness to you?" she cried in a low voice.

"Never mind that. If there's anything I can do for you, I'm here to do it."

She gulped down a sob. "No, you've done enough for me . . . too much. Joe will hear that you drove me to town. He'll make trouble for you. I know him." A faint flush of anger dyed her thin cheeks. "No, I'll go my road and you'll go yours. I'm an old woman already in my feelings. I'm burned out, seems like. But you're young. Forget there was ever such a girl as Norma Davis."

He hesitated, uncertain what to say, and, while he groped, she spoke again: "There's a girl waiting for you somewhere, Rowan. Go and find her . . . and marry her."

Beneath the tan he flushed, but his eyes did not waver. "I'm going to her now, Norma. She's waiting for me at Cheyenne. We're to be married tomorrow."

After just an instant came the woman's little, whispered cry: "Be good to her, Rowan."

He nodded, then shook hands with her. "And you be good to yourself, Norma. Better luck ahead."

She gave a little wry smile. "Good bye."

McCoy passed forward to the day coach. From the train butcher he bought a magazine and settled himself for a long ride.

At Red Gulch, a big, tanned Westerner entered the car and stopped beside the cattleman.

" 'Lo, Mac," he nodded genially.

" 'Lo, Sheriff. Ain't you off your range?"

The big man was booted and spurred. As he sat down, the gun on his hip struck the woodwork of the seat arm. "Been looking for a horse thief I heard was at Red Gulch. False alarm," he explained.

"We can't any of us strike a warm trail every time."

"That's right." The cool, hard eyes of Sheriff Matson rested quietly on those of the cattleman. "Wonder if I'm on one now. I've been asked to arrest a man eloping with another man's wife, Mac."

"I reckon Tait phoned you from Wagon Wheel."

"You done guessed it."

"He's gone crazy with the heat. False alarm, sure."

"Says his wife is aboard this train. Is she?"

"Yes."

"Says you took him by surprise and knocked him cold on the depot as the train was leaving."

"He's made a record and told the truth twice running."

"Where's she going? Missus Tait, I mean."

"To Laramie. Her sister lives there."

Again the sheriff's hard gaze searched McCoy. "Came down from Bovier's Camp with you in your car, I understand."

"Yes. I gave her a lift down." Rowan's voice was as even as that of the officer.

"Suppose you give me a bill of particulars, Mac?"

The cattleman told a carefully edited story. When he had finished, Matson made one comment: "Tait says she hadn't a dollar. Wonder where she got the money for a ticket?"

"I wonder."

The eyes of the two men met in the direct, level fashion of the country.

"Going anywhere in particular in those glad rags, Mac?"

The sheriff's question was dropped lightly, but McCoy did not miss it significance.

"Why, yes, Aleck. I'm going to Cheyenne," he assented.

"A cattle deal?"

"Not exactly . . . object matrimony, Sheriff."

Matson shot a direct, stabbing look at him. "You've told me too much or too little."

"The young lady is named Trovillion. She spent two months at the dude ranch this summer."

The sheriff rose. " 'Nough said, Mac. I wasn't elected to do Tait's dirty work for him. I get off at this crossing. So long, old scout . . . and good luck to you on that object-matrimony game."

VII

They were married. And in swift procession the months followed the weeks.

At the Circle Diamond, Ruth queened it with a naïve childishness from which her youth had not yet escaped. Eagerly she played at housekeeping for a fortnight under the amused eyes of Mrs. Stovall, who had been employed by McCoy to do the cooking, her term as postmistress having expired. The next game that drew her was the remodeling of the house. Carpenters and decorators from Wagon Wheel came up, filled the place with litter and confusion, and under the urge of the young mistress transformed the interior of the unsightly dwelling into a delightful home.

It pleased Rowan that Ruth accepted lightly all responsibility except that of having a good time. She had shipped her own piano to Wyoming, and she played a good deal. Sometimes she read a little, more often rode or hunted. Occasionally Rowan joined her on those excursions, but usually she went alone. For business more and more absorbed his time. The war between the sheep and cattle interests was becoming acute. Ranchmen, watching the range jealously, saw themselves being pushed close to bankruptcy by Tait and his associates. Already there had been sheep raids. Cattle had been found dead at the water holes. Bullets had sung back and forth.

But though Rowan could spend little time with the girl he had married, a deep tenderness permeated his thought of her. It was still a miracle to him that she had come to the Circle

Diamond as his wife.

On an August morning Ruth, dawdling over breakfast alone, glimpsed through the dining-room window a rider galloping toward the ranch. Since Rowan had been in the saddle and away long before she was awake, the young woman answered the hail from without by going to the door.

The horseman had dismounted, flung the bridle rein to the ground, and was coming up the porch steps when Ruth appeared. He lifted the broad hat from his curly head and bowed.

"Rowan at home?" he asked.

"No, he isn't."

Swift anger blazed in the eyes of the girl. She had seen this slender, black-haired stranger twice before, once in the orchard of the dude ranch, again astride a volcanic bronco in the arena at Bad Axe.

Some wise instinct warned him not to smile. He spoke gravely. "Sorry. I've got news for him. It's important. Where is he?"

"I don't know."

"Did he say when he would be back?"

"No." Ruth cut short the conversation curtly. "I'll send one of the boys to talk with you."

She turned and walked into the house, leaving him on the porch. Out of the tail of her eye she caught sight of her husband riding into the yard with his foreman. From the dining-room window she presently watched McCoy canter away in the company of Silcott.

Ruth was annoyed, even though she recognized that her vexation at Rowan was not quite fair. It was true that he had lately fallen into a habit of disappearing for a day at a time without explanation of his absence. He was worried about something, and he had not made a confidante of her. This was bad enough, but what she resented most was the fact that he was on the best of terms with the handsome young scamp who had kissed her so blithely in the orchard. Of course she had no right to blame her husband for this, since she had never told him of the episode. Yet she did. For her mind moved by impulse and not by logic.

She wandered into the kitchen and whipped together a salad for luncheon. She knitted two rows on a sweater at which she was working, and flung it aside. Restlessly she turned to a magazine, fingered the pages aimlessly, read at a story for a paragraph or two, then with a sudden decision tossed the periodical on the table and walked out of the house to the garage. Yet a minute, and she was spinning down the road to Bovier's Camp.

The car topped the rim of the saucer-shaped valley and swept down toward the little village. What Ruth saw quickened her blood. Beyond the post office a great huddle of sheep was being driven forward. At the head of them rode a man with a rifle in one hand lying across the horn of the saddle. On the porch of the store sat Larry Silcott and her husband watching the man steadily. Neither of them carried any arms exposed to view.

The young wife drove the car down the basin and stopped near the store, leaving the engine still running. None of the men even glanced her way. Their eyes were focused on each other with a tenseness that made her want to scream. She waited, breathless, uncertain what to expect.

The man with the rifle spoke thickly in a heavy, raucous voice: "I've been looking for you, Rowan McCoy. First off, I'll tell you something. I'm here with my sheep like I promised, on the way to Circle Diamond. I'm going right past the door of the ranch to Thunder Mountain. If any man tries to stop me, I'll fix his clock. Get that?"

Rowan's eyes were like chilled steel, his body absolutely

motionless. "Better turn back while you can, Tait," he advised quietly.

"I'll see you in hell first. I'm going through. But there's another thing I've got to settle with you, Rowan McCoy. That's about my wife. Stand up and fight, you white-livered coyote!" A sudden passionate venom leaped into the voice of the sheep-man. He cursed his enemy savagely and flung at him a string of vile names.

Ruth, terror-stricken, believed the man was working himself up to do murder. She wanted to cry out, to rush forward and beg him to stop. But her throat was parched and her limbs weighted with heavy chains.

"Your wife left you because you are a bully and a drunkard. I had nothing to do with her going," retorted McCoy.

"You're a liar . . . a rotten liar! You got her to run away with you. You took her in your car to Wagon Wheel. You gave her money to buy a ticket. You were seen on the train with her. I swore I'd kill you on sight, and I'm going to do it. Get out of the way, Silcott!"

The energy flowed back into Ruth's limbs. She threw in the clutch and drove forward furiously. There was the sound of a shot, then of another. Next moment she was pushing home the brake and shutting off the gas. The car slammed to a halt, its wheels hard against the porch. She had driven directly between the sheepman and his intended victim.

Out of the haze that for a moment enveloped Ruth's senses boomed a savage, excited voice: "Turn me loose, Mac! Lemme go! I'll finish the damned sheepman while I'm on the job."

The scene opened before her eyes like a moving-picture film. On the porch her husband was struggling with a man for the possession of a rifle, while young Silcott was sagging against a corner pillar, one hand clutched to his bleeding shoulder. Thirty yards away Tait lay on the ground, face down, beside his horse.

From the corral, from the store, from the adjoining doctor's office men poured upon the scene.

The place was suddenly alive with gesticulating people.

Rowan tore the rifle from the man with whom he was wrestling. "Don't be a fool, Falkner. You've done enough already. I shouldn't wonder if Tait had got his."

"He had it coming to him if ever a man had. If I'd been two seconds later, you'd have been a goner, Mac. I just beat him to it. Good riddance if he croaks, I say."

McCoy caught sight of Ruth. He moved toward her, his eyes alive with surprise and dismay.

"You . . . here!"

"He didn't hit you!" She strangled a sob.

"No. Falkner fired from the store window. It must have shaken his aim. He hit Larry." Rowan turned swiftly to his friend, who grinned feebly at him.

" 'S all right, Mac. I'll ride in a heap of roundups yet. He punctured my shoulder."

"Good! Let's have a look at it."

A fat little man with a doctor's case puffed up to the porch as McCoy was cutting away the shirt of the wounded man from the shoulder.

"Here! Here! Wha's the matter? Let me see. Get water . . . bandages," he exploded in staccato snorts like the engine of a motorcycle.

Ruth flew into the house to obey orders. When she returned with a basin of water and towels, the doctor had gone.

"Doc is over looking at Tait," explained her husband. "Says Larry has only a flesh wound. We'll take him home with us in the car. You don't mind?"

"Of course we'll look after him till he's well," Ruth agreed.

"I wouldn't think of troubling you, Missus McCoy," objected Silcott. "All I need is. . . ."

"Rest and good food and proper care. You'll get it at the Circle Diamond," the girl interrupted decisively. "We needn't discuss that. You're going with us."

She had her way, as she usually had. After Dr. Irwin had dressed the shoulder, the young ranchman got into the back seat of the car beside Ruth.

McCoy asked a question pointblank of the fussy little physician: "What about Tait? Will he live?"

"Ought to. If no complications. Just missed lower intestines . . . near thing. Lot of damn' fools . . . all of you," he snorted.

"Sure thing." Silcott grinned. "Come and see me tonight, Doc."

"Humph!"

"I'll be looking for you, Doctor Irwin!" Ruth called back from the moving car.

From the rim of the valley McCoy looked down and spoke grimly: "I notice that Tait's herders have changed their minds. They're driving the sheep back along the road they came."

"Before we're through with them they'll learn where to head in," boasted Larry querulously, for his wound was aching a great deal. "Next time they cross the deadline there'll be a grave dug for someone."

"I wouldn't say that, Larry," objected Rowan gently. "We'd better cut out threats. They lead to trouble. We don't want to put ourselves in the wrong unnecessarily. Take Falkner now. I was just in time to keep him from finishing Tait."

"Oh, Falkner? He's crazy to be a killer. But at that I don't blame him this time," commented the younger man.

Silcott went to bed in the guest chamber between clean sheets, and sank back with a sigh of content into the pillow. The atmosphere of home indefinably filled the room. The cool tints of the wallpaper, the pictures, the feminine touches visible here and there, all were contributing factors, but the light-footed girl, so quiet and yet so very much alive in every vivid gesture, every quick glance, was the center of the picture.

He knew that she had something on her mind, that she was troubled. He thought he could guess the reason, and felt it incumbent upon him to set himself right with her. When, toward evening, she brought him a dainty tray of food, he could keep away from the subject no longer.

"I was a boor," he confessed humbly.

For an instant she did not know what he meant. Then: "Yes," she agreed.

"I'm sorry. You've made me ashamed. Won't you forgive me?" he pleaded.

Ruth had plenty of capacity for generosity. This good-looking boy was ill and helpless. He appealed strongly to the mother instinct that is alive in all good women. He was the central figure, too, of an adventure that had excited her and intrigued her interest. Moreover, she was cherishing a new and more important resentment, one which made her annoyance at him of small moment.

"Do you mean it? Are you really sorry?" she asked.

He nodded. "I think so. I know I ought to be. Anyhow, I'm sorry you're angry at me," he answered with a little flare of boyish audacity.

She bit her lip, then laughed in spite of herself. She held out her hand a little hesitantly, but he knew he was forgiven.

Young Silcott's fever mounted toward evening, but when Dr. Irwin arrived he gave him a sleeping powder, and before midnight the wounded man fell asleep. Ruth tiptoed about the room while she arranged on a little table beside the bed his medicines and drinks in case he awakened later. After lowering the light, she stole away silently to her own bedroom.

Rowan knocked a few minutes later. He heard her move across the floor in her soft slippers. All day McCoy had been swept by waves of tenderness for this girl wife of his who had risked her life to save him by driving into the line of fire so pluckily. He had longed to open his heart to her, and he had not dared. Now there was a new note about her that puzzled him, one he had never seen before. The eyes that flashed into his were fierce with defiance. Her slim figure was very erect and straight.

"What do you want?" she demanded.

He was taken aback. Never before had her manner been less than friendly to him. While she was in this mood, he could not voice his surcharge of feeling for her.

"You are tired," he suggested.

A sudden gusty passion flared in her face. "Did you come to tell me that?"

"No. To thank you."

"What for?"

"For risking your life for me this morning. It was splendid."

She dismissed his thanks with a contemptuous laugh. "If that's all you have to say. . . ."

"That's all, except good night, dear."

Definitely she refused his wistfulness, definitely withdrew into herself and met his appeal icily.

"Good night." Her voice rejected flatly the love he offered.

Always he had been chary of embraces with her. To him she was so fine and exquisite that her kisses were a privilege not to be claimed of right. Now he merely hid his hurt with a patient smile.

"I hope you'll sleep well."

Her eyes flamed with scorn. She closed the door. He heard the key turn in the lock. Rowan knew that she was locking him out of her heart as well as out of the room.

VIII

Across the breakfast table next morning Rowan faced a hostile young stranger. The gay comrade who was so dear to him had vanished to give place to a cold and flinty critic. Abruptly and without notice she had withdrawn her friendship. Why? Was it that she had grown tired of him and what he had to offer? Or had he done something to displease her?

Man-like, he tried gifts.

"I've decided to have that conservatory built for you off the living room as soon as I can get the glass. Better draw up your plans right away."

"I've changed my mind. I don't want it."

Her voice was like icy water.

"I'm sorry," he said gently, and presently he finished his breakfast and left the room.

Ruth bit her lip and looked out of the window. Tears began to film her eyes. She went to her room, locked the door, and flung herself down on the bed in a passion of weeping.

Ever since the first days of her acquaintance with Rowan she had known the story of how Norma Davis had jilted him. Mrs. Flanders, of the dude ranch, was a gossip by nature and had told Ruth the history of the affair with gusto. The girl had been merely interested. But yesterday afternoon she had ridden over to the summer resort and asked Mrs. Flanders some insistent questions. The mistress of the dude ranch was a reluctant witness, but a damning one. It was true that Mrs. Tait had run away with McCoy in his car and that they had taken the train together. There were witnesses to prove that he had paid for the sleeper berth she used and that it was in his name. For once Joe Tait had told the truth.

The thing that hit Ruth like a sudden slap in the face was that this escapade had taken place while McCoy had been on his way to marry her. It was not an episode of the past, but a poisonous canker that ate into the joy of her life. If he could do a thing so vile, there was no truth in him.

All the golden hours they had spent together were tainted by his infidelity. Never in all her life had she met a man who had seemed so genuine, so wholly true. She had offered him her friendship and love, had given her young life into his keeping. His reverence for her had touched her deeply. Now she knew there was nothing but hypocrisy to it. She must leave him, of course.

On the very heel of this resolution came Mrs. Stovall with bad news about their patient. "His fever's mighty high. Looks like someone will have to nurse that boy regular for quite a while," she said.

"I'll look after him . . . anyhow till the doctor comes," Ruth volunteered.

Humph! Been crying her eyes out. What's she got to worry about . . . with the best man in the Fryingpan country crazy about her? wondered the housekeeper. *Trouble with her is that Rowan's too good to her. She needs to bump up against real grief before she'll know how well off she is.*

Once installed in the sick room, Ruth did not find it easy to get away. For three days Silcott needed pretty constant attention. After the delirium had passed, he lay and watched her, too weak to wait upon himself.

"You'll not leave me," he whispered to her once, and there was something so helpless and boyish about his dependence upon her that Ruth felt a queer little lump in her throat. Just now at least there could be no doubt of the genuineness of his need of her.

"Not till you're better," she promised.

And if there were tears in her eyes, they were less for him than for herself. She was thinking of another man who had told her how greatly he needed her, of another man whose whole relation to her had been a lie.

It was like Larry to take her emotion and her kindness as evidence of her special interest in him. Nor did Ruth resent it that he claimed it as a privilege of his invalidism to pass into immediate friendship with her. His open admiration of her was balm to the sick heart of the girl.

In the days that followed Rowan caught only glimpses of his wife. She was never up now in time for his early breakfast. All day he was away, and she contrived to be busy with her patient while Mrs. Stovall served his supper.

Whenever they did meet, Ruth encased herself instantly in a still white armor of reserve. She never called him by name and her manner was one of formal politeness. In his presence her joy was struck dead.

A less sensitive man might have come to grips with her and fought the thing out. Once or twice Rowan tried in a halting fashion to discover the cause of the change in her, but she made it plain to him that she would not discuss the matter. At the bottom of his heart he had no doubt as to the reason. She had found out that his ways were not hers. He held no resentment. It was natural that her eager youth should weary of the humdrum life he offered.

Sometimes, as he passed Silcott's room, Rowan heard the gay laughter of the young people. Later, when Larry was strong enough, McCoy met them driving, on their way to a picnic for two. If the sight of their merriment was a knife in his heart, Rowan gave no sign of it. His friendly smile did not fail.

"Better come along, Mac. You'll live only once, and then you'll be dead a long time," suggested Larry.

McCoy shook his head. "Can't . . . business." He noticed that Ruth had not seconded the invitation of her companion.

Although he never intruded, it was impossible for Rowan to live in the same house without running into them occasionally.

Ruth was in the grip of one of the swift friendships to which she was subject. She liked Larry a lot. They had many common interests. But she plunged into her little affair with him only because misery made her reckless. Quite well she knew that Larry's coaxing smile, his dancing eyes, his boyish winsomeness, cloaked a purpose of making love to her as much as he dared. She felt no resentment on that account. Indeed she was grateful to him for distracting her from her woe. To her husband she owed nothing. If she could hurt him by playing his own game, so much the better.

Because she was such a child of impulse, so candid and so frank, Rowan worried lest her indiscretions should be noticed. He did not like to interfere, but he considered dropping a hint to Larry that he was needed at the Open ANC.

It was not necessary. Over the telephone one morning came news that Miss Morgan, who was still stopping at the dude ranch, had suffered a relapse and was not expected to live. Ruth fled at once to join her, and Larry discovered a few hours later that he was well enough to go home.

As Ruth nursed her aunt through the silent hours of the night, her mind was busy with her own shattered romance. She confessed to herself that she had not really been having a good time with Larry. She had turned to him as an escape and to punish her husband. But all the while her heart had been full of bitterness and desolation.

Miss Morgan died the third day after the arrival of her niece. In accord with a desire she had once expressed, she was buried in a grove back of the pasture at the ranch.

Ruth accepted the invitation of Mrs. Flanders to stay a few days at the dude ranch as her guest. The days lengthened into weeks, and still she did not return to the Circle Diamond. Larry made occasions to come to the hotel to see Ruth. Sometimes Rowan came, but not often. The gulf between him and his young wife had widened until he despaired of bridging it. He felt that the kindest thing he could do was to stay away. The whole passionate urge of his heart swept him toward her, but his iron will schooled his impulses to obedience.

But as Rowan rode the range, he carried with him the memory of a white face, fragile as a flower, out of which dark eyes looked at him defiantly. His heart ached for her. In his own breast he carried a block of ice that never melted, but he would gladly have taken her grief, too, if that had been possible.

IX

Ruth and Mrs. Flanders sat on the porch at Elkhorn Lodge and watched a rider descend a hill trail toward the ranch. It was late in the season. Except a hunting party, only a few stray boarders remained, and these would soon take flight for the cities. But in spite of the almanac the day had been hot. Even after sunset it was pleasant outdoors.

The rider announced his coming with song. For a fortnight he had been on the roundup, working sixteen hours a day, and now that it was nearly over he was entitled to sing. The words drifted down to the women on the porch.

> *Foot in the stirrup and hand on the horn,*
> *Best damned cowboy that ever was born.*

"It's Larry Silcott," announced Mrs. Flanders.

"Yes," assented Ruth. She had known for some moments that the approaching rider was Larry.

He offered for their entertainment another selection.

> *Sift along, boys, don't ride so slow.*
> *Haven't got much time but a long round to go.*
> *Quirt him on the shoulders and rake him down the*
> *   hip,*

I'll cut you toppy mounts, boys, now pair off and rip.

The young man appeared to catch sight of the women and waved his pinched-in felt hat at them, finishing his range ditty with a cowboy cheer for a rider to the last stanza.

> *Coma ti yi youpy ya youpy ya,*
> *Coma ti yi youpy, youpy, ya.*

He cantered up to the ranch, flung himself from the saddle, grounded the reins, and came forward to the porch with jingling spurs. Ruth did not deny that he was a most engaging youth.

"Is the roundup finished?" asked Mrs. Flanders.

"They've got to comb Eagle Creek yet and the Flat Top." He fell into the drawl of the old cowman. "But I'm plumb fed up with the dust of the drag driver. Me, I'm through. The boys can finish without Larry Silcott."

> *Oh, I'm going home*
> *Bullwhacking for to spurn,*
> *I ain't got a nickel,*
> *And I don't give a darn.*

"You seem to have quite an attack of yodeling tonight," suggested Ruth.

"Yodeling nothing. Every one of 'em is a range classic. I got them from old Sam Yerby, who brought them up from Texas," defended Larry.

"Who is boss of the roundup this year?" asked Mrs. Flanders.

"Rowan is, and believe me he worked us for a fare-you-well. He's some driver, Mac is. I'm a wreck."

"What's that I hear about Falkner and Tait having some more trouble?"

"Trouble is right, Missus Flanders. They met over by the

creek at Three Willows. One thing led to another, and they both got down from their horses and mixed it. Tait had one of his herders with him, and he took a hand in the fracas. The two of them gave Falkner an awful beating. He was just able to crawl to his horse."

"Tait ought to be driven out of the country," pronounced Mrs. Flanders indignantly. "He's always making trouble."

"Joe is certainly a bad actor, but it would be some job to drive him away. If Falkner ever gets him at the wrong end of a gun. . . ." He left his sentence unfinished. The imagination could supply the rest.

"They say Tait has driven his sheep across the deadline again?" Mrs. Flanders put her statement as if it were a question.

Larry, recalling a warning he had been given, became suddenly discreet. "Do they?"

"Will the Hill Creek cattlemen stand for it?"

There was a sullen, mulish look on his face that suggested he knew more than he intended to tell. "Maybe they will. Maybe they won't."

Business called the mistress of Elkhorn Lodge into the house.

Larry settled himself comfortably on the porch against a pillar. "I want to ask your advice. I'm just a plain cowpuncher and you're a wise young lady from a city. So you can tell me all about it. I'm getting old and lonesome, and my mind has been running on a girl a heap."

Ruth's glance took in the slim, wiry youth at her feet. She smiled. "You'd better ask Missus Flanders. I'm too young to advise you."

"No. You're just the right age. I'll tell you about her. There never was anybody prettier . . . not in Wyoming. She's fresh and sweet like those wild roses we picked in Bear Creek Cañon. Her eyes are kind o' rippled by a laugh 'way down deep in them, then sometimes they are dark and still and . . . sort of tender.

She has the kindest heart in the world . . . and the cruelest. I wouldn't want a better partner, though she's as wild as an unbroken bronc' sometimes. You never can tell when she's going to bolt."

There was a faint flush of pink in her cheeks, but her eyes danced. "You don't make her sound like a really nice girl."

"Oh, she's nice enough, when she isn't a little devil. The trouble is, she isn't footloose."

"Of course she is tremendously in love with you."

"She likes me a heap better than she pretends."

"I'm sure she would adore you if she knew how modest you are," Ruth answered with amiable malice.

Silcott's gaze absorbed her dainty sweetness. He spoke with an emphasis of the cattleman's drawl.

"I'd like right well to take her up on my horse and ride away with her like that Lochinvar fellow did in the poetry book you lent me once . . . the one that busted up the wedding of the laggard guy and went a-fanning off with his girl behind him, whilst the no-'count bridegroom and her paw hollered help."

"Lochinvar? Oh, he's out of date."

"Maybe so. But it's a great thing to know when to butt in." He watched her covertly as he spoke.

"And when not to," added Ruth. "Come on. Let's go over to the mesa and look at the desert in the moonlight."

Beneath the stars this land of splintered peaks and ragged escarpments always took on a glory denied to it by day. The obscuration of detail, the vagueness of outline, lent magic to the hills. Below, the valley swam in a sheen of gleaming silver.

Ruth drew a deep breath of sensuous delight and lifted her face to the star-strewn sky. Her companion watched her, his eyes shining.

"The world's going to bed," she whispered. "It always says its prayers first . . . wonderful prayers full of the fragrance of roses and the sough of wind just touching the pines, and the far, far song of birds."

Larry slipped his big brown hand over her little one. "You're not happy," he told her bluntly.

He was one of those men whose attitude toward a young and attractive woman is always that of the lover, potential or actual. He was never quite satisfied until the talk became personal and intimate.

Ruth nodded agreement. She let her hand lie in his. Since her break with Rowan she was often the victim of moods when she craved a sympathy such as Larry offered, one that took her trouble for granted without discussing it.

"Why don't you chuck it all overboard and make a new start?" he asked her abruptly.

She looked at him, a little startled. He had never before made so direct a reference to her situation. "I don't care to talk about that."

"But you'll have to talk about it some time. You can't go on like this forever, and . . . you know I love you, that I'd do anything in the world for you."

"I know you talk a lot of foolishness, Larry," she retorted sharply. "I may be a goose, but I'm not silly enough to take you seriously all the time. Let's go back to the house."

"I don't see why you can't take me seriously," he said sulkily.

"Because you're only a boy. You think you want the moon, but you don't . . . at least the only reason you want it is because it's in somebody else's yard."

"It doesn't need to stay there always, does it?"

"That isn't a matter for you and me to discuss," she flashed at him with spirit. "Whenever I need your advice, I'll ask for it."

She led the way to the house, her slender limbs moving rhythmically with light grace. Larry walked beside her sullenly. What was the matter with her tonight? Last week she had almost let him kiss her. If she had held him back, still it had been with the promise in her manner that next time he might be more successful. But now she had pushed him back into the position of a friend rather than a lover.

Larry had no intention of being her friend. It was not in his horoscope to be merely a friend to any charming woman. Moreover, he was as much in love with Ruth as he could be with anybody except himself.

Just before they reached the porch, she asked him a question: "When will they be through with the roundup?"

"In two or three days. Why?"

"I just wondered."

Her eyes evaded his. His annoyance flashed suddenly into words.

"If it's Rowan you want, why don't you go back to him like a good, little girl and say you're sorry? I expect he would forgive you."

Anger, sudden and imperious, leaped into her eyes. "I wish you'd learn, Larry Silcott, to mind your own business." She turned and fled into the house.

X

Nowhere outside of cattle land would such a scene have been possible. The air was filled with the fine dust of milling cattle, with the sound of bawling cows and blatting calves. Hundreds of them, rounded up on the Flat Top and driven down Eagle Creek, were huddled in a draw fenced by a score of lean, brown horsemen.

Now and again one of the leggy hill steers made a dash for freedom. The nearest cowpuncher wheeled his horse as on a half dollar, gave chase, and headed the animal back into the herd. Three of the old stockmen rode in and out among the packed cattle, deciding on the ownership of stray calves. These were cut out, roped, and branded on the spot.

Everybody was busy, everybody cheerful. These riders had for weeks been in the saddle eighteen hours out of the twenty-four. They were grimy with dust, hollow-eyed from want of sleep. But every chap-clad, sun-baked horseman was hard as nails and tough as leather. To feel the press of a saddle under his knees in all this clamor and confusion was worth a month of ordinary life to a cowpuncher.

McCoy, since he was boss of the roundup, was chief of the board of arbiters. An outsider would have been hopelessly at a loss to decide what cow was the mother of each lost and bewildered calf. But these experts guessed right ninety-nine times out of a hundred.

"Goes with the big bald-faced cow . . . D Bar Lazy R brand," was the verdict of Rowan as to one roan stray.

"You done said it, Mac," agreed Sam Yerby, chewing his quid of tobacco lazily.

The third judge, Brad Rogers, of the Circle BR, nodded his head. Duncan King, whose father owned a ranch near the headwaters of Hill Creek, cut out the bawling little maverick for the branders.

While the outfit was at supper after the day's work, a man rode up to the chuck wagon and fell into the easy, negligent attitude of the range rider at rest.

"Hello, Larry! Come and get it!" shouted the cook, waving a beefsteak on the prong of a long fork.

Silcott slid from the saddle and joined the circle. He found a seat beside McCoy.

"I want to see you alone, Mac," he said in a low voice.

Rowan nodded, paid no more attention to him, and joined again in the general conversation. But presently he got up and strolled toward the remuda.

Larry casually joined him. "Tait has been across the deadline for two days, Mac. He's traveling straight for the Circle Diamond with fifteen hundred sheep. About a third of them belong to Gilroy. Joe has two herders with him."

"Where are they camped tonight?"

"At the foot of Bald Knob."

"Is Gilroy with them?"

"No. He was this morning, but he telephoned his wife from Westcliff that he would be home tonight."

The boss of the roundup looked away at the purple hills, his close-gripped jaw clamped tight, his eyes narrowed almost to slits.

"Drift back to the wagon, Larry, and tell Yerby and Rogers to drop out of the crowd and meet me here quietly."

"Sure." The younger man hung in the wind. "What are you going to do, Mac?"

"What would you do?"

Silcott broke into a sudden angry oath. "Do? I'd meet Joe Tait halfway. I'd show him whether he can spoil the range for us at his own sweet will. He wants war. By all that's holy, I'd carry it right into his camp."

Rowan did not deny to himself the seriousness of the issue as he waited for the coming of the two men. He faced the facts squarely, as he always did. Tait had again declared war. To let the man have his own way meant ruin to the cattle interests on the Fryingpan. For if one sheepman were permitted to invade the range, dozens of others would drive across into the forbidden territory. The big, fearless bully had called for a showdown. Let him win now, and it would be a question of months only until McCoy and his neighbors were sold out at a sheriff's sale.

Out of the darkness sauntered Yerby, followed presently by Rogers.

"What's on your mind, Mac?" drawled Yerby, splattering expertly with tobacco juice a flat rock shining in the moonlight.

Sam Yerby was an old cowman from Texas. As a youth he had driven cattle on the Chisholm Trail. Physically he was a wrinkled little man with a merry eye and a mild manner that was apt to deceive.

"Tait has crossed the deadline again. He is headed for the Thunder Mountain country."

Yerby rubbed a bristling cheek slowly with the palm of his hand. "Well, I'll be dog-goned. Looks like he's gone loco," he commented mildly.

The owner of the Circle BR broke into excited threats. "He'll never take his sheep back again . . . never in the world. I'll not stand for it . . . none of the boys will. Right now is when he gets all the trouble he wants."

"That your opinion, too, Sam?" asked Rowan quietly.

The faded blue eyes of the Texan had a far-away look. His fingers caressed a chin rough with gray stubbles. He was thinking of his young wife and his year-old baby. Their future depended upon his little cattle ranch.

"I reckon, Mac. We got to fight sometime. Might as well be right now."

"Tonight," agreed McCoy decisively. "We'll settle this before daybreak. We don't want too many in this thing. Five or six are enough."

"Here are three of your six," suggested Rogers.

"Larry Silcott is four. We've got to take Larry. He brought me the news."

"How about Dunc King? He's a good boy . . . absolutely on the square."

Rowan shook his head. "Let's keep Dunc out of this. You know what a good old lady Missus King is. We'll not take her only son into trouble. Besides, Dunc talks too much."

"Well, Jack Cole. He'll go through and padlock his mouth, too. I'd trust Jack to a finish."

"Cole is all right, Brad. You feel him out. Five of us are all that's needed. We'll meet at the Three Pines at midnight. Sam, you and Brad can decide to spend the night at home since we're camping so near your places. I'll drive my bunch of cows down to the Circle Diamond as an excuse to get away. I can take Jack and Larry with me to help. Probably you had better hang around till after we've gone a while."

The Circle Diamond cattle were cut out from the bunch and started homeward. Rowan, with Silcott and Cole to help him on the drive, vanished after them into the night.

"Funny Mac didn't start at sunset. What's the idea of waiting till night?" asked King of Falkner, who sat beside him at the campfire.

"Beats me." Falkner scowled at the leaping flames. His face was still decorated with half a dozen ugly cuts and as many bruises, souvenirs of his encounter with Tait. Just now he was full of suspicions, vague and indefinite as yet, but nonetheless active. For Larry had told him the news he had brought.

"Sing the old Chisholm Trail song, Sam," demanded a cowpuncher.

A chorus of shouts backed the request.

"Cain't you boys ever leave an old man alone?" complained Yerby. "I done bust my laig today when I fell offen that pinto. I've got a half notion to light a shuck for home and get Missie to rub on some o' that white liniment she makes. It's the healingest medicine ever I took."

"Don't be a piker, Sam. Sing for us."

"What'll I sing? I done sung that trail song yesterday."

"Anything. Leave it to you."

The old Texan piped up lugubriously, a twinkle in his tired eyes.

Come, all you old cowpunchers, a story I will tell,

81

And if you'll be quiet I'm sure I'll sing it well,
And if you boys don't like it, you sure can go to hell!

A shout of laughter greeted this unexpected proposition. "Fair enough."

"Go to it, Sam!"

"Give us the rest," urged the chap-clad young giants around the fire.

Yerby took up his theme in sing-song fashion, and went through the other stanzas, but, as he finished, he groaned again. "My laig sure is hurting like sixty. I'm going home. Wish one of you lads would run up a horse for me. Get the roan with the white stockings, if you can."

"I'll go with you, Sam," announced Rogers. "I'm expecting an important business letter and I expect it's waiting at the house for me. Be with you tomorrow, boys."

After they had gone, Falkner made comment to young King satirically: "What with busted legs and important letters and night drives, we're having quite an exodus from camp, wouldn't you say?"

"Looks like," agreed King. "That's the way with married men. They got always to be recollecting home ties."

"That's your notion, is it?" jeered Falkner. "Why, yes, you see, it's different here. They got a hen on. That's what's the matter with them."

"Whajamean, a hen on?" King leaned forward, eyes sparkling, cigarette half rolled. If there was anything doing, he wanted to know all about it.

"Larry let it out to me at supper. He was so full of it he couldn't hold it in. Tait crossed the deadline again."

"No?" The word was a question, not a denial. Young King's eyes were wide with excitement. This was not merely diverting news. It might turn out to be explosive drama.

"I'm telling you, boy." Falkner rapped out an annoyed

impatient oath. "They left me out of it. Why? I got as good a right to know what's doing as any of 'em. More, by God!" He touched the scars on his face, and his eyes flamed to savage anger.

"What do you reckon Mac aims to do?" asked King.

"I reckon he means to raid Tait's herd. Can't be anything else. But I mean to find out. Right now I'm declaring myself in."

The campfire circle broke up, and the cowpunchers rolled into their blankets. Falkner did not stay in his long. He slipped out to the remuda and slapped a saddle on one of his cow ponies. The explanation he gave to the night herders was that he was going to ride down to Bovier's Camp to get some tobacco.

He struck the trail of McCoy's bunch of cows and followed across the hills. Within the hour he heard the lowing of cattle, and felt sure that he was on the heels of those he followed. From the top of the next ridge he looked down upon them in the valley below.

This was enough for Falkner. Evidently Rowan intended to get the cattle to his corral before any move was made against Tait. The range rider swung to the right across the brow of the hill, dipped into the next valley, struck a trail that zigzagged up the shale slope opposite, and by means of it came, after an hour of stiff riding, to the valley where the Triangle Dot Ranch had its headquarters.

He tied his horse in a pine grove and stole silently down to the bunkhouse. This he circled, came to the front door on his tiptoes, and entered noiselessly. A man lay sleeping on one of the farther bunks, arms flung wide in the deep slumber of fatigue.

Falkner reached for a rifle resting on a pair of elk horns attached to the wall, and took from one of the tines an ammunition belt. He turned, knocked over in the darkness a chair, and fled into the night with the rifle in one hand, the belt in the other.

Reaching the pine grove, he remounted, skirted the lip of the valley, and struck at its mouth the trail to the Circle Diamond. Three quarters of an hour later he was lying on the edge of a hill pocket above that ranch with his eyes fastened to the moonlit corral in which stood two saddled horses.

The moon was just going under a cloud when Rowan and his two companions rode away from the Circle Diamond. They had plenty of time before the appointed hour at the Three Pines. Since they expected to ride hard during the night, they now took a leisurely road gait in and out among the hills.

Yerby and Rogers were waiting for them beneath the largest of the big pines.

"Better 'light, boys," suggested the Texan. "I reckon we might as well kinder talk things over. We aim to bend the law considerable tonight. If any of you lads is feeling tolerable anxious, he'd better burn the wind back to camp. Old Man Trouble is right ahead of us on the trail. Now's the time to holler. No use bellyaching when it's too late."

"Think we're quitters?" Larry demanded indignantly.

"No, son, I don't allow you are. If I did you can bet them fifteen-dollar boots of yours that you or Sam Yerby wouldn't be here. What I'm saying is that this is serious business. Take a good, square look at it before you-all go ahead."

"Sam's quite right," assented McCoy. "We're going on a sheep raid, and against a desperate man. We're going to kill his sheep . . . ride them down . . . stampede them. It's not a nice business, and the law is dead against us. I don't like it a bit, but I'm going because it is the only way to pound sense into Tait's fool head. We've got to do it or shut up shop."

Rowan spoke with a gravity that carried conviction. He was a man notable even in that country that bred strong men.

"I stand pat," said Silcott.

Cole nodded agreement.

"Good enough. But understand this . . . we're not man-killers. Tait is a bad lot, all right, but we're not out to get him. We're going to mask, surprise the camp, hold it up, do our business, then get out. Is that plain?"

"Listens fine," assented Yerby with a grin. "But what have you arranged for Tait to be doing while you-all is making him a prisoner?"

"He'll be sleeping, Sam. Here's the layout. One of the herders and the dogs will be with the sheep. We'll slip right up to the wagon and capture Tait first thing. He's a heavy sleeper . . . always was. Once we get him the rest will be easy."

The Texan nodded. "Ought to go through as per plan if the sheep are far enough from the wagon."

"They'll be far enough away so that the dogs won't bark at us."

"Who is that?" cried Rogers, pointing to the trail below.

All of them with one consent stopped to watch the horseman riding up out of the darkness.

"It's Hal Falkner," Cole cried in a low voice.

"Falkner! What's he doing here?" demanded McCoy. He whirled on Silcott. "Did you tell him where we were tonight, Larry?"

"No, I didn't."

"You told him something . . . that Tait had crossed the deadline and was heading for Thunder Mountain."

"I might have said that," admitted Silcott a little sulkily.

"Did you tell anyone else?"

"No. What's ailing you, Mac?"

"Just this, I don't want to go to the penitentiary because you can't keep your mouth shut, Larry. Falkner is the last man you ought to have told. I don't want him with us tonight. He's too anxious to get at Tait."

"Oh, well, I guess he'll be reasonable."

Falkner rode up the trail out of the shadowy gloom. "Thought you'd lose me, did you? Fine stuff, boys. How's your busted leg, Sam?"

"What do you want, Hal?" asked Rowan curtly.

"Me, Mac? Same as you. I want to shoot some pills into Mary's little lambs. Did you think I was riding for my health?"

"We don't want you along with us. Our party's made up."

"Short and sweet, Mac. What's the objection to my company?" demanded Falkner frostily.

"No personal objection whatever, Hal. But we don't want anyone along that has a grudge at Tait. We're fighting for the range, and we don't intend to settle any individual scores."

"Suits me. I expect I can square accounts with Joe Tait at the proper time without lugging all you fellows along."

McCoy looked directly at him. "This party is ducking trouble, not looking for it, Hal. We intend to get the drop on Tait and hold him prisoner till we're through. Our only targets will be sheep."

"Fine. I'll take orders from you tonight, Rowan."

"That makes everything all right then," put in Larry cheerfully.

McCoy still hesitated. He knew of Falkner's gusty and ungovernable temper.

"Oh, let him go," decided Rogers impatiently. "One more won't do any harm, and we might need him. Falkner isn't a fool. He knows we can't afford to shoot up Tait or his men."

"Sure I know it. What's the use of so much beefing? I'm going with you, whether or no."

"Looks like our anxious friend has elected himself one of us,"

Sam assented amiably.

Rowan was outvoted. He shrugged and, against his better judgment, gave up the point.

They rode hard across a rough, hilly country. The moon had gone under scudding clouds. It had turned a good deal colder, and there was a feel of rain in the air.

The time was 2:30 when Rogers struck a match and looked at his watch.

"Bald Knob is less than a mile from here," said McCoy. "We'll mask now in case we should bump into the camp sooner than we expect. Think we'd better cut out talking. We've got to surprise them. If we don't, Tait will fight and that isn't what we want."

He drew from his pocket half a dozen bandannas. Each man made and fitted his own mask from a handkerchief.

They rode cautiously now, one after the other in single file. From a ridge McCoy pointed out the sheep camp at the foot of Bald Knob.

"We'll leave our horses in that clump of pines and creep forward to the wagons," he gave directions. "Remember, boys. No shooting. We're going to get the drop on Tait and take him prisoner. If we can't do that, the raid is off. We're not killing human beings. Get that, Hal."

Falkner nodded sulkily. "I told you I was taking orders from you tonight, Mac."

Under cover of a hill they rode into the pines and tied their horses. McCoy deployed his men in such a way that they could move toward the camp in a half circle. He put Cole on the extreme left, and next to him Yerby, Rogers, Silcott, and Falkner in the order named. Rowan chose the place on the right for himself, because it was nearest the wagons. He stationed Falkner near to him so that he could keep an eye on him.

The raiders crept forward slowly through the brush. McCoy,

as he moved forward, took advantage of all the cover he could find. He could see Falkner as a dark shadow over to his left. Silcott was lost in the gloom.

The sound of a shot shattered the stillness. Falkner, the rifle in his hand smoking, let out the exultant "Yip—yip!" of a cowboy.

"Back to cover, boys!" yelled Rowan instantly. He stumbled on a clump of grass and went down. Before he reached his feet again the tragedy was under way. Another shot rang out—a third—and a fourth.

Tait, revealed by a fugitive moon that had escaped from behind scudding clouds, was in the door of the wagon, as he had often promised. The rifle in his hands was pumping lead at the foes advancing toward him from the brush. Flashes in the darkness told Rowan that the cattlemen were answering his fire.

The head of the big sheepman lurched forward, and the rifle slid from his hands out of the wagon to the ground. At the same moment another man leaped from the wagon and started to run.

"Stop firing!" ordered McCoy sharply.

He ran forward to protect the retreat of the sheepman, but he was too late. Falkner fired. The running figure doubled up like a jack rabbit and went down, headfirst.

McCoy plunged straight for the second wagon. He could hear a herder tumbling hastily out of it, and he stood directly between the man and Falkner. The runner was, he knew, scuttling into the brush for safety.

"Let him go. Don't shoot, Hal!" shouted McCoy.

Falkner, panting, eyes burning with the lust of battle, pulled up beside Rowan.

"What'd you get in my way for?" he cried excitedly. "We got to make a clean sweep now. Got to do it to save ourselves."

"No. You can't get the others without getting me first." Mc-

Coy's voice rang, sharp and dominant.

"But, man, don't you see we've got to destroy the evidence against us? Leggo my arm."

Rowan's fingers had fastened upon the wrist of the other like steel clamps. His steady eyes were deadly in their intentness "You've got to kill me before you kill them. Understand?"

Yerby had reached the wagon. He spoke up at once: "Mac is right. We've done too much killing already. Good Lord, how did it start?"

Falkner opened his lips to speak, then closed them again. He looked at McCoy and waited savagely for the accusation. But none came. Rowan said nothing.

"First I knew Tait was in the wagon door with his gun and we were all shooting. But someone fired first and brought him out from the wagon. It came from the right. Who was it, Mac?" demanded Rogers.

Cole and Silcott joined them. They had been examining the fallen men.

"Both of them are dead," said Cole.

"I can't hardly believe it. But it's so. A bullet got Gilroy right through the heart."

Rowan looked up quickly. He was white to the lips. "Gilroy? Did we kill Gilroy?" He turned to Larry. "I thought you said he went home today."

"He telephoned his wife he would be home tonight. Must have changed his mind."

"It cost him his life, poor devil," Rogers broke out.

"I ain't so sure it won't cost us ours," added Yerby quietly. "If I'd known Gilroy was here tonight, Sam Yerby wouldn't have gone riding."

"That's right," agreed Cole. "Tait is one proposition . . . Gilroy is another. This whole country is going to buzz now. He has hundreds of friends."

All of them recognized the truth of this.

The death of Tait alone would have stirred resentment. But Gilroy was an old-timer, a quiet, well-respected man who had friends.

"Who killed him?" asked Rogers again. "Who started this shooting? That's what I want to know."

Rowan answered quietly: "The less we know about that the better, boys. We're all tied up together in this. In the excitement some of us have gone too far. That can't be helped now. We've got to see it out together . . . got to stand back of each other. Before the law we're all guilty. The only thing to do is to let tonight's work be a mystery that is never solved. We'll fix up a story and all stand by it."

Yerby broke a long silence. "Well, boys, we better make our getaway. A whole passel of sheriffs will be combing these hills for us soon. I reckon we had better fix up our alibis and then burn the wind for home."

"Can't start pushing on our reins any too quick to suit me," Cole assented.

"That's the only thing to do," agreed McCoy. "Sam, you and Brad had better get back to your homes, where you've been sleeping all night if anyone asks you. Falkner, you go back with us to the ranch. We'll fix up a story about how you joined us there and bunked with Jack and Larry."

"What about these?" Rogers indicated with his hand the sprawling bodies of the sheepmen. His voice was a whisper.

"We can't do anything for them," answered Rowan. "We've got to think of ourselves. If we talk, if we make any mistakes, we're going to pay the price of what we've done. We can't explain we didn't intend to kill anyone. We're all in this. The only thing to do is to stand together and keep our mouths shut."

Everybody was in a sudden hurry to be gone. They tramped back to the pine grove, and hurriedly mounted, eager to put as many miles as possible between them and what was lying at the foot of Bald Knob.

A light snow was already falling. They welcomed it for the protection it offered.

"We've bumped into good luck to start with," said Larry to Cole. "The snow will blot out our tracks. They can't trail us now."

Cole nodded. "Yep. That's so."

But the thing that had been done chilled their spirits, and the dread as to what was to come of it rested like a weight upon their hearts. Mile after mile they rode, swiftly and silently.

The party broke up at the Three Pines after a hurried agreement as to plans. They were all to meet at the roundup. None of them was to know anything about the raid until news of it came to the camp from outside.

Yerby and Rogers rode into the hills, the rest down to the Circle Diamond.

They covered the ground fast, so as to get into the house before anyone was astir with the coming day. Already gray was sifting into the sky, a warning that the night was ending.

Larry, riding beside McCoy, looked furtively at him and asked a question just as they came in sight of the ranch.

"Who shot Gilroy, Mac?"

Rowan looked at him with bleak, expressionless eyes. "We all did."

"Yes, but. . . ." His whisper died away.

"None of us knows who fired the shot. It doesn't matter. Never forget one thing, Larry. We're all in the same boat. We sink or swim together."

"Sure. But whoever it was. . . ."

"We don't know who it was," McCoy lied. "We're not going to try to find out. Forget that, Larry."

They stabled their horses and stole into the bunkhouse.

Fortunately it was empty, Rowan's men being at the roundup. McCoy left them there and returned to the house.

He met Mrs. Stovall in the corridor. She was on her way to the kitchen to begin the day's work.

"I've been out looking at one of the horses," McCoy explained. "Colic, looks like."

The housekeeper made no comment. It passed through her mind that it was odd he should take his rifle out with him to look at a sick horse.

XI

Rowan closed the door of his bedroom with a sick heart. It was characteristic of him that he did not debate his responsibility for the death of the two sheepmen. It did not matter that he had repeatedly warned his friends not to shoot or that from the beginning to the end of the affair he had not fired his rifle. He could not escape the conviction of guilt by pleading to himself that but for the heady folly of one man the raid would have worked out as planned. Nor did it avail to clear him that he had tried to save the life of Gilroy and had protected the herder from the blood lust of Falkner. Before the law he was a murderer. He had led a band of raiders to an attack in which two men had died.

The rock upon which the venture had split was Falkner's uncontrolled venom. But for that first shot and the triumphant shout of vengeance Tait could have been captured and held safely a prisoner. Now they all stood within the shadow of the gallows.

The shock of Gilroy's death was for the time deadened to McCoy by the obligation that lay on him to look out for the safety of his associates. The cattleman did not deceive himself for an instant. The days when men could ride to lawless murder in Wyoming were past. Shoshone County would flame with

92

indignation at the outrage. A deep cry for justice upon the guilty would run from border to border.

Beyond doubt suspicion would be directed toward them on account of their absence from the roundup camp at the time of the raid. But unless some of them talked there could be no proof. The snow had turned out only a flurry of an inch or two, but it was not likely Matson could reach Bald Knob before night. This would give them till tomorrow morning, by which time the trail would be obliterated.

Rowan had collected all of the bandannas used as masks. He intended to burn them in the kitchen stove as he passed through to breakfast. It could not be proved that Rogers and Yerby had not slept at home unless their wives got to gossiping, nor that the others had not spent the night at the Circle Diamond. On the whole they were as safe as men could be who stood over a powder mine that might be fired at any moment.

When the breakfast bell sounded, McCoy descended by the back stairs to the kitchen. Mrs. Stovall was just putting a batch of biscuits into the oven.

"Would you mind stepping outside and ringing the bell, Missus Stovall?" Rowan asked. "Three of the boys are sleeping in the bunkhouse. They stayed there last night after we drove the bunch of cows home."

As soon as his housekeeper had left the room, McCoy stepped to the stove, lifted a lid, and stuffed six colored handkerchiefs into the fire. When Mrs. Stovall returned, he was casting a casual eye over the pantry.

"Not short of any supplies, are you, Missus Stovall?"

"I'm almost out of sugar and lard."

"Better make out a list. I've got to send one of the boys to Wagon Wheel with the team tomorrow."

The burden of keeping up a pretense of conversation at breakfast rested upon the host and Jack Cole. Silcott was jumpy with nerves, and Falkner was gloomy. As soon as he was alone with the men on the trail to the roundup camp McCoy brought them to time.

"This won't do, boys. You've got to buck up and act as usual. You look as if you were riding to your own funeral, Hal. You're just as bad, Larry. Both of you have criminal written all over you. Keep your grins working."

"What am I to do with this gun?" demanded Falkner abruptly. "I got it last night from the bunkhouse at the Triangle Dot."

"Did anybody see you get it?"

"No."

"We'll have to bury it. You can't take it into camp with you."

With their knives they dug a shallow ditch back of a big rock and in it hid the rifle. The ammunition belt was put beside it.

It was perhaps fortunate that by the time they reached camp the riders had scattered to comb Plum Creek for cattle. Rowan sent his companions out to join the drive, while he waited in camp for a talk with Rogers and Yerby, neither of whom had yet arrived.

About noon the two hill cattlemen rode into the draw. The men met in the presence of the cook. They greeted each other with the careless aplomb of the old-timer.

" 'Lo, Mac."

" 'Lo, Sam . . . Brad. How's every little thing?"

"Fine. Missie done fixed my game leg up with that ointment good as new. I want to tell you-all that girl is a wiz," bragged Yerby, firing his tobacco juice at a white rock and making a center shot.

McCoy breathed freer. Yerby and Rogers could be depended upon to go through the ordeal before them with cool imperturbability.

Late in the afternoon the bawling of thirsty cattle gave notice that the gathered stock was nearing camp. Not until the stars were out was there a moment's rest for anybody.

Supper was eaten by the light of the moon. During this meal a horseman rode up and nodded a greeting.

Young King caught sight of him first. "Hello, Sheriff?" he shouted gaily. "Which of us do you want? And what have we been doing now?"

Rowan's heart sank. Matson had beaten the time he had allowed him by nearly twenty-four hours. But he turned a wooden face and a cool, impassive eye upon the sheriff.

" 'Lo, Aleck. Won't you 'light?"

"Reckon I will, Mac."

The sheriff swung from his horse stiffly and came forward into the firelight. At least six pairs of eyes watched him closely, but the tanned, leathery face of the officer told nothing.

"Anything new, Matson?" demanded a young cowpuncher. "Don't forget we've been off the map 'most three weeks. Who's eloped, absconded, married, divorced, or otherwise played billiards with the Ten Commandments?"

Matson sat down, tailor fashion, and accepted the steak, bread, and coffee offered him.

"The only news on tap when I left town was that the Limited got in on time . . . yesterday. Few will believe it, but it's an honest-to-goodness fact. We had it sworn to before a notary."

It happened that Sheriff Matson had been in the hills on official business and slept at Bovier's Camp the night of the sheep raid. He was by custom an early riser. The sky was faintly pink with the warning of a coming sun when he had stepped out of the house to wash. As he dried his face there came to him the sound of dragging steps and labored breathing.

Matson had turned. A pallid little man sank down on the step and buried his face in his hands.

"What's up?" demanded the officer.

The panting man lifted to him eyes that still mirrored the fear of death. "They . . . they've killed Tait and Gilroy."

"Who?"

"Raiders."

"When?"

"This morning . . . two hours ago." A shiver shook the fellow like a heavy chill. "My God . . . it was awful!" he gasped.

The sheriff let fall a strong, brown hand on his shoulder. "Tell me about it, Purdy. You were there at the time?"

The man nodded assent. He swallowed a lump in his dry throat and explained: "I been herding for Tait. We bedded at Bald Knob last night. They . . . shot up the camp and killed Tait and Gilroy."

"Just where was the camp?"

"Right at the foot of Bald Knob."

"Did you recognize any of the raiders?"

"No. They wore masks."

"How many were there?"

"About twenty . . . maybe twenty-five." The cool, hard eyes of the sheriff narrowed to slits.

With the news that had just come to him he was a changed man. The careless good nature was sponged from his face.

A few more sharp, incisive questions told him all Purdy knew. He got Wagon Wheel on the long-distance, and rang his deputy up from sleep.

"There's been a killing at Bald Knob, Lute. Drop everything else. Get together half a dozen men and ride up to Bovier's Camp. Bring supplies for several days. Wait at the camp until you hear from me. Tait and Gilroy killed. By cattlemen, looks like. I'll know more about that later."

He ate a hurried breakfast and struck across country for the raided sheep camp.

As soon as he came in sight of the sheep camp, Matson dismounted and tied his horse. He had to pick up a cold trail covered with snow. The fewer unnecessary tracks the better.

The bodies of the sheepmen lay where they had fallen, a light mantle of snow sheeting the still forms. Three empty shells lay close to the rifle of Tait, but Gilroy's gun had not been fired. It was lying in the wagon.

The sun had already melted most of the snow, and for hours Matson quartered over the ground, examining tracks that the untrained eye would never have seen.

The boot tracks, faint though they were, led him to the pine grove where the horses had been tethered.

With amazing pains he traced the retreat of the raiders to the Three Pines. It was a very difficult piece of trailing, for the snow had wiped out the tracks entirely for stretches of hundreds of yards. Once it was a splash of tobacco juice on a flat rock that told him he was still on the heels of those he wanted. In Shoshone County men will still tell you that Aleck Matson's feat of running down the night raiders in spite of an intervening snowstorm was the best bit of trailing they ever knew.

From the Three Pines the tracks of most of the party took the sheriff straight to the Circle Diamond Ranch. He dropped in just in time to join Mrs. Stovall at her midday dinner.

They exchanged the casual gossip of the neighborhood. Presently he steered the talk in the direction he wanted.

"Mac is up at the roundup, I reckon."

"Yes. He drove a bunch of cattle down last night."

"So? Any of the boys with him?"

"Three of them. They stayed in the bunkhouse."

"I've been wanting to see Art Philips. Was he one of them?"

"No. Young Silcott and Jack Cole and Hal Falkner."

"Went back this morning, did they?" asked Matson casually.

"Right after breakfast."

"Jack Cole was talking about trading me a Winchester. Don't suppose he had it with him."

"No. Hal Falkner had one. A deer had been seen near camp, and he brought it on the chance he might see it again."

"Oh, yes, Mac was going to show me one of his guns next time I came up to the ranch. I don't suppose. . . ."

"All his guns are in that little room off the living room, as Missus McCoy calls the parlor. Go in and look 'em over if you like."

The sheriff thanked her and availed himself of the chance. When he came out, he found Mrs. Stovall clearing off the table.

"I'll be moving along, Missus Stovall. Much obliged for that peach cobbler like Mother used to make."

On his way to the stable Matson dropped in at the bunkhouse. He made the discovery that at least one of McCoy's guests had lain on top of the blankets and not under them. Nor had he taken the trouble to remove his boots.

The officer smiled, thinking: *Just made a bluff of lying down . . . figured it wasn't worthwhile taking off his boots for a few minutes. I'll bet that was Falkner. He's a roughneck, anyhow.*

Matson rode back to the Three Pines, and from there followed the trail of the two horses that had turned into the hills at this point. By the middle of the afternoon it brought him to the Circle BR, a ranch that nestled at the foot of the big peaks in a little mountain park.

It took no clairvoyant to see that Mrs. Rogers was not glad to see him. Unless her face libeled her, she had been weeping. Her eyes flew a flag of alarm as soon as they fell upon him.

" 'Afternoon, Missus Rogers. Brad home?"

"No. He's at the roundup."

"Gone back, has he?"

She considered a moment before a reluctant yes fell from her lips.

The sheriff smiled grimly as he rode across the hills. He had five of the raiders identified already—five out of either six or seven, he wasn't quite sure which.

He intended that this should be the last night raid ever made in Shoshone County. Unless the district attorney fell down on his job, more than one of the Bald Knob raiders would end with a rope around his throat.

Yet Matson was puzzled. McCoy had been the leader of the group. There could be no doubt about that. His was far and away the strongest personality. And McCoy usually thought straight. He did not muddle his brain with false reasoning. How, then, had he come to do such a thing?

As the sheriff sat by the campfire at the roundup later, it was even more difficult to think of this clean, level-eyed boss of the roundup as an ambusher by night. The whole record of the man rose up to give the lie to the story that he had ridden out to kill his foe in the dark. While Sam Yerby entertained the boys with one of his trail songs, Matson's mind was going over the facts he had gathered.

> *Whoopie ti yi yo, git along, little dogies,*
> *It's your misfortune and none of my own.*
> *Whoopee ti yi yo, git along, little dogies,*
> *For you know Wyoming will be your new home.*

Sam looked around carefully, selected a flat rock at the edge of the fire, and slashed the center of it accurately with tobacco juice. Give him a chew of tobacco as a weapon and the Texan was the champion shot of Wyoming.

Matson was no longer thinking of McCoy. From the shadow where he lounged, his narrow eyes watched Yerby intently.

He had not moved a muscle of his big body, but every nerve had suddenly grown taut. For he guessed now who the sixth man was that had ridden on the sheep raid. Sam's habit of selecting a rock target for his tobacco juice had betrayed him.

XII

Like wildfire the news spread through western Wyoming that Tait and Gilroy had been shot down in their sheep wagon by night raiders. Soon there was no ranch so deep-hidden in the hills, no herder's camp so remote that the story had not been carried there.

Furtive whispers of names began to be heard. That of Falkner was mentioned first. Then the murmured gossip took up the name of McCoy, added shortly to it those of Cole and Silcott. It was known that all four of the suspected men had been absent from the roundup the night of the killing. By their own statements they had all been together during the hours when the raid took place.

Meanwhile, Sheriff Matson moved about his business of gathering evidence with relentless singleness of purpose. He, too, heard whispers and followed them to sources. He rode up and down the country piecing this and that together until he had a net of circumstance encircling the guilty ones.

From one of the herders who McCoy had saved he gathered valuable information. The man had been awakened by the sound of firing. He had run to the door of the wagon in time to see Gilroy shot down. The herder had been saved by one of the attackers who had stood between him and another and prevented the second man from murdering him. The first man had called the other one Hal. The raiders were all masked and he had not recognized any of them.

One of the whispers Matson heard took him to Dunc King. That young man had, as usual, been talking too much. The sheriff found him at his mother's ranch mending a piece of broken fence.

" 'Lo, Dunc. How's everything?" the officer asked by way of greeting.

The young man looked at him with suspicion and alarm. "Why, all right, I reckon. How's cases with you, Sheriff?"

"I hear you had a little talk with Hal Falkner the night of the raid. Do you remember exactly what he said to you?"

"Why, no. I don't remember a thing about it," the young man returned uneasily. He knew his tongue had once more tripped him up.

"Better sharpen up your memory. How about it, Dunc? You want to be an accessory to this crime?"

"No, sir, an' I ain't aiming to be, either. If I knew anything I'd tell you, but I can't tell you what I don't know, can I?"

The young man was no match for the sheriff. Before Matson had left the place he knew all that King did.

Forty-eight hours later the sheriff with a posse rode up to the Circle Diamond Ranch. Rowan McCoy was sitting on the porch, oiling a gun. The first glance told him that Matson had two prisoners, the second that they were Falkner and Silcott.

Matson swung from the saddle and came up the steps to the porch.

"I've got bad news for you, Mac," he said bluntly. "You're under arrest."

The cattleman did not bat an eye. "What for?" he asked evenly.

"For killing Gilroy and Tait."

"The damn' fool's going around arresting everybody he knows, Mac," broke in Falkner.

McCoy observed that Falkner was handcuffed and that Silcott was not.

He asked the sheriff a question. "Do I understand that you've arrested Hal an' Larry for this, too?"

"Yes, Mac. Larry behaved sensible an' promised not to make any trouble, so I aim to be as easy on him as I can. Falkner had other notions. He tried to make a gun play."

"You taking us to Wagon Wheel, Aleck?"

"Yes."

"You have a warrant for my arrest?"

The officer showed the warrant and Rowan glanced over it.

"All right," said McCoy. "I'll saddle up an' be ready in a jiffy."

"No need for that, Mac. Fact is, I'm not quite ready to start. Got a little more business to do first. If you don't mind, I'll make the Circle Diamond my headquarters for a few hours," Matson proposed amiably.

The owner of the ranch answered pleasantly but perhaps with a touch of sarcasm. "Anything you say, Aleck. If your boys are here at dinnertime, I expect Missus Stovall can fix you-all up."

"Sure, Mac, an' if he needs horses or guns, probably you can lend him a few," Falkner added with an oath.

"No use getting annoyed, Hal," the ranch owner said quietly. "Aleck has to make his play. He's not arresting us for pleasure. I reckon he thinks he's got some evidence, or maybe he wants to scare us into thinking he has some."

"You'll find I've got evidence aplenty, Mac," the sheriff answered mildly. "No hard feelings, you understand. All in the way of business. I'm leaving three of the boys here, Mac. Be back here myself in a few hours, I reckon. If I don't get back, I've arranged for you to make a start for town about two o'clock. That agreeable to you?"

"Any time that suits you," McCoy answered.

The sheriff was back within the specified time limit. He brought with him Rogers and Yerby. From a remark he dropped later McCoy learned that Cole had been arrested earlier in the day at Wagon Wheel.

"You're making quite a gather, Aleck," said Rogers. "There are several other ranchmen up here you've overlooked. How about them?"

"I've got all I want for the present, Brad," the sheriff replied.

His manner was not reassuring, nor was the fact that he had picked out and arrested just the six men who had been engaged in the night raid.

Silcott was plainly down-hearted. McCoy maneuvered so that he rode beside him when they took the road.

"Don't you worry, Larry," the older man said in a cheerful voice, but one so low that it carried only to the ears of the man it addressed. "He can't make his case stick, if we all stand pat on our story."

"I'm not worried, Mac, but he must know something or he wouldn't be arresting us. That's a cinch."

"He knows a little, an' guesses a lot more, an' figures probably that there's a quitter among us. That's where his case will break down. All we've got to do is to keep mum. In a week or so we'll be riding the range again."

"Yes," agreed Larry, but without conviction.

Yet though the public was in a measure prepared, there was a gasp of surprise when the word spread that Sheriff Matson had arrested and brought to Wagon Wheel six cattlemen from the Hill Creek district. McCoy and Rogers were so well and favorably known that the charge of murder against them set tongues buzzing far and wide. Yerby had not been so long in the district, but he, too, bore the best of reputations. By reason of his riding and his gay good-fellowship Larry Silcott was a favorite with the young people. In the cattle country, where he was best known, Jack Cole's character was as good as a letter of credit. Of the six, Falkner alone bore a rather doubtful reputation.

When the news of the arrests reached the dude ranch, Ruth was out on the mesa doing a sketch of the sunset. She was not really painting to any purpose, but had come out to be alone. Just below the mesa the valley lay in a golden harmony of color beneath a sky soft with rain clouds. It was a picture that just now filled Ruth with deep peace. The brush lay idle in her fingers, and on the face of the girl was a soft and rapt exaltation.

She had a secret. Sometimes it filled her with a wild and tremulous delight. Again she stood before it with awe and even terror. More than once in the night she had found herself weeping with poignant self-pity. There were hours when her whole soul cried out for Rowan, and others when she hated him with all the passionate intensity of her untutored heart.

A chill wind from the snow peaks swept the mesa. Ruth gathered up her belongings and walked back to the house. She slipped in quietly by the back door, intent on reaching her room unnoticed. As she passed the door of the big lounging room, the voice of Tim Flanders boomed out: "I tell you that if McCoy led that raid, there was no intention of killing Tait and Gilroy. I've known Mac twenty-five years. He's white clear through."

Ruth wheeled into the room instantly. She went straight to Flanders. "Who says Rowan led that raid?" she demanded, white to the lips.

There was a long moment of silence. Then: "He'll clear himself," Flanders replied lamely.

The young wife had not known her husband was even suspected. She caught the back of a chair with a grip so tight that the knuckles lost their color.

"Tell me . . . tell me what you mean."

He tried to break it gently, but blundered out that the sheriff had to arrest somebody and had chosen McCoy among others.

"Where is he?" And when she knew: "Take me to him!" she ordered.

Flanders wasted no words in remonstrance. He agreed at once, and had his car waiting at the door before Ruth had packed her suitcase. Through the darkness he drove down the steep mountain road to Wagon Wheel.

By the time they reached town it was too late to get permission of the sheriff to see her husband that night, but Tim made arrangements by which she was to be admitted to his cell as soon as breakfast was over next morning.

The limbs of the girl trembled as she followed the jailer. The pulse in her throat was beating fast.

At sight of her standing in the shadow of his cell, Rowan drew a deep, ragged breath. The tired eyes in the oval of her pale face held the weariness of woe. The youth in her was quenched. He had ruined her life.

His impulse was to sweep her into his arms and comfort her, but he lacked the courage of his desire. The tragic gravity of her told him that she had come as a judge and not as a lover.

When the guard had gone, she asked her question: "You didn't do it, did you?"

His throat ached with tightness. There was nothing he could say to comfort her. He could not even, on account of the others, tell her the truth and let her decide for herself the extent of his guilt.

"Tell me you didn't do it!" she demanded.

Beneath the tan he was gray. "I'm sorry. I wish I could tell you everything. But I can't talk . . . even to you."

"Can't talk?" she echoed. "When you are accused of . . . of this horrible thing, aren't you going to tell everybody that it is a lie?"

He shook his head. "It isn't so simple as that. I can't talk

105

about the case because. . . ."

"I'm not asking you to talk about the case. I'm asking you to tell me that you're innocent . . . that it's all an awful mistake," she ended with a sob.

"If you'll only trust me . . . and wait," he began desperately. "Someday I'll tell you everything. But now . . . I wish I could tell you . . . I wish I could."

"You mean that you don't trust me."

"No. I trust you fully. But the charge against me lies against others, too. I can't talk."

"You can't even tell me that you didn't murder two men in their sleep?" Her voice was sharp. All the pain and torture of the long night rang out in it.

He winced. "I'll have to trust to your mercy to believe the best you can of me."

"What can I believe when you won't even deny the charge? What else is there to think but that. . . ." She broke off and began to whimper.

He took a step toward her, but a swift gesture of her hand held him back. "No . . . no! You can't trust me. That's all there is to it . . . except that you're guilty. I'd never have believed it . . . never in the world . . . not even after what I know of you."

Rowan longed to cry out to her to have faith in him. He wanted desperately to bridge the gulf that was growing wider between them, to have her see that he had closed the door behind him and must follow the course he had chosen. But he was dumb. It was not in him to express his feeling in words.

Into the delicate white of her cheeks excitement had brought a stain of pink. Eagerly she poured out her passionate protest: "You don't mean me to think . . . surely you can't mean . . . that . . . that . . . you did this horrible thing. You couldn't have done it. The thing isn't possible. Tell me you had nothing to do with it."

He felt himself trapped in a horrible ambuscade. He would not lie to her. He could not tell the truth. If she would only have faith in him. . . .

But there was no chance of that. To look at the hostile, accusing gaze of this girl was to know that he had lost her.

"I'm sorry," he began.

Her affronted eyes stabbed him. "That's all you have to tell me?"

"If you only knew."

The dumb appeal of him might have moved her, but it did not. She was too full of her wrongs.

"But I don't know, and you won't tell me. So there's nothing more to be said."

Suddenly she broke down, turned away with a sob, and through the blindness of her tears groped to the door. She had rushed to him—to tell him that she knew he was innocent, and he had repulsed her, had made a stranger of her. In effect, he had told her that he did not want her help, that he would go through his trouble alone. If he had really loved her—if he had loved her, how differently he would have acted. A great lump filled her throat and choked her.

Rowan watched her go, his fingers biting into the palms of his hands. The hunger of his soul stared out of his eyes.

XIII

Matson nodded a pleasant good morning, offered his prisoner a cigar, and sat down on the bed.

"How's everything, Mac?"

The cattleman smiled ironically. "Fine as silk, Aleck. How are they a-coming with you?"

Matson looked out of the barred window at the warm sunshine flooding the yard. When his gaze returned to McCoy it was grave and solicitous.

"I'm going to give you straight talk, Mac. Don't fool yourself. Shoshone County has made up its mind. The men that killed Dan Gilroy are going to hang."

"Sounds cheerful, Aleck."

"I'm here for the last time to ask you to come through. If you'll give evidence for the state, I can save you, Mac."

McCoy looked straight at him from cold, bleak eyes. "We discussed this subject once before, Sheriff. Isn't once enough?"

"No," returned the officer doggedly. "I've been talking with Haight. Inside of twelve hours he's going to get a confession out of . . . well, never mind his name. But the man's weakening. He'll come through to save his skin. Mac, beat him to it."

The cattleman laughed without mirth. "I reckon this confession talk is come-on stuff. Even if any of the boys knew anything, he wouldn't tell it."

"Wouldn't he? You ought to know that there's always a weak link in every chain. In every bunch of men there's a quitter."

"So you're offering me the chance to be that quitter. Fine, Aleck. You've got a high opinion of me. But why give me the chance? By your way of it, I led the raid."

"I'm not a fool, Mac. I know you didn't set out to kill. If you ask me who started the gun play, I can come pretty near giving his name. One of your party has been talking, and the rumor is that you saved the herders. Anyhow, I don't want to see you hang if I can help it."

"Good of you," derided the prisoner.

"But that's what is going to happen if you don't take my offer. You are going to trial first . . . and for the killing of Gilroy. You'll be convicted. Last call, Mac. Will you come through?"

"No, Aleck. I don't admit I have anything to tell, but, if I had, I expect I'd keep my mouth shut."

"Then you'll hang."

"Maybe I will . . . maybe I won't," answered Rowan coolly.

Matson rose. "No use spilling words. Are you going to be reasonable or not?"

The men looked at each other with direct, level gaze.

"I aim always to try to be," replied McCoy.

"Well, will you come through with what I want, or will you hang?"

"Since you put it that way, Sheriff, I reckon I'll hang."

"You damn' fool!" exploded the sheriff.

But there was no censure in his voice. The cattleman had done what he would have done under the same test—come clean as a whistle from the temptation to betray his accomplices.

"I knew you wouldn't do it," continued Matson. "But I've given you your chance. Don't blame me."

Later in the day the sheriff tried out another of his prisoners. He had told McCoy the truth. One of the six was weakening. Matson had his own favorites and wanted to give them a chance before the state's attorney was pledged. By sunset a confession would be in the hands of Haight, and it would be too late to save his friends.

He found Yerby whittling out a boat for his baby. The Texan looked up with a faint, apologetic smile in his faded blue eyes.

"I was making a pretty for my little trick at home, Sheriff. He's the dad-blamedest kid you ever saw . . . keeps his old dad humping to make toys for him to bust. Don't you blame Steve for loaning me this two-bit Barlow. He takes it back every night. Steve's a good jailer all right."

The Southerner was a shabby little man, tobacco-stained, with a week's growth of red stubble on his face. But it was impossible to deny him a certain pathetic dignity.

"I've come to talk to you for that little kid, Sam. You don't want him to be an orphan, do you?"

"I reckon that don't rest with me."

Matson cut straight to business. "That's just who it rests

with. Sam, it's a showdown. Will you come through with the evidence I want, or won't you?"

"I won't. We done talked that all out, Aleck." He offered the officer a chew of tobacco to show that he was not peevish about the matter.

The sheriff waved the plug aside impatiently. "One of the boys can't stand the gaff. He's breaking, Sam. But you've got a wife and a kid. He hasn't. I want you to have first chance. Come clean and I'll look out for you. After the trial I'll see you get out of the country quietly. You can take your folks back to Texas."

Sam looked out of the window. The little boat and the jack-knife hung limply in his hands. In a cracked, falsetto voice he took up a song of the range that he had hummed a hundred times in the saddle.

> *I woke one mo'ning on the old Chisholm Trail,*
> *Rope in my hand and a cow by the tail.*

He thought of the rough and turbulent life that had come at last to the peaceful shoals of happy matrimony. A vision rose before him of his smiling young wife and growing baby. They needed him. Must he give them up for a point of honor? If someone was to go clear, why not he?

"We have evidence enough. It isn't that. I'm giving you a chance, Sam. That's all."

The lips of the Texan murmured another stanza, but his thoughts were far afield.

> *Oh, a ten-dollar hoss and a forty-dollar saddle . . .*
> *And I'm goin' to punchin' Texas cattle.*

"Never again, Sam. Not unless you take your chance now." The sheriff put a hand on his shoulder. "For the sake of the wife and the little man. You're not going to throw them down, are you?"

We hit Caldwell and we hit her on the fly,
We bedded down the cattle on the hill close by.

The faded eyes were wistful. It was his chance for freedom, perhaps his chance for life, too. What would Missie and the baby do without him? Who would look after them?

No chaps, no slicker, and it's pourin' down rain,
And damn my skin if I night herd again!

Matson said nothing. The Texan was building up for himself a vision of the life he loved in the wind and the sunshine of the open range. The old Chisholm Trail song he sang must bring to his memory a hundred pictures of the past. These would be arguments more potent than any the sheriff could use.

Stray in the herd and the boss said kill it,
So I shot him in the rump with the handle of the
*   skillet.*

The cracked voice became clearer.

I'll sell my outfit soon as ever I can,
I won't punch cattle for no damned man!

"You don't want your kid to grow up and learn that his dad was hanged," insinuated Matson. "That would be a fine thing to leave him."

Foot in the stirrup and hand on the horn . . .
Best damned cowboy that ever was born!

The voice of the singer rang like a bell at last. He turned serene eyes on the tempter.

"What do you think I am, Aleck? If I hang, I hang, but I'm damned if I'll be a traitor."

The sheriff gave him up. "All right, Sam. It's your say-so, not mine. Got everything you want here so you're fixed comfortable?"

"You're treating me fine. I ain't used to being corralled so close, but I reckon it would be unreasonable to ask for a horse and a saddle and an open range in your calaboose."

As the sheriff passed down the corridor, he heard Sam's tin-pan voice chirruping bravely.

> There's hard times on old Bitter Creek
> That never can be beat;
> It was root, hog, or die,
> We cleared up all the Indians,
> Drank all the alkali,
> Under every wagon sheet.
> And it's whack the cattle on, boys . . .
> Root, hog, or die!

XIV

Not for years had Shoshone County been so interested in any public event as it was in the trial of Rowan McCoy for the murder of Dan Gilroy. Scores of ranchmen had driven in from the hills to be present either as witnesses or spectators.

The sentiment of the people was strong for a conviction. Rowan had many friends, and the cattle interests were anxious to see him acquitted. But the killing of Gilroy had been so unprovoked that it had aroused widespread resentment. The feeling of those not involved in the cattle and sheep war was that an example must be made.

Haight, the new district attorney, was a young man, almost a stranger in the country, and he wanted a record for convictions.

Therefore he brought McCoy to trial for the murder of Gilroy rather than Tait. Gilroy had many friends and no personal enemies. He was a quiet peaceable man. Apparently he had been shot while unarmed and trying to escape. His killing had been wanton and unprovoked.

The courtroom was crowded to the windows. Two bailiffs stood at the door and searched every man that entered, for the feeling was so intense that the authorities did not want to take the chance of any possible outbreak. A gun in a hip pocket was too easy to reach.

In his opening statement the district attorney told the story of the sheep and cattle war. He traced the source of the bad feeling between the prisoner and Tait, and showed that the bitterness extended to Silcott and Falkner, two others charged with this murder, one of whom had been wounded and the other beaten up by the sheepman. The prosecution would prove that both Silcott and Falkner had made threats against Tait, that Falkner had been seen to take a rifle from a ranch bunkhouse in the dead of night, and that McCoy had led the party that had killed the two sheepmen. The testimony would show that McCoy with three of his companions rode back to the Circle Diamond Ranch, pretended to the housekeeper that they had spent the night there, and after breakfast returned to the roundup camp, burying on the way the rifle that Falkner had been seen to take the night before.

Bit by bit, with the skill of the trained lawyer, Haight used his witnesses to spin a web around the accused man. He showed how, after the arrival of Silcott at the camp the night of the raid, McCoy decided unexpectedly to drive the Circle Diamond cattle home and took with him Cole and Silcott. Shortly afterward Rogers and Yerby had departed with flimsy excuses. Falkner had stolen away without any assigned reason. They had not been seen again at camp until late next morning. Hans

Ukena, a rider for the Triangle Dot, testified that he had been sleeping in the bunkhouse the night in question and was wakened by a noise. By the light of the moon he saw Falkner pass through the open door, carrying a rifle in one hand and an ammunition belt in the other.

The interest grew tense when Sheriff Matson took the stand. As he told the story of how he had followed the trail of the raiders foot by foot from the scene of the crime to the Circle Diamond Ranch the hopes of the defense sank.

It had taken three days to select a jury and four more to examine witnesses to date. Wagon Wheel buzzed with gossip. The rumor would not go down that one of the prisoners had turned state's evidence and was to be put on the stand next morning.

Ruth, torn by conflicting emotions, had been present with Mrs. Flanders all through the trial. The testimony of Matson had left her shaken with dread. She felt now that Rowan was guilty, and she believed he would be convicted. But it was impossible for her not to admire his courage under fire. His nerve was so cool and steady, his frank face so open and friendly.

Immediately after court was declared in session next morning, Haight turned to the bailiff.

"Call Larry Silcott."

A murmur swept like a wave through the courtroom. Men and women craned their necks to see the young cowman as he passed to the witness stand. Ruth noticed that Larry's face was gray and that he kept his eyes on the floor. But even then she had no premonition of what he was about to do.

But Rowan knew. While Silcott answered nervously the first routine questions of the lawyer, the prisoner watched him steadily with a scornful little smile. Rowan had taught him the practical side of his business, had looked after his cattle, given him his friendship. Once he had dragged him out of the Fryingpan when he was drowning. His feeling for the younger man was like that of an older brother. He had felt an affectionate pride in his pupil's skill at roping and at riding. Now Larry, to save his own skin, was betraying him and the rest of his companions.

Haight was very gentle and considerate of his star witness. But Silcott was in hell nonetheless. Dry-lipped and pallid, with tiny sweat beads on his damp forehead, he faced row upon row of tense, eager faces all hanging on what he had to tell. Not one of them all but would despise him. His stripped and naked soul writhed, the vanity for once burned out of him. He shivered with dread. It was being driven into him that although he had bought his life he must pay for his treachery with years of isolation and contempt.

The prosecuting attorney led him over the story of the night when he had ridden with the sheep raiders. Step by step the witness took the party from the roundup to the camp at Bald Knob.

"Who had charge of your party?" continued Haight.

"McCoy."

"Who assigned you positions before the attack?"

"McCoy."

"In what order did he place you?"

"Counting from the left, Cole, Yerby, Rogers, myself, Falkner, McCoy."

"Which of you was nearest the camp?"

"McCoy was closer than the rest of us."

"When was the first shot fired?"

"I judge we were about a hundred yards from the wagons."

"Did it come from the camp or was it fired by one of your party?"

"By one of us."

"Were any of the sheepmen then in sight?"

"No."

"Who fired that shot, Mister Silcott?"

Larry's eyes went furtively about the room, met those of Mc-Coy, and dropped to the floor. "It . . . it came from the right."

"Did you see who fired it?"

"Falkner or McCoy . . . I wasn't sure which."

Rowan's lawyer objected and was sustained. The judge cautioned the witness to tell only what he knew.

Silcott went over the story of the shooting of Tait with great detail. The prosecuting attorney made another dramatic pause to let the audience get the significance of his next lead.

"Were you where you could see Dan Gilroy when he ran from the wagon?"

"Yes."

"Will you tell exactly what happened when Gilroy ran from the wagon?"

"He ran out from the back and started for the brush."

"Was he armed?"

"No."

"Proceed. What happened?"

"He had run about thirty feet when somebody fired. He fell."

"Were any more shots fired?"

"No. That was the last."

"From what direction did it come?"

"From my right."

"How do you know?"

"By the sound and the smoke."

"Where did the smoke rise with relation to the defendant?"

Silcott moistened his dry lips with his tongue. He was sweating blood. "It was close to him."

Haight threatened him with his forefinger. "Won't you swear that the defendant fired that shot? Don't you know he fired it?"

"I . . . I can't swear to it."

"Weren't you convinced that it was McCoy who . . . ?"

The defense objected angrily: "The witness has answered the question. Is the prosecuting attorney trying to change that answer?"

When at last Haight was through with him the witness dripped with perspiration. But his troubles were only beginning. The lawyers for the defense took him in hand. Two points they developed in favor of their client—that he had repeatedly warned his friends against shooting and that he had saved the lives of the herders from Falkner.

But although Silcott was left a rag, his story stood the fire of cross-examination. When he stepped down from the stand, he left behind him a net of evidence through which McCoy could not break.

As Larry moved down the aisle someone in the back part of the room broke the silence: "You damned Judas!"

Instantly echoes of the word filled the courtroom. The judge pounded with his gavel for silence, but that low-hissed—"Judas! Judas!"—pursued the young cowman down the stairs. It would be many years before he could recall without scalding shame that moment when the finger of public scorn was pointed at him in execration.

XV

Murder in the first degree.

Not a muscle of the prisoner's face moved as the clerk of the court read the verdict.

Into the dead silence of the courtroom was lifted the low, sobbing wail of a woman. Ruth had collapsed into the ample bosom of Mrs. Flanders.

The face of the convicted man twitched, but he did not look around. He knew who had broken down under the strain, whose game will had weakened at the blow. In that moment he thought wholly of her, not at all of himself.

A grizzled old cattleman pushed his broad shoulders through the crowd toward the condemned raider. "This ain't the end, boy. We'll work like sixty to get you a new trial. This will never go through . . . never in the world." His strong arm fell with frank affection across the shoulders of his friend. "It don't matter what names they call you, son. You're the same old Mac to all of us."

"This is when a fellow finds out who his friends are, Roswell," answered Rowan simply.

He had many of them. They rallied to him by scores—long, loose-jointed, capable men with leathery brown faces, men who had fought with him against Wyoming blizzards for the lives of cattle, men who had slept beside him under the same tarp by many a campfire. From Rawlins and Caspar and Cheyenne, and even far-away Denver, came words of good cheer. They stressed the point that the fight for his life was just beginning and that the verdict of the jury would not be accepted as final.

Mrs. Stovall, who had been a very unwilling witness for the prosecution, brought a cake and a cherry pie to the jail for him. Incidentally she delivered a message with which she had been commissioned.

"Norma says for me to tell you that this trial doesn't fool her any. She knows you're being punished for some of the other boys. She wanted I should tell you that she knows you didn't intend to kill Joe."

This was an opinion becoming every day more widespread. Men began to say that McCoy was the victim of evil chance.

The financial side of the affair was troubling the officials of the county. The trial had been a long and expensive one. It had cost many thousand dollars, and there was talk of grounds for an appeal. With four other trials yet to come, it became apparent that Shoshone County would be bankrupt long before the finish.

Roswell, acting for a group of friends, went to the prosecuting attorney.

"Look here, Haight. You're up against it. Maybe you've got evidence to convict these boys. Maybe you haven't."

"There's no maybe about that . . . I have," Haight broke in grimly.

"Well, say you have. That ain't the point. The county can't stand the expense of all those trials. You know that. What are you going to do about it?"

"Go right ahead with the trials. We begin with Brad Rogers tomorrow."

"Oh, well. We got to be reasonable . . . all of us. Now here's my proposition . . . let me talk with the boys and their lawyers. If I could get them to plead guilty, it would save a heap of trouble all around."

Haight had looked at the matter from this angle before. He nodded. "All right. See what you can do, Mister Roswell. If they will save us the expense of trying them, I think I can arrange for life imprisonment."

"For all of them?" demanded the cattleman shrewdly.

"For all the rest of them."

"How about Rowan?"

"He's not included. We've got to make an example of him. He led the raid."

Roswell fought it out with the lawyer for an hour, but on this point Haight stood firm. McCoy had to pay the extreme penalty for his crime. That was not even open to argument.

The old cattleman called at once upon the leading lawyer for the defense, and with him visited the cell of Yerby. The Texan was greatly depressed at the issue of the trial. He could not get over his bitterness at the part Silcott had played.

William MacLeod Raine

"I reckon he's up at the hotel eating fried chicken and water-melon. Well, he's welcome. I wouldn't swap places with him. Neither would Mac. We all had our chance to do like he done."

"No, Silcott's still in jail. He asked Matson to keep him there till the trials are over and he can light out. I expect he don't like to trust himself outside." Roswell came abruptly to the object of his call. "Sam, we got to face facts. Haight has the goods on you boys. He'll sure convict you."

"Looks like," agreed the Texan dejectedly.

"We'll have to fix up a compromise. If you'll all plead guilty, Haight is willing to call it life imprisonment."

"What do the other boys say?"

"They are willing, I reckon, to take the best terms they can get."

"I'd as lief be dead as locked up in jail for the rest of my life."

"We'll get you out on parole in two or three years. The worst of it is that Mac ain't included in the arrangement. Haight swears he has got to hang." Eyes narrowed to slits, Roswell watched the Texan while he fired his next shot. "Mac was the leader. There wouldn't have been any killing except for him. He's the responsible party. So Haight says that. . . ."

"Got it all figured out, have you? Mac did the killing. Mac was to blame. I'll tell you this . . . if Mac had had his way there wouldn't have been any killing. Just because he shuts his mouth and stands the gaff. . . . Dog-gone it, you and Haight can take your compromise plumb to hell!" decided the Texan, his anger rising.

Roswell gave a low whoop and fell upon him. "That's the way to talk, old-timer. We've got Haight on the hip. The county's busted high and dry. Folks are beginning to holler already about the expense of the trials. Haight's ready to talk turkey. If you lads will stand pat, it's an even bet that he'll have to crawfish

120

about Mac."

"I 'low we'll stay hitched . . . all of us that haven't a big yellow streak up our backs. Why-for should we let Mac get the worst of the deal? You go tell Haight he can't stack the cards that-a-way."

Rogers, coming up for trial next day, was anxious to get the matter settled. But he, too, declined the terms.

Cole and Falkner in turn were visited. The former refused flatly to consider any arrangement that did not include McCoy.

To satisfy his own curiosity Roswell ventured on debatable ground with Falkner.

" 'Course you don't owe Mac anything. He led you into the trouble. The whole thing is his fault. Now by accepting Haight's proposition, Mac will be hanged and you other lads. . . ."

"Mac will be hanged, will he?" growled Falkner.

"Sure thing. Nothing can save him if you accept Haight's terms. But, after all. . . ."

The prisoner looked at the old cattleman blackly. Whatever faults he had, Falkner was not a sneak. McCoy had kept quiet when he might have told the others who had done the killing. McCoy had stood pat from start to finish. If Mac had given the word, it would have been Falkner who would have been hanged while the others got off with prison sentences. Hard citizen though he was, the man was game to the core.

"Who in hell wants to accept Haight's offer?" he snarled. "I've lived a wolf, by some folks' way of it. I reckon I'll die one."

Roswell grinned. To the prosecuting attorney he carried back word that his offer had been rejected. No compromise would be considered that did not include McCoy.

The hotel where Roswell and his friends stayed became active as a hive of bees. From it cowpunchers and cattlemen issued to make a quiet canvass of the leading citizens of Shoshone County. The result was that Haight and his political friends were besieged for twelve hours by taxpayers who insisted on a compromise being arranged.

"What's the idea, Haight?" asked a prominent irrigation engineer in charge of a project under construction. "We stand for the law. We want to see every man punished that was in the sheep raid. But there's no object in starting trouble with the cattlemen, and that's what it will amount to if you hang Rowan McCoy. Tait and Gilroy weren't blameless. They knew what they were going up against. They didn't have to cross the deadline and ruin the ranchmen on the Fryingpan. A prison sentence all around hits me as about right. I've talked with lots of people, and that's the general sentiment."

Just before Rogers was to be brought into the courtroom for trial Haight gave way. He had a long conference with the lawyers for the defense and the presiding judge. As a result of this it was announced that the prisoners would plead guilty.

Before sunset each of the five had been sentenced to life imprisonment.

XVI

With the news that Rowan would not have to pay with his life, Ruth's anxiety took on another phase. Their happiness had come to grief. It was likely that the tentative separation caused by her anger at his unfaithfulness would prove to be a final one. But her imperative need was to demand the truth about the sheep-raid killings. At the bottom of her heart was still a residuum of deep respect for him. It was impossible to believe that Rowan was a common murderer who had stolen up at night to shoot down his enemy from cover. Moreover, there was a reason—a vital, urgent, compelling one—why she must think the best she could of the man she had married.

This reason took her to Sam Yerby's cell at the county jail. She and the Texan had struck up one of the quick, instinctive friendships that were scattered along Ruth's pathway. The girl had completed her conquest of him by taking a great interest in Missie and the baby. She had embroidered for the little fellow a dress that Sam thought the daintiest in the world.

The tired eyes of the old cattleman lit when she came to the door of his prison.

"It's right good of you, Miss Ruth, to come and see the old man before he goes over the road."

"I'm so sorry, Mister Yerby." She choked up. "But everybody tells me you won't have to stay in very long, and I'm going to look out for Missie and the boy."

Tears filmed his eyes. The muscles of the leathery face worked with emotion.

"I cain't thank you, Miss Ruth, but I reckon you know what I'm thinking."

"Missie is going to teach the boy what a good man his father is, and when you come out, you and he will be great friends."

He nodded. Speech at that moment was beyond him.

"All the boys are going to look after your stock just as if it belonged to them."

"That's right kind of them. I sure do feel grateful." He looked shyly at his visitor. Sam knew that all was not well between her and Rowan. "What about you, Miss Ruth? You-all are losing a better man than Missie ever had. He's a pure, Mac is."

Her eyes fixed themselves on him. "There's something I want to know, Mister Yerby . . . something I have a right to know. It's . . . it's about the sheep raid."

"Why don't you-all go to Mac and ask him?"

"I've been to him. He wouldn't tell me . . . said he couldn't."

A puzzled expression of doubt lifted his eyebrows. "I don't reckon I can tell you then."

"You've got to tell me. I've a right to know. I'm going to know."

"O' course in regards to what took place. . . ."

"Did you start that night intending to kill Joe Tait?"

"No, ma'am, we didn't. Rowan told the boys time and again there wasn't to be any killing. He planned it so it wouldn't be necessary."

"Then how was it?"

"I'll tell you this much . . . someone went out of his haid and began shooting. Inside of three minutes it was all over."

"Did . . . did Rowan kill either of them?" she whispered.

"I don't know who killed Tait. Several of the boys were firing. Mac didn't kill Gilroy. I'm 'most sure of that."

"You're not dead sure," she insisted.

"I'm what you might call morally certain. But there's one man can set your mind at rest, if you can get him to talk."

"Who?"

"Hal Falkner. He knows who started the shooting and who killed Dan Gilroy."

"I've hardly met him. Do you think he would tell me?"

"Maybe he would." He smiled a little. "I notice you mostly get your way. Hal's rough and ready. Don't you mind it if he acts gruff. That's just his way."

"I'll go see him."

"I reckon it won't do any harm. But I can tell you one thing, anyhow. If you give Mac the benefit of all the doubts, it will be about what's right. If Mac wouldn't tell you all what happened, it was because we had all made a solemn agreement not to talk."

"Do you think that is it?"

"I shorely do."

"I'm so glad."

"An,' Miss Ruth?"

"Yes, Mister Yerby?"

He hesitated before he made the plunge. "I won't see you-all again for a long time, maybe never. You're young and proud and high-heeled, like you-all got a perfect right to be. But I want to say this . . . if you live to be a hundred, you'll never meet anyone that's more of a man than Rowan McCoy."

A wistful little smile touched her face. "He has one good friend, anyhow."

"He has hundreds. He deserves them, too."

"I've got to say good bye now, Mister Yerby." She gave him both hands. Tears blurred her eyes so that she could scarcely see him. "Good bye. Heaps of luck . . . oh, lots of it. And don't worry about Missie and your boy."

"I'll not worry half so much now, little friend. And I'm hoping all that luck will come to you, too."

From Sheriff Matson Ruth secured a permit to see Falkner.

The cowpuncher was brought, handcuffed, into the office of the jailer. It was an effect of his sudden, furious temper that his guards never took any chances with him. None of the friendly little privileges that fell to the other prisoners came his way.

"Missus McCoy wants to talk with you, Hal," explained Ackerman, the jailer. "Don't make any mistake about this. I'll be in the outer room there with a gat. I've got a guard under the window. This is no time to try for a getaway."

Falkner looked at him with an ugly sneer. "Glad you mentioned it, Steve. But when the time comes, I'm going."

Ackerman shrugged his shoulders and left the room.

"I've come to ask a favor of you, Mister Falkner," Ruth blurted out.

Her courage was beginning to ebb. The man looked so formidable now that she was alone with him. His reputation, she knew, was bad. More than once, when she had met him on horseback in the hills, the look in his burning black eyes had sent little shivers through her.

"A favor of me, Missus McCoy. Ain't that a come-down? Didn't know you knew I was on the map. You're sure honoring me," he jeered.

It was his habit to take note in his sullen fashion of all good-looking women. When he had seen her about the ranch or riding with her husband or Larry Silcott, he had resented it that this slender, vivid girl who moved with such quick animal grace, whose parted lips and shining eyes were so charmingly eager, had taken him in apparently only as a detail of the scenery.

Now his dark eyes, set deep in the sockets, narrowed suspiciously. What did she want of him?

"I want to know about the Bald Knob raid," she hurried on. "Maybe I oughtn't to come to you. I don't know. But I've got to know the truth of what happened that night."

"Why don't you go to your husband, then?" he demanded. "Mac knows as much about it as I do."

"I went to him. He wouldn't tell me . . . said it wouldn't be right to tell anything he knew."

"That so?" From his slitted eyelids he watched her closely, not at all certain of what was her game. "Then if it wouldn't be right for Mac to tell you, it wouldn't be right for me, would it?" The strong white teeth in his coffee-brown face flashed in a mocking grin.

"That was before the trial. Mister Yerby said he wouldn't talk then because you had agreed not to."

"Oh! So you've been to Yerby?"

"Yes. He couldn't tell me what I want to know."

"And what is it you want to know particularly?"

"You know what Mister Silcott testified about . . . about where the shooting started from and about where the shot came from that killed Mister Gilroy. I want you to tell me that it wasn't Rowan who fired those shots."

He considered her a moment warily, his mind loaded with suspicions. Was this a frame-up of some sort? Was she trying to trap him into admissions that would work against him later?

"Well, the trial is past now. Mac can talk if he wants to. Why don't you go to him?" he asked.

"I'd rather you would tell me."

He grinned. "Nothing doing today, my dear."

Then Falkner met one of the surprises of his life. Fire flashed from this slim slip of a girl. Her eyes attacked him fearlessly. "You wouldn't dare say that if you and Rowan were free," she blazed.

He let slip a startled oath. "That's right. I wouldn't." The cowpuncher laughed hardily. He could afford to make this admission. Nobody had ever questioned his courage. "All right, ma'am. Objection sustained, as the judge said. I'll take back that 'my dear'."

"And will you tell me what I want to know?"

"That's another proposition. You got to give me better reasons than you have yet why I should. Do you reckon I'm going to put my cards on the table while you pinch yours up close? What's the game? What are you aiming to do with what I tell you?"

"Nothing. I just want to know."

"What for?"

A little wave of pink beat into her cheeks. "I don't want . . . if I can help it . . . to think of my husband as . . . as a. . . ."

"A murderer. Is that it?" he flung at her brutally.

She nodded her head twice. The word hit her, in his savage voice, like a blow in the face.

"Then why don't you ask Mac? Are you afraid he'd lie to you?"

"I know he wouldn't," she answered with spirit.

"Well, then?" He watched her with hard eyes, still doubtful of her.

"I'm his wife. Isn't it natural I should want to know the truth?"

"What are you trying to put over on me? Why don't you go to Mac and ask him?"

She threw herself on his mercy. "We . . . we've quarreled. I can't go to him. There's nobody else to tell me but you."

There were dark shadows under the big eyes in the colorless face. She had suffered, he guessed, during these last weeks as she never had before.

Something in the dreariness of her stricken youth touched him. He spoke more gently: "According to Silcott's story it lies between me and Mac. If he didn't fire those shots, I did. Do you reckon I'm going to tell you that he didn't fire them? Why should I?"

Her eyes fell full in his. "Because I'm entitled to know the truth. I'm in trouble and you can help me. You're no Larry Silcott. You're a man. You stood firm at the risk of your life. Even if it is at your own expense, you'll tell me. Rowan would do as much for your wife if you had one."

Ruth had said the right word at last, had in two sentences touched both his pride and his gratitude.

"I reckon that beats me, ma'am," he said. "I owe Mac a lot, and I'll pay an installment of it right now. Your husband never fired his gun from start to finish of the Bald Knob raid."

The light in her eyes thanked him more than words could have done.

"While I'm at it, I'll tell you more," he went on. "Mac laid the law down straight that we weren't gunning for Tait. He didn't want to take me along because he knew I was sore at the fellow, but when I insisted on going, the others overruled him. After the killing Mac never once said I told you so to the others for letting me go along. What's more, when they asked questions about who killed Gilroy and who started the shooting, he gave them no satisfaction. He let the boys guess who did it. If Mac had said the word, the rest would have rounded on me. I would have been hanged, and they would have got short sentences. Your husband is a prince, ma'am."

"Thank you."

"I got him and the other boys into all this trouble. He hasn't flung it up to me once. What do you know about that?"

"I'm so glad I came to see you. It's going to make a great difference to me." There was a tremor in her voice that told of suppressed tears.

Ackerman came to the door: "About through?"

The prisoner lifted his upper lip in a sneer. "Better throw your gat on me, Steve. I might make trouble, you know."

Akerman followed Rowan into the sheriff's office. Matson looked up from the desk where he was working.

"All right, Steve. You needn't wait."

When he had signed his name to the letter he was writing, Matson turned to his prisoner.

"We're going to start on the eleven-thirty, Mac. Your wife is down at the house with Missus Matson. She wants to say good bye there instead of at the depot. I've got considerable business to clean up before train time, so I'll stay on the job. Be back here in an hour."

"You mean that I'm to go there alone?"

"Why not? I'll ask you to go through the alleys if you don't mind. I don't want the other boys to feel that I'm playing favorites."

"I'll not forget this, Aleck."

"Sho! You never threw a man down in your life, Mac. I don't reckon you're going to begin now. Hit the dust. I'm busy."

Rowan crossed the square to a street darkened by shade trees, and followed it to the alley. Down this he passed between board fences. He took his hat off and lifted his face to the star-strewn sky. It would be many years before he walked again a free man beneath the Milky Way.

McCoy was suffering poignantly. He was on his way to say good bye to the wife he loved. It was his conviction that when he emerged from the shadow now closing in upon him Ruth would have passed out of his life. Already she had wearied of what he had to offer. There was no likelihood that she would waste her young years waiting for a man shut up in prison for his misdeeds. Far better for her to cut loose from him as soon as possible. He intended to advise her to sell the ranch, realize what she could in cash from it, and then file an action for divorce. The law would operate to release her almost automatically from a convict husband.

Mrs. Matson met him at the back door. She led the way to a living room and stood aside to let him pass in. Then she closed the door behind him, shutting herself out.

The parlor was lit only by shafts of moonlight pouring through the windows. Ruth stood beside the mantel. She wore a white dress that had always been a favorite of Rowan's.

Neither of them spoke. He noticed that she was trembling. From out of the darkness where she stood came a strangled little sob.

Rowan took the distance between them in two strides. He gathered her into his arms, and she hid her face against his woolen shirt. She wept, clinging to him, one arm tight about his neck.

He caressed her hair softly, murmuring the sweetheart words his thoughts had given her through all the days of their separation. Not for many years had he been so near tears himself.

Presently the sob convulsions that shook her slight body grew less frequent. She dabbed at her eyes with a lace handkerchief.

"I've not been a good wife to you, Rowan," she whispered at last. "You don't know how sometimes I've . . . hated you . . . and distrusted you. I've thought all sorts of bad things about you, and some of them aren't true."

His arms tightened. The wild desire was in him to hold her against the world.

"I flirted with Larry Silcott," she confessed. "I did it to . . . to punish you. I've been horrid. But I loved you all the time. Even while I hated you I loved you."

The blood sang through his veins. "Why did you hate me?"

"I . . . I can't tell you that. Not yet . . . someday maybe."

"Was it something I did?"

"Y-yes. But I don't want to talk about that now. They're going to take you away from me. We've only got a few minutes. Oh, Rowan, I don't see how I'm going to let you go."

His heart overflowed with tenderness and pride. Every one of her broken little endearments filled him with joy. Her dear sweetness was balm to his wounded soul.

"Let me tell you this, Ruth. I'm happier tonight than I've been for a long time. They can't separate us if we keep each other in our hearts. I thought I'd lost you. I've been through hell because of it, my dear."

"You do . . . love me," she murmured.

He did not try to tell her in words how much. His reassurance was in the lover's language of eyes and lips and the soft touch of hands.

They came again to the less perfect medium of words, and she told him of her visits to Yerby and Falkner.

"I knew all the time you couldn't have done what Mister Haight said you did . . . 'way down deep in my heart I knew it. But I wanted to hold a grudge against you because you didn't confide in me. I wanted to think bad things about you, and yet they made me so dreadfully unhappy, Rowan. And all the time you were sacrificing yourself for the man who brought you into the trouble. I might have known it."

He shook his head. "No, honey. I wasn't doing any more than I had to do. We were all partners in the raid. What one did all did. I couldn't throw Falkner down just because he was the instrument. That wouldn't have been square."

"I don't agree with you at all. If he had done as you said, there wouldn't have been any lives lost. They've no right to hold you for it, and I'm going to begin working right away to get you out. I went to school with the governor's wife, you know. They have just been married . . . oh, scarcely a year. He's a lot older than she is and very much in love with her, Louise says. So she'll make him give you a pardon."

Rowan smiled. "I'm afraid it isn't going to be so easy as that, dear. The governor couldn't pardon me on account of public opinion even if he wanted to do it."

"He's got to. I'll show you. I want you home." She broke down and sought again the sanctuary of his shoulder.

While she cried he petted her.

After a time she began to talk in whispered fragments.

"I'm going to need you so much. I can't stand it, Rowan, to have you away from me now. I want my man. I want you . . . oh, I want you so badly. It isn't fair. It isn't right . . . now."

Something in her voice startled him. He took her by the shoulders and held her gently from him while he looked into her eyes.

"You mean. . . ."

She broke from his hands and clung to him. He knew her secret now. His heart beat fast as he held her in his strong arms. Joy, exultation, humility, fear, infinite tenderness—he tasted them all. But the emotion that remained was despair.

He groaned. Ruth heard him murmur: "My love. My precious lamb." She read the burning misery in his eyes. Woman-like, she flew to comfort him.

"I'm glad . . . oh, you don't know how glad I am . . . now that we are together again. I wouldn't have it any other way, Rowan. If it weren't for what's going to happen . . . I couldn't stand it to wait for you. Don't you see? I'll have a pledge of you with me all the time. When I'm loving it, I'll be loving you."

What she said was true. There had been forged a bond irrevocable between them. He recognized it with a lifted heart.

"I've made my plans," she went on. "I know just what I'm going to do . . . if you'll let me. I want to go back to the ranch and run it."

"I'm afraid that isn't possible. This trial has cost me a lot of money. I'm mortgaged and in debt. Besides, ranching takes expert knowledge. It's doubtful whether I could have held the ranch, anyhow. The government is creating forest reserves up in the hills. That will cut off the free range. Sheep are pushing in, and they'll get what is left. We'd better sell out and save for you what little we can. It won't be much, but, if the stock brings a good price, it will be something."

"Please, Rowan. I want so much to try it," she pleaded. "I haven't ever been any help to you . . . thought of nothing but having a good time. But now I'm going to be such a tip-top manager, if you'll only let me."

"I would, dear . . . if it were any use," he told her gently. "But you would have all your worry for nothing. The new conditions make the old ways impossible. I'm sorry."

Her coaxing smile refused to accept his decision. "My aunt left me her money, you know. I don't know how much it is yet. Most of it is property that must be sold. But I can use it when it comes to save the ranch. I'd love to. I want to be helping you."

"Ask Tim Flanders if I'm not right, sweetheart. He has a

level head. He'll tell you just what I'm telling you."

"All right. I'll ask him. We don't need to decide my future now. There will be lots of time after you have gone."

Rowan drew her to a chair and sat down with her in his arms. For once his tongue was not tied. The ten minutes that were left he packed full of all the love that had so long been waiting in his heart for expression.

When she said good bye to him it was with a wan, twitchy little smile on her face. But as soon as he was out of the room she flung herself down, weeping, beside the lounge.

She was still lying crouched there when McCoy climbed to the vestibule of the through train. He moved awkwardly because his left wrist was shackled to the right one of Cole.

XVII

Rowan's decision to sell the ranch was on the face of it a wise one. Ruth recognized this. She knew nothing of cattle, nothing of farming.

But she told herself she could learn. Her interest was very greatly engaged in saving the Circle Diamond for Rowan. Other women had done well homesteading. She knew one widow who raised cattle, another who made money on sheep. Why should she not do the same?

She talked it all over with Flanders, a long-headed business-man who knew cattle from hoof to horn.

"The cattleman sure has his troubles aplenty," he told her. "Short summers, long winters, deep snows, blizzards, bad roads, heavy railroad rates, a packers' trust to buck, drought, and now sheep. A cowman has got to bet before the draw . . . he can't ever tell whether he's going to finish with a hand all blue or a busted flush."

"Yes, but I've heard you say yourself that cattle-raising used to be a gamble and that from now on it's going to be a business, instead," she reminded him.

He took off his big white hat and rubbed a polka dot handkerchief over his bald head.

"Tha's right, too. Government reports show there's several million fewer cattle in the country than there was five years ago. That spells good prices. There's a good side to this forest-reserve business, too. It keeps the range from being overcrowded, and it settles the sheep and cattle war."

"Well, then?" she demanded triumphantly.

"That ain't saying *you* could make money. Jennings is a good foreman, but it takes a boss to run any she-bang right."

"When the boss is in doubt she could telephone to you."

Ruth had always been a favorite of Flanders's. It pleased him that he could help her in her affairs, and it flattered him to think that he could help her make a success of the Circle Diamond. The conspiracy she proposed intrigued his interest. She had some money. Why not use it to save the ranch for Rowan? Why not let her have the pleasure of showing her husband later how well she had done in his absence? It would give a zest to her life that would otherwise be lacking. Moreover, it would be another tie to bind her to McCoy.

He yielded to the temptation, fell into her plans, even grew eager over them.

In a letter, Ruth wrote her husband that Flanders thought it better not to sell out just yet, but she gave no details of what she was doing in a business way. There was, she felt, no use worrying him about the venture she was making.

Her interest in the ranch developed amazingly. Jennings was an experienced cattleman and devoted to Rowan. It had been his curt opinion that McCoy was a fool for marrying this feather-footed girl from the East. Her gaiety and extravagance had annoyed him. The flirtation with Silcott had set him flatly against her. But now he began to revise his estimate. He liked the eagerness with which she flung herself into this exciting game of saving the Circle Diamond. He liked the deference she paid his judgment, and he admired the courage with which once or twice she decided flatly against him.

There were hours, of course, when the loneliness of her life swept over Ruth in waves, when she fought desperately for a footing against despair. It was her inheritance to tread the hilltops or the valleys rather than the dusty road. But in general she was almost happy. A warm glow flushed her being when she thought of Rowan. Some sure voice whispered to her that however long he might be kept from her the flame of love would burn bright in his heart.

He had sinned against her pride and self-esteem, and she had forgiven him. He had brought to her trouble and distress by breaking the law of the land. All her Eastern friends pitied her. They pelted her with letters beginning: *Poor dear Ruth.* But she refused to feel humiliated. Rowan was Rowan, the man she loved, no matter what wrong he had done. There burned bright in him a dynamic spark of self-respect that would never be quenched. She clung to this. She never let herself doubt it now, even though one memory of him still stung her to shame.

Ruth lay snuggled up on the lounge in her sewing room, one foot tucked comfortably under her, half a dozen soft pillows piled at her back. She was looking rather indolently over the two days' old Wagon Wheel *Spoke* to see if it gave any beef quotations. The day had been a busy one. In the morning she had ridden across to Pine Hollow to inspect a drift fence. Later she had come home covered with dust after watching the men fan oats. Getting out of her serviceable khaki, she had reveled in a hot bath and put on a loose morning gown and slippers. Tonight she was content to be lazy and self-indulgent.

An advertisement caught and held her eye. It was on the

back page and boxed to draw more attention.

The open ANC Ranch, together with all cattle and personal property pertaining thereto, is offered for sale by me at a figure much below its value to an immediate purchaser.

I shall be at the ranch, ENTIRELY UNARMED, for a week beginning next Monday. Prospective buyers may see me there.

LAWRENCE SILCOTT

The young woman read the announcement with contemptuous interest. She had expected Silcott to leave the country. It was not to be looked for that a man weak enough to betray his friends would run the risk of living in the neighborhood of those who had suffered from his treachery. At the two capitalized words she smiled bitterly. They were both a confession and a shield of defense. They admitted fear, and at the same time disarmed the righteous anger of his former neighbors.

Inevitably she compared him with Rowan. Her imagination pictured McCoy as he had sat through the strain of the trial— cool, easy, undisturbed, master of whatever fate might be in store for him. She saw in contrast Silcott, no longer graceful and debonair, smiles and gaiety all wiped out, a harried, irritable wretch close to collapse. It was the first time she had ever seen two men's souls under the acid test. One had assayed pure gold, the other a base alloy.

Yet all these years Silcott had been accepted in the community as a good fellow. Ruth was deeply ashamed that she had let him go as far with her as he had.

Her thoughts went back to Rowan. They never wandered very long from him these days. He was the center of her universe, although he was shut up behind bars in a dingy prison. She knew she was not responsible for the thing he had done, but she reproached herself that she had not been a greater comfort to him in the dark days and nights of trial.

Some sound on the porch outside attracted her attention. A loose plank creaked. It seemed to her she heard the shuffling of furtive feet. Then there was silence. Ruth sat up. The curtains were drawn, so that she could not see out without rising.

Fingers fumbled at the latch of the French window she had had made. She was not afraid, but she felt a curious expectant thrill of excitement. Who could be there?

Slowly the casement opened. A man's head craned forward. Eyes searched the room warily and found the young woman.

Ruth rose. "You . . . here!"

Larry Silcott put his finger to his lips, came in, and closed the window carefully.

"What do you want?" demanded the girl, eyes flashing.

The man looked haggard and miserable. All his gay effrontery had been wiped out.

"I want to see you . . . to talk with you," he pleaded.

"What about?" Her manner was curt and uncompromising.

"I want to explain. I want to tell you how it was."

"Is that necessary?" asked Ruth, her scornful eyes fully on him.

"Yes. I don't want you to blame me. You know how . . . how fond I am of you."

She threw out a contemptuous little gesture. "Please spare me that."

"Don't be hard on me, Ruth. Listen. They had the goods on us. We were going to hang . . . every one of us. They kept at me day and night. They pestered me . . . woke me out of my sleep to argue and explain. If it hadn't been me, it would have been one of the others that gave evidence for the state."

"I don't believe it."

"It's true. Both Haight and Matson told me so. The only question was who would come through first."

"If that was the only question for you, then it shows just what you are. Did you never hear of such things as honor and decency and fair play? If anybody was entitled to the benefit of state's evidence, it should have been the married men, poor Sam Yerby or Mister Rogers. They have children dependent on them. Anybody with the least generosity could see that. But you're selfish to the core. You never think of anybody but yourself."

"How can you say that when you know that I love you, Ruth?"

Her eyes blazed. "Don't say that. Don't dare say it!" she cried.

"It's true."

"Nothing of what you say is true. You don't know the truth when you see it. They picked you, Haight and Matson did, because they knew you had no strength or courage. Do you suppose that the others didn't get a chance to betray their friends, too? All of them did. Every one of them. But they were *men*. That was the difference. So the prosecution focused on you. And you weakened."

"Why not? I didn't kill Tait or Gilroy. Why should I be hanged for it? I wasn't guilty."

"You are as guilty as Rowan was."

"I dunno about that. He shot Gilroy, if Falkner didn't," Silcott said sulkily.

"Never! Never in the world!" she cried. "Don't tell me so, you cowardly Judas!"

"You can talk. That's easy. But you've never had a rope around your neck. You've never awakened in the night from a dream where they were taking you out to hang you. You've never been hounded till your nerves were ragged and you wanted to scream out."

"I don't care to discuss all that. You had no business to come here. You made your choice to save yourself. That was your privilege, just as it is mine to prefer never to see you again."

His voice rose. "Why do you say that? I'm not a leper. I'm

still Larry Silcott, your friend. Say I did wrong. Don't you suppose I've paid? Don't you suppose I've lived in hell ever since? Have I got to spend all the rest of my life an outcast?"

She wouldn't let herself sympathize with his wretchedness. He had betrayed the man she loved, had struck at his life. The harsh judgment of youth condemned him.

"You should have thought of that before you sold out the men who trusted you," she told him coldly.

"I didn't sell them out. I didn't get a penny for it. I told the truth. That's all," he cried wildly.

"You had forfeited the right to tell the truth. And you did sell them out. You wouldn't be here tonight if you hadn't."

Silcott shifted his defense. "I'm sick and tired of things tonight, Ruth. Let's not quarrel," he begged.

"I'm not quarrelling. I don't quarrel with anyone except my friends, and I'm trying to make it clear that Mister Lawrence Silcott is not one of them. You are not welcome here, sir. I ask you to leave."

"You've got to forgive me, Ruth. I . . . oh, you don't know what I've been through!" He broke down and brushed his hand across his eyes. "I haven't slept for a week. It's been hell every hour."

"You'd better go away somewhere," she suggested. "Leave your affairs with an agent. You ought not to stay here."

"No. My nerves are all jumpy. I've got to get away." He took a long breath and plunged on: "I'm going to begin all over again in Los Angeles or San Francisco. I've had my lesson. I'll run straight from now on. I'm going to work hard and get ahead. If you'd only stand by me, Ruth. If you'd. . . ."

"I can't be a friend of the man who betrayed my husband, if that's what you mean."

"You'd have to choose between him and me. That's true. Well, Rowan is in the penitentiary for life. You're young. You can't wait forever. It wouldn't be right you should. Besides, you and Rowan never did get along well. I'm not saying a word against him but. . . ."

"You'd better not!" she flamed, the lace on her bosom rising and falling fast with her passionate anger. "You say he is in the penitentiary. Who put him there?"

"That isn't the point, Ruth. Hear me out. You can get free from him without any trouble. The law says that a convict's wife can get a divorce any time. . . ."

"I don t want a divorce. I'd rather be his wife, if he stays in prison forever, than be married to any other man on earth. I . . . I never heard such insolence in my life. I've a good mind to call the men to throw you off the place. Every moment you stay here is an insult to me."

He moistened his parched lips with the tip of his tongue. "There is no use getting excited, Ruth. I came here because I love you. If you'd only be reasonable. Listen. I'm going to California. If you change your mind and want to come out there. . . ."

Ruth marched past him and flung the door open. She turned on him eyes that blazed. "If you've not gone in five seconds, I'll turn the men loose on you. They've been aching for a chance."

His vanity withered before her wrath. For the moment he saw himself as she saw him, a snake in the grass, hateful to all decent human beings. It was a moral certainty that she would keep her word and call the Circle Diamond riders. What they would do to him he could guess.

He went without another word.

Presently she heard him galloping down the road and out of her life.

The anger died out of Ruth almost instantly. She was filled with a sense of desolating degradation. There had been a time in her life when she had put this weakling before Rowan, when

141

her laughter and her friendliness had been for him instead of for the man to whom she was married.

The feeling that floored her now was almost a physical nausea.

XVIII

As Tim Flanders had predicted, the establishment of government forest reserves changed the equation that faced the cattleman. The open range was doomed, but federal supervision brought with it compensations. One of these was that the man who ran cattle on the reserve need not fear overstocking or the competition of Mary's Little Lamb. The market was in a better condition than it had been for years. The price of beef was high, and was still on the rise. Nor was there any prospect of a slump, since the supply in the country was not equal to the demand.

Ruth had every reason to feel satisfied. Her shipment of beef steers had brought a top price at the Denver stockyards. The opportune sale of a house from her aunt's estate made it possible for her to pay the debts that had accumulated from Rowan's trial and to reduce a little of the mortgage on the Circle Diamond. The hay-cutting in the meadow had run to a fair average, and already she had in one hundred acres of winter wheat.

She had worked hard and steadily, so that when one afternoon Jennings brought back from the post office a letter from Rowan his young mistress decided to ride up into the hills and read it where she could be alone among the pines.

As the pinto—one that Rowan himself had gentled for his bride—picked his way into the cañon mouth through blue-spiked larkspur and rabbitbrush in golden splashes the girl in the saddle was nearer happy than she had been for many a day. Her lover's letter lay warm against her breast, all the joy of reading it still before her.

In a pine grove on a sunny slope Ruth read his letter. To read what he had written was to see the face of love. It filled her with deep joy, brought with it a peace that was infinitely comforting. She wept a little over it thankfully, although every word carried good cheer.

Dusk had fallen before Ruth rode down the trail to the ranch, her spirit still with Rowan up in the pines.

Mrs. Stovall was on the porch speeding a parting guest, a dark-eyed, trim young woman of unobtrusive manners.

"Missus McCoy, I want you should meet an old friend of mine . . . Missus Tait," said the housekeeper by way of introduction.

It was like a blow in the face to Ruth. She drew herself up straight and stiff. A flush of indignation swept into her face. With the slightest of bows she acknowledged the presentation, then marched into the house and to her bedroom.

All the sweet gladness of the day was blotted out for her. Just as she and Rowan were coming together again the woman who had separated them must intrude herself as a hateful reminder of the past. She had forgiven her husband—yes, but her forgiveness did not extend to the woman who had led him into temptation. And even if she had pardoned him, she had not forgotten.

She did not deny that she was jealous. All of Rowan she could hold fast would not be too much to carry her through their years of separation. Except for this one deadening memory, she had nothing to recall but good of him. Why must this come up now to torment her?

A knock sounded on the door. "Supper's ready," announced Mrs. Stovall tartly.

"I don't want any tonight."

After a moment's silence Ruth heard retreating footsteps. A few minutes later there came a second knock.

"I've brought you supper." The housekeeper did not wait for an invitation, but opened the door and walked in. Never before had she done this.

Ruth jumped to her feet from the chair where she was sitting in the dusk. "I told you I didn't want any supper," she said, annoyed.

Mrs. Stovall had promised Rowan to look after Ruth while he was away. In her tight-lipped, sardonic fashion she had come to be very fond of this girl who was the victim of the frontier tragedy that had so stirred Shoshone County. Silently she had watched the flirtation with Larry Silcott and the division between husband and wife. It was her firm opinion that Ruth needed a lesson to save her from her own foolishness. But what had occurred on the porch a half hour since had given her a new slant on the situation. Martha Stovall prided herself on her plain speaking. She had a reputation for it far and wide. She proposed to do some of it now.

"Why don't you want any supper?" The housekeeper set the tray down on a little table and faced her mistress. Every angular inch of her declared that she intended to settle this matter on the spot.

Ruth was too astonished for words. Mrs. Stovall did not miss the opportunity.

"What ails you at the supper? Are you sick?" The thin lips of the woman were pressed together in a straight line of determination.

"I'm not hungry."

"Fiddle-dee-dee! It's Norma Tait that's spoiled your appetite. What call have you to be so highty-tighty? Isn't she good enough for you?"

"I would rather not discuss Missus Tait," answered Ruth stiffly. "I don't quite see why you should come into my room and talk to me like this, Missus Stovall."

"Don't you? Well, maybe I'm not very polite, but what I've got to say is for your good . . . and I'm going to say it, even if you order me off the place when I get through."

The answer of Ruth was rather disconcerting. She said nothing.

"When I introduced you to Norma Tait, you 'most insulted her. I'd like to know why," demanded the housekeeper.

"I think I won't talk about that," replied the young woman with icy gentleness.

"Then I'll do the talking. You've heard that fool story about Norma and Mac. I'll bet a cookie that's what is the matter with you." The shrewd little eyes of Martha Stovall gimleted the girl. "It's all a pack of lies. I ought to know, for it was me that asked Mac to drive Norma down to Wagon Wheel in his car."

"You!" The astonishment of the girl leaped from her in the word.

The housekeeper nodded. "Want I should tell you all about it?" The acidity in her voice was less pronounced.

"Please."

"You know that Mac used to be engaged to her and that after a quarrel Norma ran away with Tait and married him?"

"Yes."

"Joe Tait was a brute. He bullied Norma and abused her. When she couldn't stand it any longer, she ran away and phoned me to get a rig to have her taken to Wagon Wheel, so's she could go to Laramie, where her sister lives."

It was as though a weight were lifting from Ruth's heart. She waited, her big eyes fixed on those of Mrs. Stovall.

"But folks didn't want to anger Joe Tait," went on the housekeeper. "He was always raising a ruckus with someone. Folks knew he'd beat the head offen any man that helped Norma get away from him. So they all had excuses. When I was at my wit's end, Mac came along in his car, headed for Wagon Wheel. I asked him to take Norma along with him. Well, you know Mac. He said . . . 'Where is she?' And I told him. And he took her."

Ruth nodded urgently, impatiently. She could not hear the rest too soon.

"Mac stands up on his own hind legs. He didn't need to ask Joe Tait's permission to help a woman when she was in trouble," explained Mrs. Stovall. "So he took Norma down and fixed it with Moody so's he lent her the money for her ticket. Mac had phoned down to the depot agent and got the last vacant berth to Cheyenne. He gave it up to Norma and went into the day coach. That's exactly what he did. There's been a lot of stuff told by them that ought to've known Mac and Norma better, and o' course Tait spread a heap of scandal, but Bart Mason, the Pullman conductor, told me this his own self. Mac never even sat down beside Norma. He talked with her a minute, and then walked right through to the chair car."

Not for an instant did Ruth doubt that this was the true version of the story she had heard. It was like Rowan to do just that, quietly and without any fuss. How lacking in faith she had been ever to doubt him.

Her heart sang. She caught Mrs. Stovall in her arms and kissed the wrinkled face. "I've been such a little fool," she confided. "And I've been so dreadfully unhappy . . . and it's all been my own fault. I got to hating Rowan, and I was awfully mean to him. Before he went away we made it all up, but I wasn't any help to him at all during the trial. I'm so glad you told me this." She laughed a little hysterically. "I'm the happiest girl that ever had a lover shut up in prison for life. And it's all because of you. Oh, I've acted hatefully, but I'll never do it again."

Mrs. Stovall, comforting the young wife after the fashion of her sex, forgot that she was the cynic of the settlement, and mingled her glad tears with those of Ruth.

XIX

The long white fingers of winter reached down through the mountain gulches to the Circle Diamond. Ruth looked out of her windows upon a land grown chill and drear. She saw her line riders returning to the bunkhouse crusted with snow and sleet. The cattle huddled in the shelter of haystacks, and those on the range grew rough and thin and shaggy.

The short days were too long for the mistress of the ranch. She began to mope, and her loneliness was accented by the bitter wind and the deep drifts that shut her from the great world outside.

When the winds died down she made Jennings show her how to travel on snowshoes, and after that there was seldom a day during which she could not be outdoors about the place for at least a little while.

Her fragility had always been more apparent than real. Back of her slenderness was a good deal of wiry strength. As the months passed she took on flesh, and by spring was almost plump. The open life she cultivated did not help her pink-and-white complexion, but brought solidity to her frame and power to her muscles.

The boy was born in early April. Norma Tait and Mrs. Stovall nursed her back to health, and in a few weeks she was driving over the ranch in consultation with Jennings.

Rowan, Jr. was king of the Circle Diamond from his birth. He ruled imperiously over the hearts of the three women. It was natural that Ruth should love him from the moment that they put him in her arms and his little heel kicked her in the side. He was the symbol of the love of Rowan that glowed so steadfastly in her soul. So she worshipped him for his own sake and for the sake of the man she had married. The small body that breathed so close to her, so helpless and so soft, filled her with everlasting wonder and delight.

147

In every letter she wrote Rowan the baby held first place, but she was careful to show him that the boy was his son as well as hers, a bond between them from the past and a promise for the future. In one letter she wrote:

While I was putting Rowan, Jr. to bed I showed him your picture— the one the Denver Times *photographer took just after you won the championship last year—and he reached out his dimpled fingers for it and spluttered, "Da-da-da-da-da." I believe he knows you belong to him. Before I put his nightie on, I kissed his dear little pink body for you.*

Do you know that we are about to entertain distinguished visitors at the Circle Diamond? Louise McDowell and the governor are going to stay with us a day on their way to Yellowstone Park. I can't help feeling that it is a good omen. Last year when I went to Cheyenne he would not give me any hope—said he could not possibly do anything for me. But there has been a great change of sentiment here. Tim Flanders talked with the governor not long since, and urged a parole for you. I feel sure the governor would not visit me unless he was at least in doubt.

So I'm eager to try again, with Rowan, Jr. to plead for me. He's going to make love to the governor, innocently and shamelessly, in a hundred darling little ways he has. Oh, you don't know how hard I'm going to try to win the governor this time, dear.

Governor McDowell was a cattleman himself. His sympathies were much engaged in behalf of the Bald Knob raiders. All the evidence at the trial tended to show that Tait had forced the trouble and had refused all compromise. From his talk with the prisoners the governor had learned that the tragedy had flared out unexpectedly. Personally he liked Rowan McCoy very much. But he could not get away from the fact that murder had been done. As a private citizen, McDowell would have worked hard to get his friend a parole; as governor of the state of Wyoming he could not move in the matter without a legitimate excuse.

It was his hope of finding such an excuse that led him to diverge from the direct road to Yellowstone for a stop at the Circle Diamond Ranch. On the way he called at the ranches of several old-timers who he had long known.

"It's like this, Phil," one of them told the governor. "The government has stepped in and settled this whole sheep and cattle war. We don't aim to go night raiding any more . . . none of us. Sheep are here, and they're going to stay whether we like it or not. So we got to make the best of it . . . and we do. What's the use of keeping Mac and Brad and the other boys locked up for an example when we don't need one any more? Everybody would be satisfied to see 'em paroled . . . even the sheepmen would. You couldn't do a more popular thing than to free the whole passel of 'em."

The governor made no promises, but he kept his ears open to learn the drift of public opinion. Even before he reached the Circle Diamond, he knew that there would be no strong protest against a parole from the western part of the state.

Ruth did not make the mistake of letting the governor see her in the rough-and-ready ranch costume to which she was accustomed. She dressed her hair with care and wore a simple gown that set off the slender fullness of her figure. When she came lightly and swiftly to meet them as the car drew up at the Circle Diamond, her guests were impressed anew with the note of fineness, of personal distinction. There was, too, something gallant and spirited in the poise of the small head set so fastidiously upon the rounded throat.

Mrs. McDowell always admired tremendously her school companion. She was more proud of her than ever now, and, as she dressed for dinner, she attacked her husband.

"You've got to do something for her, Phil. That's all there's to it. I can't look that brave girl in the face if you don't let her husband out of prison."

He was wrestling with a collar and a reluctant button. A grunt was his only answer.

Ruth and Tim Flanders showed the guests over the ranch, and afterward in the absence of the mistress, who was in the kitchen consulting with Mrs. Stovall about the dinner, the owner of the dude ranch sang her praises with enthusiasm.

"I never saw her beat, Phil. That slim little girl you could break in two over your knee has got more git-up-and-dust than any man I know. Mac wanted her to sell the ranch and live off the proceeds. Did she do it? Not so you could notice it. She grabbed hold with both hands, cleared off the debts of the trial, wiped off the mortgage, got a permit to run a big bunch of cattle on the reserve, and has made money hand over fist."

McDowell smiled dryly. "She's doing so well it would be a pity to let Mac come home and gum up the works."

But in his heart the governor was full of admiration for this vital young woman who had thrown herself with such pluck and intelligence into the task of saving the ranch for her imprisoned husband. The situation troubled him. He wanted to do for her the most that he legitimately could, but he came up always against the same barrier. Rowan McCoy had been convicted of first-degree murder. He had no right to pardon him within fifteen months without any new extenuating evidence.

The governor was a warm-souled Scotch Irishman. Until the past year he had been a bachelor. He was very fond of children. Rowan, Jr. walked right into his heart.

Nonetheless, he was glad when the time came for him to go. It made the big, simple cattleman uncomfortable not to be able to relieve the sorrow of this girl who his wife loved.

Ruth made her chance to see him alone and let him know at

once what was in her heart. She stood before him white and tremulous.

"What about Rowan, Governor?"

He shook his head. "I wish I could do what you want. In a couple of years I can, but not yet."

She bit her lip. The big tears came into her eyes and splashed over.

"Now don't you . . . don't you," he pleaded, stroking her hand in his big ones. "I'd do it if I could . . . if I were free to follow my own wishes. But I'm not."

Softly she wept.

"Get me some new evidence . . . something to prove that Mac didn't shoot Gilroy himself . . . and I'll see what I can do. You see how it is, Ruth. Someone shot him while he was unarmed. All five of them pleaded guilty. If Mac's lawyers can find the man that did the killing, I'll parole the others. That's the best I can do for you."

With that promise Ruth had to be content.

XX

During the second winter Ruth left the ranch only twice, except for runs down to Wagon Wheel. Late in January she went to Cheyenne with her boy to make another appeal to the governor. He was full of genuine homely kindness to her, and renewed at once his allegiance to Rowan, Jr. With the large hospitality of the West, he urged her to spend the next few months as their guests, to postpone her return at least until the snow was out of the hills. But in the matter of a parole he stood firm against the entreaties of his wife, the touching wistfulness of her friend, and the tug of desire at his own big heart.

Her other visit was in April to the penitentiary. McCoy was away as a trusty in charge of a road-building gang near Casper. But it was not her husband that Ruth had come to see. She wanted to make a plea to the one man who could help her.

The hour she had chosen was inauspicious. Falkner, sullen and dogged, was brought in irons to the office of the warden. His face was badly swollen and cut. He pretended not to recognize Ruth, but stood, heavy and lowering, his sunken eyes set defiantly straight before him.

"He's been in solitary for a week," explained the warden. "Makes us more trouble than any two men here. This time he hit a guard over the head with a shovel."

The prisoner had the baited look of a hunted wild animal.

"I'm so sorry," breathed Ruth. It was plain to her at a glance that he was much more of a wild beast than he had been when she last saw him.

"You needn't be sorry for him. He brings it all on himself." The warden turned curtly to Falkner. "This lady wants to talk to you. See you behave yourself."

But when she was alone with this battered hulk her carefully prepared arguments all fell away from her. She hesitated, uncertain how to proceed. The best she could do was to repeat herself.

"I'm sorry they don't treat you well, Mister Falkner. Is there anything I can do for you . . . tobacco, or anything like that?"

He gave her a sulky sidewise look, but did not answer.

"We're all hoping you'll get out soon," she went on bravely. "They are talking of getting up a petition for all of you."

She was stuck again. His whole attitude was unfriendly and hostile. "I . . . I've come to ask another favor of you. Perhaps you don't know that I have a little baby now. I'm trying to get Rowan out on parole, but the governor won't do anything unless we bring evidence to show that he did not kill Mister Gilroy."

He clung still to his obstinate silence. His eyes were watching her now steadily. It came to her that her suffering pleased him.

"So I've come to you, Mister Falkner. You are the only man that can help me. If you'll make a statement that you shot Mister Gilroy, the governor will give me back my husband. I'm asking it for the sake of my little baby." A pulse beat fast in her throat. A tremor passed through her body.

He laughed, and the sound of his laughter was harsh and cruel. "I'd see the whole outfit of you in hell first."

"I'm sure you don't mean that," she said gently. "You haven't been treated well here, and naturally you feel hard about it. Anybody would. But I'm sure you want to be fair to your friends."

"My friends!" he jeered bitterly. "That's a good one. My friends!"

"Isn't Rowan your friend? You told me yourself that he had stood by you to the finish, though it almost cost him his own life. You said as much to me that day down at Wagon Wheel. Won't you say as much to the governor now? It can't hurt you, and it would bring happiness to so many people."

"You want me to be the goat, eh?"

"I want you to tell the truth. Rowan would in your place. He'd never let women and children suffer for his wrongdoing. I don't think you would if you thought of it."

"You're wasting your breath," he told her sulkily.

"I wish you could see Missie Yerby and her little boy. They get along somehow because the neighbors help with the cattle. She doesn't complain. But she does miss Sam dreadfully. So does the little boy. He's a nice manly little chap, but he needs a father. He often asks when his dad is coming home."

"I ain't keeping him here," he growled.

"And Missus Rogers will be an old woman soon if Brad doesn't get out. I can see her fading away. It seems to me that, if I could help them by saying a few words, by just telling the truth, that it would give me pleasure to make them happy."

"Different here," he snarled. "It's everyone for himself."

"Kate is still waiting for Jack Cole. She won't look at any other man."

"Makes no difference to me if she waits till Kingdom Come."

"That's three women who are unhappy, and Jack's mother is another, and I'm the fifth. Five women and two children you could make glad by confessing that you started the shooting and killed Mister Gilroy. Not many men have an opportunity like that. We would bless you in our prayers, Mister Falkner."

"Keep right on soft-soaping me. See where it gets you," he taunted.

She ignored his retort. "We'd do more for you than that. We'd all work for your pardon, too. Pretty soon we'd get you out, too."

"The hell you would! Don't I know? I'd stand the gaff for all of 'em. Ain't I doing it now? Rowan's out somewhere bossing a road gang. Rogers is in the warden's office. Sam Yerby putters around the garden. An' me . . . I live in that damned dark hole alone. They're warden's little pets. I'm the one that gets the whip. By God, if I ever get a chance at one of these slave-drivers. . . ." He broke off, to grind his teeth in fury of impotent rage.

"Don't! Don't feel that way," she begged. "You get all the worst of it. Don't you see you do? And it makes you unhappy. Let me tell the warden that you'll try not to break the prison rules. It would be so much better for you."

"Tell him I'll cut his black heart out if I ever get a chance."

She was appalled at his venomous hatred. She knew that prison discipline was harsh. Falkner was refractory and undisciplined. No doubt he had broken rules and been insubordinate. It came to her that there had been some contest of stubborn will between this lawless convict and the guards who had charge of him. His face was scarred with wounds not yet healed. She did not know that ridges crossed and recrossed his back where the lash had cut away the skin with cruel strokes that had burned like fire. But she did know that he was untamed and unbroken, that nothing short of death could make that wild spirit quail before his tormentors.

"I wish I could help you," she said. "But I can't. All I can do is ask you to help me. Won't you think about it, please?"

"I don't need to think about it. I'm playing my own hand."

"The governor says that if I can get any evidence, any proof that Rowan did not start the shooting or kill Gilroy, he will give him a pardon. It lies with you, Mister Falkner."

"Well, I've given you my answer. I'm for myself, an' for nobody else. That's the bedrock of it."

For Rowan's freedom Ruth would have gone a long way. She had humbled herself to plead with the convict. But she had known it would be useless. When she left the prison it was with the knowledge that she had not advanced her husband's cause one whit.

In front of the warden's house a convict was wheeling manure and scattering it on the lawn. Some trick of gesture caught the attention of Ruth. Her arrested eyes fixed themselves on the man. His shoulders drooped, and his whole attitude expressed dejected listlessness, but she was sure she knew him. Deserting the warden's wife she ran forward, with both hands outstretched.

"Oh, I'm so glad to see you!"

For an instant a puzzled expression lifted the white eyebrows and slackened the lank jaw of Sam Yerby. Then his shoulders straightened. He had been caught with his guard down, detected in the mood of hopelessness into which he often fell now.

He came gamely to time. "Well, well, Miss Ruth. I'm sure proud to see you, ma'am."

"They told me you were at a road camp. One of the guards said so."

"I was, but I'm back. You're looking fine, ma'am. Missie writes me you-all done got a little baby of your own now."

She nodded. "Yes, I'll tell you all about it. But how are you? Missie will ask me a hundred questions."

"I'm tol'able, thank you." Yerby, looking across her shoulder, saw a guard moving toward them. He did not mention to her that he was liable to ten days' solitary confinement for talking to a visitor without permission. "How's Missie ... and my son?"

"Missie is prettier than ever. She's always talking about you. And the boy ... he's the dandiest little chap ... smart as a whip and good as gold. You'll be awfully pleased with him when you come home."

"Yes'm ... when I come home."

His voice fell flat. Its lifelessness went to the heart of his friend. She saw that hope was dead within him. He was getting into the fifties, and the years were slipping away.

"That won't be long. We're getting up a petition to. . . ."

The guard pushed between Ruth and the convict. "You know the rule, Yerby," he said curtly.

"Yes, sir, and I most generally aim to keep it. But when a lady speaks to me ... an old friend. . . ."

"Come along with me."

The old cowman dropped his shovel and shambled off beside the guard.

Ruth turned in consternation to the wife of the warden. "What have I done?"

"He oughtn't to have talked with you. That's the rule. He knew it."

"You won't let him be punished because I made a mistake, will you? He's a Texan, you know. He thinks it wouldn't be courteous not to answer a lady. It would make me very unhappy if I had got him into trouble."

The warden's wife smiled. "I think it can be arranged this time. We all like him. We're all sorry for him. I wish the governor would pardon him. If he stays much longer, he'll become an old man with no hope in his heart."

"I'll tell his wife that you are good to him. It will be a great comfort to her."

The meeting with Yerby depressed Ruth more even than her encounter with Falkner. She took home with her a memory of a brave man slowly having the zest of life pressed out of him.

But of this she said little when next she wrote to Rowan. Always her letters had running through them the red thread of hope. She told him that Flanders was getting up a petition for a parole that had been signed by half the county, including the judge who had tried him, every member of the jury, the prosecuting attorney, and the sheriff. But she did not mention that Ruth McCoy was the motive power behind the petition, that she in person had won the signatures of Haight, Matson, and the judge, as well as hundreds of others.

XXI

Again spring bloomed into summer and summer yellowed into autumn. During the daytime Ruth was busy with business details of the roundup, of the fall beef shipment, of planting and of harvesting. As soon as dusk fell she devoted herself to the baby until he went to sleep for the night. In the evening she took up the accounts of the ranch, wrote to Rowan, held a conference with Jennings, or did a little desultory reading. The housekeeping she left almost entirely in the competent hands of Mrs. Stovall.

In addition to the business of the Circle Diamond and superintending the care of a year-old baby, Ruth had other claims upon her time that she could not ignore. One of these was to promise to Sam Yerby to look after Missie and the boy. It was her custom to have them down for a day every other month and to visit the Yerby place between times.

On a day in mid-November, with Rowan, Jr. beside her, Ruth set out in the car for the little mountain ranch. It was a cool, crisp morning. The sting of frost was in the air, and the indigo mountains were ribbed with white in the snow-filled gulches. To the nostrils came the tang of sage and later of pine.

After she had driven from the foothills into the cañon, Ruth stopped to wrap an extra blanket around the baby, for the sun was painting only the upper walls as yet, and down by the creek there was an inch-thick ice at the edges. The early fall snows were melting on the sunny slopes above, and Hill Creek was pouring down in a flood. The road crossed the creek twice, but after she was on it Ruth discovered that the second bridge was very shaky. The car got over safely, but she decided to take the high-line road home, even though it was a few miles longer.

Robert E. Lee Yerby came running down to the gate to meet them.

"Oh, Auntie Rufe!" he shouted. "Momma's peelin' a chicken for dinner."

Ruth caught the youngster up and hugged him. He was an attractive little chap, with the bluest of eyes and the most ingenuous of smiles.

"I like you, Auntie Rufe. You always smell like pink woses," he confided with the frankness of extreme youth.

"I've brought Budda to play with you, Bobbie." Budda was the nearest Robert could come to the word brother at the time Rowan was born, and the word had stuck with him.

"Now let me go. I must get out and shut the gate."

"No, it don't hurt if it's open. Momma said so, tos every-fing's in the pasture."

As she went into the house with Missie, stripping the driving gauntlets from her hands, Ruth noticed that clouds were banking in the sky over the summit of the range. It looked like snow.

The days she spent with Ruth were red-letter ones for Mrs. Yerby. Missie was a simple mountain girl, born and bred in the Wyoming hills. What little schooling she had had was of the country-district kind. It did not go far, and was rather sketchy even to the point she had gone. But this radiant, vital girl from the city, so fine and beautiful, and yet so generous of her friendship, so competent and strong and self-reliant, but so essentially feminine—Missie accepted what she offered with a devotion that came near worship.

The women chatted and worked while the youngsters played on the floor. Just before dinner a cowpuncher from the Triangle Dot rode up and trailed into the house with spurs a-jingle. He had come to tell Mrs. Yerby about one of her yearlings he had rescued from the swamp and was keeping in the corral for a day or two. His nostrils sniffed the dinner in the kitchen, and it was not hard to persuade him to stay and eat.

"Have you ladies heard about Hal Falkner?" he asked.

Ruth, putting a platter of fried chicken on the table, turned abruptly to him. "What about him?"

"He escaped from the pen four days ago . . . beat up a guard 'most to death and made his getaway. Four prisoners were in the jailbreak, but they've got 'em all 'cept Hal. He reached the hills somehow."

The eyes of Ruth McCoy asked a question she dared not put into words.

"No, ma'am. None of the rest of our boys mixed up in it a-tall," he told her quickly.

The young woman drew a deep breath of relief. The hope was always with her of a day near at hand when the Bald Knob raiders would be paroled, but she knew if they joined such an undertaking as this it would be fatal to their chances.

"Do you think Mister Falkner will get away?" Ruth asked.

"I reckon not, ma'am. You see, he's got the telephone against him. Whenever he shows up at a ranch, the news will go out that he was there. But he got holt of a gun from a farmer. It's a cinch they won't take him without a fight."

Snow was already falling when the cowpuncher took his departure. He cast a weather eye toward the hills. "Heap much snow in them clouds. If I was you, Missus McCoy, I'd start my gasoline bronc' on the home trail so's not to run any chances of getting stalled."

Ruth thought this good advice. It took a few minutes to wrap Rowan for the journey and to say good bye. By the time she was on the way the air was full of large flakes.

The storm increased steadily as she drove toward home. There was a rising wind that brought the sleet about her in sharp gusts. So fierce became the swirl that when she turned into the high-line drive she was surrounded by a white, stinging wall that narrowed the scope of her vision to a few feet.

The temperature was falling rapidly, and the wind swept the hilltops with a roar. The soft flakes had turned to powdered ice. It beat upon Ruth with a deadly chill that reached to the bones.

The young mother became alarmed. The boy was well wrapped up, but no clothing was sufficient protection against a blizzard. Moreover, there were dangerous places to pass, cuts where the path ran along the sloping edge of the mountain with a sheer fall of a hundred feet below. It would never do to try to take these with snow heavy on the ledge and the way blurred so that she could not see clearly.

Ruth stopped and tried to adjust the curtains, but her fingers were like ice, and the knobs so sleet-encrusted that she could not fasten the buttons. It was her intention to drive back to the Yerby Ranch, and she backed the car into a drift while trying to turn. The snow was so slippery that the wheel failed to get a grip. She tried again and again without success, and at last killed the engine. Her attempts to crank it were complete failures.

It was a moment for swift decision. Ruth made hers instantly. She took the baby from the front seat, wrapped him close to her in all the blankets she had, and started forward toward a deserted miner's cabin built in a draw close to the trail.

Half a mile is no distance when the sun is shining and the path is clear. But near and far take on different meanings in a blizzard. Drifts underfoot made the going slow. The pelting wind, heavy with the sting of sleet, beat upon her, sifted through her clothes, and sapped her vitality. More than once her numbed legs doubled under her like the blades of a jackknife.

Ruth knew she was in deadly peril. She recalled stories of how men had wandered for hours in the white whirl, and had lain down to die at last within a stone's throw of their own houses. A young schoolteacher from Denver had perished three years before with one of her hands clutching the barbwire strand that led to safety.

But the will to live was strong in the young mother. For the sake of that precious young life in her arms she dared not give up. Indomitably she fought against the ice-laden wind that flung sleet waves at her to paralyze her energy, benumb her muscles, and chill the blood in her arteries. More than once she went down, her frozen legs buckling under her as she moved. But always she struggled to her feet again and plowed forward.

Out of the whirling snow loomed a log wall within reach of her hand. She staggered along it to the door, felt for the latch, found it, and stumbled into the hut.

Ruth, weak and shaken from her struggle with the storm, stood in bewildered amazement near the door. A man was facing her, in his hands a rifle. He stood crouched and wary, like a wolf at bay.

The man was Falkner.

"Any more of you?" he demanded. Not for an instant had his eyes relaxed.

"No."

"Sure of that?"

She nodded, much too exhausted for speech.

"Fine," he went on, lowering his gun slowly. "We'll be company for each other. Better shut the door."

She staggered forward to the table and put down the bundle of shawls. Her arms were as heavy as though they were weighted. She sank down on the long bench in front of the table.

"Stormbound, I reckon," suggested the man, watching her with narrowed lids.

"Yes," she panted. "Going home from the Yerbys."

From outside came the shriek of the rising storm.

"It's an ill wind that blows nobody good, my dear." He grinned with a flash of his broken teeth.

Ruth looked around at him, her steady eyes fixed in his. There came to her a fugitive memory of meeting him on a hill trail with that look in his eyes that was a sacrilege to her womanhood. She remembered once before, when he had used those words *my dear*. Since then the wolf in him had become full grown, fed by the horrors of his prison life. He was a hunted creature. His hand was against society and its against him. The bars that had restrained him in the old days were down. He was a throwback to the cave man, and, what was worse, that primitive animal with enemies hot on his trail.

If this adventure had befallen her two years earlier, the terror-stricken eyes of the girl would have betrayed her, the blood in her veins would have chilled with horror. But she had learned to be captain of her soul. Whatever fear she may have felt, none of it reached the surface.

A little wail rose from the bundle of shawls. Falkner, his nerves jumpy from sleepless nights and the continuous strain of keeping his senses alert, flashed a quick, suspicious look around the room.

Ruth turned and unloosened the wraps. The convict, taken by sheer astonishment, moved forward a step or two.

"Well, I'll be dog-goned. You got a kid in there," he said slowly.

At sight of his mother the face of the youngster cleared. Through all the fight with the storm, snug and warm in his nest, he had slept peacefully. But now he had wakened, and objected to being half smothered.

"Don't you remember?" Ruth asked the man. "I told you I had a baby. Do you think he is like me or Rowan?" She walked straight to him, and held the baby up for his inspection.

Falkner murmured something that sounded like an oath. But it happened that Rowan, Jr. took to men. He smiled and stretched out his arms. Before the outlaw could speak, before he could voice the sullen rejection of friendliness that was in his mind, Ruth had pushed the boy into his arms.

The soft little hands of the baby explored the rough face of the man. Rowan, Jr. beamed with delight.

"You da-da," he announced confidently.

Ruth managed a little laugh. "He's claiming you already, Mister Falkner, even though he doesn't know that meeting you has probably saved our lives."

For years Falkner had fought his snarling way against those who held the upper hand. Hatred and bitterness had filled his soul. But the contact with this soft, helpless bit of gurgling humanity sent a queer thrill through him. It was not alone a physical sensation that reached him. Somehow the little tot, so absolutely sure of his welcome, twined those dimpled fingers around the heartstrings of the callous man. Not since his mother's death had any human being come to him with such implicit trust. The Adam's apple in the convict's throat shot up and registered emotion.

"The blamed little cuss. See him grab a-holt of my ear."

Ruth left the baby in his arms, took off her coat, and walked to the stove. She held out her hands and began to warm them.

"We were in the car," she explained. "I took the high-line back because I was afraid of the upper bridge. The machine stalled in a drift."

"You don't ask me how-come I'm here," he growled.

"I know," she said simply. "Art Philips dropped in while at was at the Yerbys' and stayed for dinner. He told us you escaped four days ago."

"Did he tell you I killed a guard?"

"No. He said you wounded one."

"First I knew he wasn't dead. Wish I'd been more thorough. If ever a man needed killing, he did."

"They abused you a good deal, didn't they?" she ventured.

He ripped out a sudden furious oath. "If ever I get a chance at two or three of them. . . ."

"Better not think of that now. The question is how you are going to get away."

"What's that to you?" he demanded, his suspicions all alert.

"I thought if you'd come down to the Circle Diamond, you could get a horse. That would give you a much better chance."

"And how do I know you wouldn't phone to Matson?" he sneered.

She looked at him. "Don't you know me better than that, Mister Falkner?" she said gently.

He mumbled what might be taken either for an apology or for an oath.

"That's all right. I dare say I wouldn't be very trustful myself if I had been through what you have." Ruth tossed him a smiling nod and dismissed the subject. "But we're not down at the ranch yet. How long is this storm likely to last, Mister Falkner?"

"It will blow itself out before morning. Too early in the season for it to last."

"You don't think there will be any trouble about getting down tomorrow, do you?" she asked anxiously. "I'm not worried about myself, but I've got to get food for the baby."

"Depends on the snow," he said sulkily. "If it keeps on, you can't break trail and carry the kid."

"Perhaps you could go with me . . . then you could cut out a horse and ride away after dark."

"I don't have to go down there. I can pick up a horse at the Yerbys'." He added grudgingly in explanation: "Me for the hills. I don't want to get down into the valleys, where too many people are."

At midnight the storm outside was still howling and the sleety snow was beating against the window. The wind, coming straight from the divide above, buffeted the snow clouds in front of it. Drifts sifted and shifted as the snow whirled with the changing gusts.

The young mother, crouched behind the stove with her baby asleep across her knees, drowsed at times and wakened again with a start to see half-shuttered eyes shining across at her from the other side of the fire. In the darkness of the night she was afraid. Those gleaming points of light, always focused on her, were too suggestive of a beast of prey. With that blizzard raging outside she was a thousand miles from help, beyond the chance of human aid in case of need.

Again her instinct served Ruth well. She rose stiffly and carried the baby across to the man.

"Would you mind holding him for a while? I've been still so long my muscles are stiff and numb."

Grudgingly Falkner took the baby, but, as the warm body of the sleeping child nestled close to him, he felt once more that queer tug at his heart. A couple of inches of the fat, pink little legs were exposed where the dress had fallen back. The man's rough forefinger touched the soft flesh gently. To the appeal of this amazing miracle—a helpless babe asleep in his arms—everything that was good and fine in him responded. He had lived a harsh and bitter life, he had cherished hatred and dwelt with his own evil imagination, but, as he looked down and felt the clutch of those small fingers on his wrist, the devil that had been in his eyes slowly vanished.

Ruth tramped the floor till the pin pricks and the numbness were gone from her limbs. Then she returned to her place against the wall back of the stove. Her eyes closed drowsily, opened again. She told herself that she must not fall asleep—dare not. Falkner was sitting motionlessly with Rowan in his arms, his whole attention on the child. The woman's head nodded. She struggled to shake off the sleep that was stealing over her.

When she wakened, it was broad day. A slant of sunshine made a ribbon of gold across the floor. Rowan was crying a little fretfully, and the convict was dancing him up and down as a diversion from his hunger.

XXII

"Can't you do something for this kid?" the man asked gruffly.

Ruth took the baby. "He's hungry," she said.

"Then we'd better be hitting the trail."

Falkner walked to the door and flung it open. He looked out upon a world of white-blanketed hills. The sun was throwing from them a million sparkles of light.

"Gimme that kid," the outlaw said roughly. "We gotta get him down to breakfast. Here! You take my gun."

Ruth wrapped up the baby warmly and handed him to Falkner. The man broke trail to the point where the draw struck the road. He looked to the right, then to the left. Safety lay for him in the mountains; for her and Rowan, Jr. at the Circle Diamond, which was three miles nearer than the Yerby Ranch. The way up the cañon would be harder to travel than the way down. There was a chance that they could not make it through the snow, even a probability.

"Which way?" asked Ruth.

He turned to the left toward the Circle Diamond. The heart of the girl leaped. The convict had put the good of the child before his own.

The day had turned warm, so that before they had traveled half an hour the snow was beginning to get soft and slushy. The going was heavy. Ruth was not wearing her heavy, high-laced boots, but the shoes she was accustomed to use indoors. Soon her stockings were wringing wet and the bottoms of her skirts were soaked. It was mostly downhill grade, but within the hour she was fagged. It cost an effort to drag her foot up for each step. She did not want to be a quitter, but at last she had to speak.

"I can't go any farther. Leave me here and send the boys to get me. Missus Stovall will look after the baby."

The outlaw stopped. There was grudging admiration in the glance he gave her.

"You can make it. We're through the worst part. Soon we'll be in the foothills, and there the snow is real light."

He brushed the snow from a rock and told her with a wave of his hand to sit down. After a few minutes' rest she rose and told him she was ready to try again.

Falkner's prediction of a lighter snowfall down in the foothills proved correct. They rounded a rocky point, which brought them within sight of the Circle Diamond. It looked very near and close, but the deceptive air of the Rockies could no longer fool Ruth. They still had two miles to go. The descent to the valley was very rapid from here, and she could see that a scant two inches would measure the depth of the snow into which they were moving.

The young woman sloshed along behind. She was very tired, and her shoulders sagged from exhaustion. But she set her teeth in a game resolve to buck up and get through somehow.

They came to the Circle Diamond line fence, crawled between the strands, and tramped across the back pasture toward the house.

Ruth must by this time have been half asleep. Her feet moved almost of their own volition, as if by clockwork.

A startled shout brought her back to life abruptly. A man with a raised rifle was standing near the bunkhouse. He was covering Falkner.

Swift as a panther, Falkner rid himself of the baby and turned to Ruth. He ripped out a sudden furious oath. She was empty-handed. Somewhere between the spot where she stood and the line fence the rifle had slipped unnoticed from her cramped fingers.

The outlaw was trapped.

"Throw up your hands!" came the curt order.

Instantly the convict swerved and began running to the right. Ruth stood directly in the line of fire. The man with the gun took a dozen quick steps to one side.

"Stop or I'll fire!" he shouted.

Falkner paid no attention. He was making for a cottonwood arroyo back of the house.

The rifleman took a long aim and fired. The hunted man stumbled, fell, scrambled to his feet again, ran almost to the edge of the gulch, and sank down once more.

The man who had fired ran past Ruth toward the fallen man. She noticed that he was Sheriff Matson. It is doubtful if he saw her at all. Men emerged from the bunkhouse, the stable, the corral, and the house. Some were armed, the rest apparently were not. One had been shaving. He had finished one cheek, and the lather was still moist on the other.

The half-shaved man was her foreman, Jennings. At sight of the mistress of the ranch he stopped. She had knelt to pick up the crying baby.

"What's the row?" he asked.

"Sheriff Matson has just shot Mister Falkner." She could hardly speak the words from her dry throat.

"Falkner! How did he come here?"

"Baby and I were snowbound in the old Potier cabin. He broke trail down for us and carried the baby."

"Gad! And ran right into Matson."

"What is the sheriff doing here?"

"Came in late last night with a posse. Word had been phoned him that Falkner had been seen in the hills heading for the Montana line. He aimed to close the passes, I reckon."

Mrs. Stovall bore down upon them from the back door of the house. Ruth cut her off without allowing the housekeeper a word.

"No time to talk now, Missus Stovall. Feed the baby. He's about starved. I'll look after this business."

With Jennings striding beside her, Ruth went across to the group surrounding the wounded man.

"Is he badly hurt?" she demanded.

One of her own cowpunchers looked up and answered gravely: "Looks like, ma'am. In the leg. He's bleeding a lot."

The sight of the blood trickling down to the white snow for an instant sickened Ruth. But she repressed at once any weakness. Matson she ousted from command.

"Stop the bleeding with a tourniquet, Jennings, then have him carried to the house . . . to Rowan's room. Sheriff, phone Doctor Irwin to come at once. Better send one of your men to meet him."

Ruth herself flew to the house. She forgot that she was exhausted, forgot that she had had neither supper nor breakfast. The call for action carried her out of her own needs. Before the men had arrived with the wounded outlaw she was ready with sponges, cold water, and bandages.

After Falkner had been made as comfortable as possible, Ruth left him in the charge of Norma Tait and retired to the pantry in search of food. When she had eaten, she left word with Mrs. Stovall that she was going to sleep, but wanted to be called when Dr. Irwin arrived at the ranch.

At the housekeeper's knock she awoke three hours later, refreshed and fit for anything.

Having examined the patient, Dr. Irwin retired with Ruth and Sheriff Matson to the front porch.

"What do you think?" asked the young woman anxiously.

"*Humph!* Think . . . just missed a funeral," he snorted. "Bullet struck half inch from an artery."

"But he'll get well?"

"I reckon. Know better later."

"When can I move him?" asked Matson.

"Don't know. Not for a week or two, anyhow. You in a hurry to get him back to that hell where he came from, Sheriff?" bristled the old doctor.

"I'm not responsible for the pen, Doc," answered Matson evenly. "But I'm responsible for turning him over to the warden. If I could get him down to Wagon Wheel. . . ."

"Well, you can't!" snapped Irwin. "He'll stay right here till I think it safe to move him."

"Sure. And while he's at the Circle Diamond, I'll leave a couple of men to help nurse him," the sheriff announced with a grim little smile.

Ruth was head nurse herself. For years she had held a bitter resentment against Falkner, but it could not stand against the thing that had happened. Put to the acid test, the man had sacrificed his chances of escape to save her and the baby. Because of his choice he lay in Rowan's room, wounded, condemned to return to Rawlins.

Never in his rough and turbulent life had the man been treated with such gentle consideration. Here were kindness and friendly smiles and an unimaginable tenderness. All three of the women were good to him in their own way, but it was for Ruth that his hungry eyes watched the door. She brought the baby with her one day, after the fever had left him, and set the youngster on the bed, where the invalid could watch him play.

Falkner did not talk much. He lay quietly for hours, scarcely moving, unless little Rowan was in the room.

Ruth, coming in silently one afternoon, caught the brooding despair in his eyes.

He turned to her gently. "What makes you so good to me? You know you hate me."

Her frank, friendly smile denied the charge. "No, I don't hate you at all. I did, but I don't now."

"I'm keeping Rowan away from you. It was my fault he went there in the first place."

"Yes, but you saved our son's life . . . and mine, too. If you had looked out only for yourself, you wouldn't be lying here wounded, and perhaps you would have got away." She flashed deep, tender eyes on him. "I'll tell you a secret, Mister Falkner. You're not half so bad as you think you are. Can't I see how you love Rowan, Junior, and how fond he is of you? You're just like the rest of us, but you haven't had a fair chance. So we're going to be good to you while we can, and, after you come back from prison, we're going to be friends."

The ice that had gathered at his heart for years was melting fast. He turned his face to the wall and lay there till dusk. Perhaps it was then that he fought out the final battle of his fight with himself.

When Mrs. Stovall came in with his supper, he told her hoarsely that he wanted to see Matson at once on important business.

The sheriff drove his car in the moonlight out from Wagon Wheel. Ruth took him in to Falkner.

"Send for Jennings and Missus Stovall. She's a notary, ain't she?" said the convalescent.

Ruth's heart beat fast. "Yes. She was one when she was postmistress. Her term hasn't run out yet."

"All right. Get her. I want to make a sworn statement before witnesses."

Matson took down the statement as Falkner dictated.

I want to tell some facts about the Bald Knob sheep raid that did not come out at the trial of Rowan McCoy. When the party was made up to ride on that raid, I wasn't included. They left me out because I had a grudge at Tait. But I horned in. I followed the boys for miles, and insisted on going along. McCoy objected. He said the party was going to drive off the sheep and not to do any killing. I promised to take orders from him. He laid out a plan by which we could surprise the camp without bloodshed, and made it plain there was to be no shooting. Afterward he went over it all very carefully again, and we agreed not to shoot.

I lost my head when we was crawling up on the camp and shot at the wagon. That was the first shot fired. Tait came out and began shooting at us. Two or three of us were shooting. I don't know who killed him. Gilroy ran out of the wagon to escape. McCoy hollered to stop shooting, and ran forward. I must have been crazy. I shot and killed Gilroy.

Then McCoy ran to protect the herders. He wrestled with me for the gun to keep me from shooting. None of the other boys had anything to do with the killing of Gilroy except me.

It was so dark that nobody knew whether McCoy or I shot Gilroy. McCoy protected me, and said we were all to blame since we had come together. He never did tell who did the shooting. I looked at his gun a little later, and saw that he had not fired a shot from first to last.

I am making this statement of my own free will, and under no compulsion whatever. I am of sound mind and body, except for a bullet wound in my leg that is getting better. My only reason for making it is that I want to see justice done. The others have suffered too much already for what I did.

Falkner signed the statement. It was witnessed by Jennings and the two deputies. Mrs. Stovall added the notarial seal of her office to it.

Ruth put her head down on the little table where the medicines were and cried like a child. At last—at last Rowan would be free to come home to her. Her long, long waiting was at an end. She could begin to count the days now till her lover would be with her again.

XXIII

Ruth telephoned a message down to Wagon Wheel to be wired to Governor McDowell that night. It was impossible for her to sleep, and, after she had packed, she lay awake for hours planning the fight for Rowan's freedom.

The sheriff drove her and the baby to town next morning. From there she sent Louise a telegram to tell her they were on the way to Cheyenne. Matson, with strong letters in his pocket from Haight and the district judge recommending clemency, took the noon train also to add the weight of his influence.

When the train rolled into the station at Cheyenne, Louise was waiting for them in her car. She and Ruth, after the manner of their sex, shed a few happy tears together in each other's arms, while Matson, raw-boned and awkward, stood near, holding Rowan, Jr.

"The board of pardons is to meet this afternoon in Phil's office, and you and Mister Matson are to have a hearing before it," her friend told Ruth.

"What does Phil say?"

"He says that if Falkner's statement is as strong as your wire claimed, the board will have to free all four. Phil wants to push the whole thing through as quick as he can for you."

"That's fine," commented Matson. "Will it be a parole or a pardon?"

"Depends on the confession, Phil says," Louise declared.

This was not the first time that Ruth and her attorney had appeared before the board of pardons. From the very day of his conviction she had missed no possible chance that might help her husband. The members of the board had been very kind to her. She had read admiration in their glances. But the majority of them had voted against her request. Today, somehow it was different. As soon as she entered the inner office of the governor with Sheriff Matson and Rowan, Jr., she knew that victory was in sight.

Little Rowan prevented the meeting from being a formal one. He wriggled free from his mother and ran forward with arms outstretched to his friend the governor.

Ruth forgot all about the arguments she had meant to present. Instead she told, between tears and smiles, the story of the blizzard and its consequences.

Just before leaving his office for the night, Governor McDowell called Louise on the telephone. That young woman beamed at what he said, and beckoned Ruth.

"Phil wants to talk with you."

Ruth took the receiver, her hand trembling. "Hello," she said.

"Yes, it's Ruth."

"I have good news for you, my dear," the voice at the other end of the wire said. "Rowan and his three friends are to be paroled at once. I am going to make it a full pardon for Rowan and for the others, too."

For years Ruth had been waiting for this news. Now that it had come she did not weep or cry out or do anything the least dramatic. She just said: "Oh, I'm so glad. Thank you."

"I've been instructed by the board to tell you how much it appreciates the game fight you made and to add that it gives this pardon with more pleasure than any it has ever granted."

"When can I see Rowan? And when will he be out?"

"He'll be out just as soon as the papers can be prepared, my dear. I'm coming right home to tell you all about it."

Two more telegrams were flashed westward from Ruth that night. One was to McCoy, the second to Tim Flanders. The message to Flanders laid upon him the duty of notifying the families of the paroled men. Early next morning Ruth sent still another telegram. It was addressed to Jennings, and gave him instructions that made him get busy at once, looking after horses, saddles, pack saddles, a tent, and other camping outfit.

Later in the day Rowan, Jr. and his mother entrained for Rawlins. The adventure before her tremendously intrigued the interest of the young wife. It was immensely more significant than her marriage had been. All the threads of her life for years had been converging toward it.

XXIV

Sam Yerby strolled up and down the station platform. His wife clung to him on one side and on the other trotted her son, hand in hand with his new-found father. Outwardly Rogers and Cole took their good fortune philosophically, but the Texan could not hide his delight at Missie, the boy, and freedom. As the old

cowman grinned jauntily at Ruth, who had come down to see
the party off, he chirruped out a stanza of a range song:

> *Goin' back to town to thaw my money,*
> *Goin' back home for to see my honey.*

"Only I don't have to go home to see her. She done come to
see the old man. I tell you it's great, Miss Ruth. This air now!
Lordee, I jus' gulp it down!"

Ruth smiled through her tears. "Good days ahead, Mister
Yerby, for all of us. We know just how you feel, don't we, Missie?"

"When do you-all expect Mac to get in?"

"Some time this afternoon. Here comes your train. We'll see
you soon."

After the train had gone, Ruth walked back to the hotel where
she was staying. Governor McDowell had given a complete
pardon to all four of the cattlemen, but Rowan had not yet
reached town from the distant road camp where he was working. The clerk handed the young woman a letter. It was from
Jennings and was postmarked at a small town seventy miles
farther up the line.

Ruth reclaimed the baby from the nursemaid with whom she
had left him and went up to her room. A man came swinging
with crisp step along the dark corridor. She would have known
that stride anywhere. A wave of emotion crashed through her.
In another moment she was in his arms.

"Oh, Rowan . . . at last!" she cried.

Presently they moved into the room and he held her from
him while he searched her face. Since last he had seen her she
had endured the sting of rain, the bluster of wind, and the heat
of sun. They had played havoc with her wild-rose complexion
and the satin of her skin. She was no longer the hothouse flower
he had married, a slip of a girl experimenting with life, but a

woman as strong as tested steel. Here was a mate worthy of any man, one with a vigorous, brave spirit clad in a body of exquisite grace, young and lissome and vital.

An incomparable mate for some man. But was he the man that could hold her? His old doubts asserted themselves in spite of the white dream of her his heart had held through the years of their separation. She had been loyal—never a woman more so. But he wanted more than loyalty.

Perhaps it was from him she got it. At any rate, an unexpected touch of shyness lowered her lashes. She caught up the baby and handed him to the father.

"Here is your son," she said, the color glowing in her cheeks.

Rowan looked at the little being that was flesh of his flesh and blood of his blood, and his heart went out to the child in complete surrender. The child was his—and Ruth's. If he lived to be a hundred, he would never again know quite the ecstasy of that moment.

To escape the tension of her feeling Ruth hurried into explanations. "I've made all our arrangements for the next three days. You're not to ask me anything about them. You're going to be personally conducted by me and the baby, and you'll have to do whatever we tell you to do. Do you understand, sir?"

He smiled and nodded. This particular Ruth—the one that gave gay, imperious orders—was an old friend of his. His heart welcomed her.

Apparently her plans included an automobile journey. Within an hour they were driving through a desert of sand and sagebrush toward the mountains.

Rowan asked no questions. He wondered where she was taking him, but he was content to await developments so long as he could sit beside Ruth with the youngster on his lap.

As for Ruth her blood began to beat faster with excitement. She was trying an experiment. If it proved a failure, she knew she would be very greatly disappointed. Just now it seemed to her that she had set the whole happiness of her life at stake. For if Rowan did not look at it as she did, if his joy in it did not equal her hopes, they would fail by just so much of the unity of mind for which she prayed.

They had left Rawlins before noon. It was well into the middle of the afternoon before the driver of the car stopped at a little two-store village deep in the hills.

"We get out here," Ruth told her husband.

She settled with the owner of the car, and the man started back to Rawlins. Opposite the store where they had stopped was a corral. Ruth led the way to it. Three horses were eating hay from a rack.

Rowan looked at them, then at Ruth. He had recognized two of the animals, and the third one showed on the flank the Circle Diamond brand.

"Am I to ask questions yet?" McCoy wanted to know.

"If you like." She smiled.

"Are we to ride home on the pinto and old Duke?"

"Yes."

"And the sorrel?"

"For a pack horse."

"You have supplies and a tent?"

"Jennings brought them."

He took a deep breath of delight. For three days and nights they would be alone, buried together in the eternal hills. Such a homecoming as this had been beyond his dreams.

"Are you . . . glad?" she asked, and her voice was tremulous.

"Glad!" He spoke a little roughly to hide his deep feeling. "If I could only let you know how I feel. If I could!"

Her heart jumped with a sudden gladness. Rowan did not want to meet his friends yet. He wanted to be alone with her and the baby. This was to be, then, their true honeymoon, the seal of their love for each other.

They camped far up beside a mountain lake. He pitched tent in a beautiful grove of wide-spaced pines through which a brook sang its way down to the lake. While he unpacked and made preparations for supper, Ruth took the rod to try her luck. When she returned half an hour later, the tent was pegged down, young pine boughs cut and spread for a bed, and the fire going for their meal. Rowan had the water on to boil for coffee, and slices of bacon in the frying pan ready to set upon the rocks that hedged in his coals.

Rowan cleaned the fish in the brook and cooked them in the pan when the bacon grease was ready. They ate with the healthy appetite of outdoor animals in the hills.

Ruth told him the gossip of the neighborhood. She retailed to him what she knew of the politics of the county. It pleased her that his interest in these far-away topics was as yet perfunctory. His world just now consisted of three persons, and of the three she was the most important.

"You're going to lose Jennings," she told him.

"Isn't he satisfied?"

Little imps of mischief danced in her eyes. "Not quite, but I think he's going to be. He has notions of marrying a handsome widow with a sheep ranch."

Rowan looked at her quickly. "You don't mean Norma Tait?"

"Don't I? Why not?"

"I'm glad. Life plays some queer tricks. But maybe in the end things even up."

From where she was cuddling the romping boy, Ruth looked up and made a confession. "At first I thought I wouldn't bring him with us. I wanted these first days to be ours . . . just yours and mine. But that was selfish. Now I'm glad he's here. You won't think him in the way, will you?"

It did not seem to him necessary to answer that in words. He took little Rowan into his arms and held him there till the child fell asleep.

When the baby was safely tucked up in the tent, Ruth and Rowan walked to the brow of the hill and watched the mist settle down into the mountain cañons. They saw the stars come out one by one until the heavens were full of them.

"The day is dead," he said at last.

She knew that in his thoughts he was breasting again the troubled waters that had swept them so far apart. Her warm, strong little hand slipped into his. Cheerfully she took up his words. "Yes, the day is dead . . . the long day so full of sorrow. But now the night has dotted out our grief. We are at peace . . . alone . . . beneath the stars."

He could not yet quite escape the net. "I've been a poor makeshift of a husband, Ruth. I've brought you much worry and sorrow. And I've put a stain on you and the boy that never can be wiped out."

"You've brought me all that makes life brave and beautiful." She turned her buoyant head, and in the white moonlight her smile flashed radiant upon him. "A new day is on the way to us, Rowan."

The man caught his breath sharply. She was so fine! With superb courage and patience she had fought for him. All good things that life had to offer should be hers. Instead, he brought her the poison of the penitentiary record to stain her future.

Something of this he tried to tell her. "I'm a pardoned convict. Your friends will never let you forget that . . . never."

"Your friends are my friends. I have no others," she told him, eyes aglow. Then added, in a murmur: "Oh, my dear, as if what anybody says matters now between you and me."

Her faith was enough to save them both. He threw away his prudent doubts and snatched her to him. In his kisses the lover spoke.

Presently they walked back to the camp through the gathering darkness. A great peace lay over their world.

★ ★ ★ ★ ★

ROBBER'S ROOST

★ ★ ★ ★ ★

I

She had been aware of him from the moment of his spectacular entrance, though no slightest sign of interest manifested itself in her indolent, disdainful eyes. Indeed, his abundant and picturesque area was so vivid that it would have been difficult not to feel his presence anywhere, let alone on a journey so monotonous as this was proving to be.

It had been at a water tank, near Socorro, that the Limited, churning furiously through red New Mexico in pursuit of a lost half hour, jarred to a sudden halt that shook sleep from the drowsy eyes of bored passengers. Through the window of her Pullman the young woman in Section 3 had glimpsed a bevy of angry train officials eddying around a sturdy figure in the center, whose strong, lean head rose confidently above the press. There was the momentary whirl of a scuffle, out of the tangle of which shot a brakeman as if propelled from a catapult. The circle parted, brushed aside by a pair of lean shoulders, muscular and broad. Yet a few moments and the owner of the shoulders led down the aisle to the vacant section opposite her a procession whose tail was composed of protesting trainmen.

"You had no right to flag the train, Sheriff Collins, and you'll have to get off . . . that's all there is to it," the conductor was explaining testily.

"Oh, that's all right," returned the offender easily, making himself at home in Section 4. "Tell the company to send in its bill. No use jawing about it."

"You'll have to get off, sir."

"That's right . . . at Tucson."

"No, sir. You'll have to get off here. I have no authority to let you ride."

"Didn't I hear you say the train was late? Don't you think you'd arrive earlier at the end of your run if your choo-choo got to puffing?"

"You'll have to get off, sir."

"I hate to disoblige," murmured the owner of the jingling spurs, the dusty corduroys, and the big, gray hat, putting his feet leisurely on the cushion in front of him. "But doesn't it occur to you that you are a man of one idea?"

"This is the Coast Limited. It doesn't stop for anybody . . . not even for the president of the road."

"You don't say! Well, I certainly appreciate the honor you did me in stopping to take me on." His slight drawl was quite devoid of concern.

"But you had no right to flag the train. Can't you understand *anything?*" groaned the conductor.

"You explain it again to me, sonny. I'm surely thick in the haid," soothed the intruder, and listened with bland good humor to the official's flow of protest.

"Well . . . well! Disrupted the whole transcontinental traffic, didn't I? And me so innocent, too. Now, this is how I figured it out. Here's me in a hurry to get to Tucson. Here comes your train a-fogging . . . also and likewise hitting the high spots for Tucson. Seemed like we ought to travel in company, and I was some dubious she'd forget to stop unless I flagged her. Wherefore, I aired my bandanna in the summer breeze."

"But you don't understand." The conductor began to explain anew as to a dull child. "It's against the law. You'll get into trouble."

"Put me in the calaboose, will they?"

"It's no joke."

"Well, it does seem to be worrying you," Mr. Collins conceded. "Don't mind me. Free your mind proper."

The conductor, glancing about nervously, noticed that passengers were smiling broadly. His official dignity was being chopped to mince meat. Back came his harassed gaze to the imperturbable Collins with the brown, sun-baked face and the eyes blue and untroubled as an Arizona sky. Out of a holster attached to the sagging belt that circled the corduroy trousers above his hips gleamed the butt of a revolver. But in the last analysis the weapon of the occasion was purely a moral one. The situation was one not covered in the company's rule book, and in the absence of explicit orders the trainman felt himself unequal to that unwavering gaze and careless poise. Wherefore, he retreated, muttering threats of what the company would do.

"Now, if I had only known it was against the law. My thick haid's always roping trouble for me," the plainsman confided to the Pullman conductor, with twinkling eyes.

That official unbent. "Talking about thick heads, I'm glad my porter has one. If it weren't iron-plated and copper-riveted, he'd be needing a doctor now, the way you stood him on it."

"No, did I? Certainly an accident. The fellow must have been in my way as I climbed into the car. Took the kink out of his hair, you say? Here, Sam!" He tossed a bill to the porter, who was rolling affronted eyes at him. "Do you reckon this is big enough to plaster your injured feelings, boy?"

The white smile flashed at him by the porter was a receipt for indemnity paid in full.

Sheriff Collins's perception of his neighbor across the aisle was more frank in its interest than the girl's had been of him. The level, fearless gaze looked at her unabashed, appreciating swiftly her points as they impinged themselves upon his admiration. The long, lithe lines of the slim, supple body, the languid grace missing hauteur only because that seemed scarce worthwhile, the unconscious pride of self that fails to be offensive only in a young woman so well equipped with good looks as this one indubitably was—the rider of the plains had appraised them all before his eyes dismissed her from his consideration and began a casual inspection of the passengers.

Inside of half an hour he had made himself *persona grata* to everybody in the car except his dark-eyed neighbor across the way. That this dispenser of smiles and cigars decided to leave her out in the distribution of his attentions perhaps spoke well for his discernment. Certainly responsiveness to the geniality of casual fellow passengers did not impress Mr. Collins as likely to be an outstanding quality in her. But with the drummer from Chicago, the young mining engineer going to Sonora, the two shy little English children just in front of him traveling to meet their father in California, he found intuitively common ground of interest. Even Major Meredith, the grim, gray-haired paymaster of the new road being run into Mexico as a feeder to the Transcontinental Pacific, relaxed at one of the plainsman's humorous tales.

It was after Collins had half depopulated the car by leading the more jovial spirits back in search of liquid refreshments that an urbane clergyman, now of Boston but formerly of Pekin, Illinois, professedly much interested in the sheriff's touch-and-go manner as presumably a fine characteristic of the West, dropped into the vacant seat beside Major Meredith.

"And who might our energetic friend be?" he asked with an ingratiating smile.

The young woman in front of them turned her head ever so slightly to listen.

"Val Collins is his name," said the major. "Sometimes called Bear-Trap Collins. He has always lived on the frontier. At least, I met him twelve years ago when he was riding mail between

Aravaipa and Mesa. He was a boy then, certainly not over eighteen, but in a desperate fight he killed two men who tried to hold up the mail. Cowpuncher, stage driver, miner, trapper, gambler, sheriff, rough rider, politician . . . he's past master at them all."

"And why the appellation of Bear-Trap, may I ask?" The smack of pulpit oratory was not often missing in the edifying discourse of the Reverend Peter Melancthon Ward.

"Well, sir, that's a story. He was trapping in the Tetons about five years ago thirty miles from the nearest ranch house. One day, while he was setting a bear trap, a slide of snow plunged down from the tree branches above and freed the spring, catching his hand between its jaws. With his feet and his other hand he tried to open that trap for four hours, without the slightest success. There was not one chance in a million of help from outside. In point of fact, Collins had not seen a human being for a month. There was only one thing to do, and he did it."

"And that was?"

"You probably noticed that he wears a glove over his left hand. The reason, sir, is that he has an artificial hand."

"You mean . . . ?" The Reverend Peter Ward paused to lengthen his delicious thrill of horror.

"Yes, sir. That's just what I mean. He hacked his hand off at the wrist with his hunting knife."

"Why, the man's a hero!" cried the clergyman with unction.

Meredith flung him a disgusted look. "We don't go much on heroes in the Army. He's game, if that's what you mean. Think I'll have a smoke, sir. Care to join me?"

But the Pekin-Bostonian preferred to stay and jot down in his notebook the story of the bear trap, to be used later as a sermon illustration. This may have been the reason he did not catch the quick look that passed without the slightest flicker of the eyelids between Major Meredith and the young woman in Section 3. It was as if the old officer had wired her a message in some code the cipher of which was known only to them.

But the sheriff, returning at the head of his cohorts, caught it, and wondered what meaning might lie back of that swift glance. Major Meredith and this dark-eyed beauty posed before others as strangers, yet between them lay some freemasonry of understanding to which he had not the key.

Collins did not know that the disdain in the eyes of Miss Wainwright—he had seen the name on her suitcase—gave way to horror when her glance fell on his gloved hand. She had a swift, shuddering vision of a grim-faced man, jaws set like a vise, hacking at his wrist with a hunting knife. But the engaging impudence of his eye, the rollicking laughter in his voice shut out the picture instantly.

The young man resumed his seat, and Miss Wainwright her listless inspection of the flying stretches of brown desert. Dusk was beginning to fall, and the porter presently lit the lamps. Collins bought a magazine from the newsboy and relapsed into it, but before he was well adjusted to reading, the Limited pounded to a second unscheduled halt.

Instantly the magazine was thrown aside, and Collins's curly head thrust out of the window. Presently the head reappeared, simultaneously with the crack of a revolver, the first of a detonating fusillade.

"Another of your impatient citizens eager to utilize the unspeakable convenience of rapid transit," suggested the clergyman with ponderous jocosity.

"No, sir . . . nothing so illegal." The cattleman smiled, a whimsical light in his daredevil eyes. He leaned forward and whispered a word to the little girl in front of him, who at once led her younger brother back to his section.

"I had hoped it would prove to be more diverting experience for a tenderfoot," condescended the gentleman of the cloth.

"It's certainly a pleasure to be able to gratify you, sir. You'll be right pleased to know that it is a train hold-up." He waved his hand toward the door, and at the word, as if waiting for his cue, a masked man appeared at the end of the passage with a revolver in each hand.

II

"Hands up!"

There was a ring of crisp menace in the sinister voice that was a spur to obedience. The unanimous show of hands voted "aye" with a hasty precision that no amount of drill could have compassed.

It was a situation that might have made for laughter had there been spectators to appreciate. But of whatever amusement was to be had one of the victims seemed to hold a monopoly. Collins, his arm around the English children by way of comfort, offered a sardonic smile at the consternation his announcement and its fulfillment had created, but none of his fellow passengers were in the humor to respond.

The shock of an earthquake could not have blanched ruddy faces more surely. The Chicago drummer, fat and florid, had disappeared completely behind a buttress of the company's upholstery.

"God bless my soul!" gasped the Pekin-Bostonian, dropping his eyeglasses and his accent at the same moment. The dismay in his face found a reflection all over the car. Miss Wainwright's hand clutched at her breast for an instant, and her color ebbed till her lips were ashen, but her neighbor across the aisle noticed that her eyes were steady and her figure tense.

Scared stiff, but game, was his mental comment.

"Gents to the right and ladies to the left . . . line up against the walls . . . everybody waltz!" called the man behind the guns with grim humor.

191

The passengers fell into line as directed, Collins with the rest.

"You're calling this dance, son . . . it's your say-so, I guess," he conceded.

"Keep still, or I'll shoot you full of holes," growled the autocrat of the artillery.

"Why, sure. Ain't you the real thing in Jesse Jameses?" soothed the sheriff.

At the sound of Collins's voice, the masked man had started perceptibly, and his right hand had jumped forward an inch or two to cover the speaker more definitely. Thereafter, no matter what else engaged his attention, the gleaming eyes behind the red bandanna never wandered for a moment from the big plainsman. He was taking no risks, for he remembered the saying current in Arizona that, after Collins's hardware got into action, there was nothing left to do but plant the deceased and collect the insurance. He had personal reasons to know the fundamental accuracy of the colloquialism.

The train conductor fussed up to the masked outlaw with a ludicrous attempt at authority. "You can't rob the passengers on this train. I'm not responsible for the express car, but the coaches. . . ."

A bullet grazed his ear and shattered a window on its way to the desert.

"Drift, you red-haired son of a Mexican!" ordered the man behind the red bandanna. "Git back to that seat real prompt."

The conductor drifted.

The minutes ticked themselves away in a tense strain marked by pounding hearts. The outlaw lounged on the arm of a seat, watching the sheriff alertly.

"Why doesn't the music begin?" volunteered Collins, by way of conversation, and quoted: "On with the dance. Let joy be unconfined."

A dull explosion answered his question. The bandits were blowing open the safe in the express car with dynamite, pending which the looting of the passengers was at a standstill.

A second masked figure joined his companion at the end of the passage and held a hurried conversation with him. Fragments of their low-voiced talk came to Collins.

"Only a hundred thousand in the express car. . . . Thirty thousand on the old man himself. Where's the rest?" The irritation in the newcomer's voice was pronounced.

Collins slewed his head and raked the man with keen eyes that missed not a detail. He was certain that he had never seen the man before, yet he knew at once that the trim, wiry figure, so clean of build and so gallant of bearing could belong only to Dolf Leroy, the most ruthless outlaw of the Southwest. It was written in his jaunty insolence, in the flashing eyes. He was a handsome fellow, white-toothed, black-haired, lithely tigerish, with masterful mouth and eyes of steel, so far as one might judge behind the white mask he wore. His hand was swarthy in hue, almost to the shade of a Mexican's. Alert, cruel, fearless from the head to the heel of him, he looked the very devil to lead an enterprise so lawless and so desperate as this. His vigilant eyes swept contemptuously up and down the car, rested for a moment on the young woman in Section 3, and came back to his partner.

"*Bah!* A flock of sheep ·. . . tamest bunch of spring lambs we ever struck. I'll send Scotty in to go through them. If anybody gets gay, drop him." And the outlaw turned on his heel. Another of the highwaymen took his place—a short, sturdy figure in the flannel shirt, spurs, and chaps of a cowpuncher.

"Come, Scotty, get a move on you," Collins implored. "This train's due at Tucson by eight o'clock. We're more than an hour late now. I'm holding down the job of sheriff in that same town, and I'm awful anxious to get a posse out after a bunch of train robbers. So turn the wind, and go through the car on the jump. Help yourself to anything you find. Who steals my purse takes trash. 'Tis something, nothing. 'Twas mine . . . 'tis his. That's right, you'll find my roll in that left-hand pocket. I hate to have you take that gun, though. I meant to run you down with that same old Colt. Oh, well, just as you say. No, those kids get a free pass. They're going out to meet papa at Los Angeles, boys. See?"

Collins's running fire of comment had at least the effect of restoring the color to some cheeks that had been washed white and of snatching from the outlaws some portion of their sense of dominating the situation. But there was a veiled vigilance in his eyes that belied his easy carelessness.

"That lady across the aisle gets a pass, too, boys," continued the sheriff. "She's scared stiff now, and you won't bother her, if you're white men. Her watch and purse are on the seat. Take them, if you want them, and let it go at that."

Miss Wainwright listened to this dialogue silently. She stood before them, cool and imperious and unwavering, but her face was bloodless and the pulse in her beautiful soft throat fluttered like a caged bird.

"Who's doing this job?" demanded one of the hold-up men, wheeling savagely on the impassive officer. "Did I say we were going to bother the lady? Who's doing this job, Mister Sheriff?"

"You are. I'd hate to be messing the job like you . . . holding up the wrong train by mistake." This was a shot in the dark, but it seemed to hit the bull's-eye. "I wouldn't trust you boys to rob a hen roost, the amateur way you go at it. When you get through, you'll all go to drinking like blue blotters. I know your kind . . . hell-bent to spend what you cash in, and every mother's son of you in the pen or with his toes turned up inside of a month."

"Who'll put us there?" gruffly demanded the walking arsenal.

Collins smiled at him with impudence superb. "I will . . .

those of you that are left alive when you get through shooting each other in the back. Oh, I see your finish to a fare-you-well."

"Cheese it, or I'll bump you off." Scotty drove his gun into the sheriff's ribs.

"That's all right. You don't need to punctuate that remark. I line up with the sky pilot and chew the cud of silence. Merely wanted to frame up to you how this thing's going to turn out. Don't come back at me and say I didn't warn you, Scotty."

"You make my head ache . . . and my name ain't Scotty," snapped the bandit sourly as he passed down the aisle with his sack, accumulating tribute as he went.

The red-kerchiefed robber whooped when they came to the car conductor. "Dig up, Mister Pullman. Go 'way down into your jeans. It's a right smart pleasure to divert the plunder of your bloated corporation back to the people. What! Only a hundred fifty-seven dollars. Oh, dig deeper, Mister Rockefeller."

The drummer contributed to the sack $87, a diamond ring, and a gold watch. His hands were trembling so that they played a tattoo on the sloping ceiling above him.

"What's the matter, Fatty? Got a chill?" inquired one of the robbers as he deftly swept the plunder into the sack.

"For . . . God's sake . . . don't shoot. I have . . . a wife . . . and five children," he stammered with chattering teeth.

"No race suicide for Fatty. But why-for do they let a sick man like you travel all by his lone?"

"I don't know . . . I. . . . Please turn that weapon another way."

"Plumb chuck full of malaria," soliloquized the owner of the weapon, playfully running its business end over the Chicago man's anatomy. "Here, Fatty. Load up with quinine and whiskey. It's sure good for chills." Scotty gravely handed his victim back $1. "Write me if it cures you. Now, for the sky pilot. No white chips on this plate, parson. It's a contribution to

195

the needy heathen. You want to be generous. How much do you say?"

The man of the cloth reluctantly said $80.35, and a silver-plated watch inherited from his father. The watch was declined, with thanks, the money accepted without.

The Pullman porter came into the car under compulsion of a revolver in the hand of the outlaw leader. His trembling finger pointed out the satchel and suitcase of Major Meredith, and under orders he carried out the baggage belonging to the retired Army officer. Five minutes later three shots in rapid succession rang out in the still night air.

Scotty and his companion, who had apparently been waiting for the signal, retreated backward to the end of the car, still keeping the passengers covered. They flung rapidly two or three bullets through the roof, and, under cover of the smoke, slipped out into the night. A moment later came the thud of galloping horses, more shots, and when the patter of hoofs had died away—silence.

The sheriff was the first to break it. He thrust his brown hands deep into his pockets and laughed—laughed with the joyous, rollicking abandon of a tickled schoolboy.

"Hysterics?" ventured the mining engineer sympathetically.

Collins wiped his eyes. "Call 'em anything you like. What pleases me is that the reverend gentleman should have had this diverting experience so prompt after he was wishing for it." He turned, with concern, to the clergyman. "Satisfied, sir? Did our little entertainment please, or wasn't it up to the mark?"

But the transported native of Pekin was game. "I'm quite satisfied, if you are. I think the affair cost you a hundred dollars or so more than it did me."

"That's right," agreed the sheriff heartily. "But I don't grudge it . . . not a cent of it. The show was worth the price of admission."

The car conductor had a broadside ready for him. "Seems to me you shot off your mouth more than you did that big gun of yours, Mister Sheriff."

Collins laughed, and clapped him on the back. "That's right. I'm a regular phonograph when you wind me up." He did not think it necessary to explain that he had talked to make the outlaws talk, and that he had noted the quality of their voices so carefully that he would know them again among a thousand.

III

The clanking car took up the rhythm of the rails as the delayed train plunged forward once more into the night. Again the clack of tongues, set free from fear, buzzed eagerly. The glow of the afterclap of danger was on them, and in the warm excitement each forgot the paralyzing fear that had but now padlocked his lips. Courage came back into flabby cheeks and red blood into hearts of water.

The sheriff, presuming on the new intimacy born of an exciting experience shared in common, stepped across the aisle, flung aside Miss Wainwright's impedimenta, and calmly seated himself beside her. She was a young woman capable of a hauteur chillier than ice to undue familiarity, but she did not choose at this moment to resent his assumption of a footing that had not existed an hour ago. Picturesque and unconventional conduct excuses itself when it is garbed in picturesque and engaging manners. She had, besides, other reasons for wanting to meet him, and they had to do with a sudden suspicion that flamed like tow in her brain. She had something for which to thank him—much more than he would be likely to guess, she thought—and she was wondering, with a surge of triumph, whether the irony of fate had not made his pretended consideration for her the means of his undoing.

"I am sorry you lost so much, Miss Wainwright," he told her.

"But, after all, I did not lose so much as you." Her dark, deep-pupiled eyes, long-lashed as Diana's, swept around to meet his coolly.

"That's a true word. My reputation has gone glimmering for fair, I guess." He laughed ruefully. "I shouldn't wonder, ma'am, when election time comes around, if the boys ain't likely to elect to private life the sheriff that lay down before a bunch of miscreants."

"Why did you do it?"

His humorous glance roamed around the car. "Now, I couldn't think it proper for me to shoot up this sumptuous palace on wheels. And wouldn't some casual passenger be likely to get his lights put out when the band began to play? Would you want that Boston church to be shy a preacher, ma'am?"

Her lips parted slightly in a curve of scorn. "I suppose you had your reasons for not interfering."

"Surely, ma'am. I hated to have them make a sieve of me."

"Were you afraid?"

"Most men are when Dolf Leroy's gang is on the warpath."

"Dolf Leroy?"

"That was Dolf who came in to see they were doing the job right. He's the worst desperado on the border . . . a sure enough bad proposition, I reckon. They say he's part Spanish and part Indian, but all p'isen. I don't know about that, for nobody knows who he really is. But the name is a byword in the country. People lower their voices when they speak of him and his night riders."

"I see. And you were afraid of him?"

"Very much."

Her narrowed eyes looked over the strong lines of his lean face and were unconvinced. "I expect you found a better reason than that for not opposing them."

He turned to her with frank curiosity. "I'd like real well to have you put a name to it."

But he was instantly aware that her interest had been sidetracked. Major Meredith had entered the car, and was coming down the aisle. Plainer than words his eyes asked a question, and hers answered it.

The sheriff stopped him with a smiling query: "Hit hard, Major?"

Meredith frowned. "The scoundrels took thirty thousand from me, and a hundred thousand from the express car, I understand. Twenty thousand of it belonged to our road. I was expecting to pay off the men next Tuesday."

"Hope we'll be able to run them down for you," returned Collins cheerfully. "I suppose you lay it to Dolf Leroy's gang?"

"Of course. The work was too well done to leave any doubt of that." The major resumed his seat behind Miss Wainwright.

To that young woman the sheriff repeated his unanswered question in the form of a statement. "I'm waiting to learn that better reason, ma'am."

She was possessed of that spice of effrontery more to be desired than beauty. "Shall we say that you had no wish to injure your friends?"

"My friends?"

Her untender eyes mocked his astonishment. "Do I choose the wrong word?" she asked with an audacity that was insolent in its aplomb. "Perhaps they are not your friends . . . these train robbers? Perhaps they are mere casual acquaintances?"

His bold eyes studied with a new interest her superb, confident youth—the rolling waves of splendid Titian hair, the lovely, subtle eyes with the depths of shadowy pools in them, the alluring lines of long and supple loveliness. Certainly here was no sweet, ingenuous youth all prone to blushes, but the complex heir of that world-old wisdom the weaker sex has shaped to serve as a weapon against the strength that must be met with the wit of Mother Eve.

"You certainly have a right vivid imagination, ma'am," he said dryly.

"You are quite sure you have never seen them before?" her velvet voice asked.

He laughed. "Well, no . . . I can't say I am."

"Aren't you quite sure you *have* seen them?" Her eyes rested on him very steadily.

"You're smart as a whip, Miss Wainwright. I take off my hat to a young lady so clever. I guess you're right. About the identity of one of those masked gentlemen I'm pretty well satisfied."

She drew a long breath. "I thought so."

"Yes," he went on evenly, "I once earmarked him so that I'd know him again in case we met."

"I beg pardon. You . . . what?"

"Earmarked him. Figure of speech, ma'am. You may not have observed that the curly-headed person behind the guns was shy the forefinger of his right hand. We had a little difficulty once when he was resisting arrest, and it just happened that my gun fanned away his trigger finger."

"They knew you . . . at least, two of them did."

"I've been pirooting around this country boy and man for fifteen years. I ain't responsible for every yellow dog that knows me," he drawled.

"And I noticed that when you told them not to rob the children and not to touch me they did as you said."

"Hypnotism," he suggested with a smile.

"So, not being a child, I put two and two together and draw an inference."

He seemed to be struggling with his mirth. "I see you do. Well, ma'am, I've been 'most everything since I hit the West, but this is the first time I've been taken for a train robber."

"I didn't say that!" she cried quickly.

"I think you mentioned an inference." The low laugh welled out of him and broke in his face. "I've been busy on one, too. It's a heap nearer the truth than yours, Miss . . . Meredith."

Her startled eyes and the swift movement of her hand toward her heart showed him how nearly he had struck home. How certainly he had shattered her cool indifference of manner.

He leaned forward, so close that even in the roar of the train his low whisper reached her. "Shall I tell you why the hold-ups didn't find more money on your father or in the express car, Miss Meredith?"

She was shaken, so much so that her agitation trembled on her lips.

"Shall I tell you why your hand went to your breast when I first mentioned that the train was going to be held up, and again when your father's eyes were firing a mighty pointed question at you?"

"I don't know what you mean," she retorted, again mistress of herself.

Her gallant bearing compelled his admiration. The scornful eyes, the satirical lift of the nostrils, the erect, graceful figure all flung a challenge at him. He called himself hard names for putting her on the rack, but the necessity to make her believe in him was strong within him.

"I noticed you went right chalky when I announced the hold-up, and I thought it was because you were scared. That was where I did you an injustice, ma'am, and you can call this an apology. You've got sand. If it hadn't been for what you carry in the chamois skin hanging on the chain around your neck, you would have enjoyed every minute of the little entertainment. You're as game as they make them."

"May I ask how you arrived at this melodramatic conclusion?" she asked, her disdainful lip curling.

"By using my eyes and my ears, ma'am. I shouldn't have

noticed your likeness to Major Meredith, perhaps, if I hadn't observed that there was a secret understanding between you. Now, why-for should you be passing as strangers? I could guess one reason, and only one. There have twice been hold-ups of the paymaster on the Elkhorn branch. It was to avoid any more of these that Major Meredith was appointed to the position. He has made good up till now. But there have been rumors for months that he would be held up either before leaving the train or while he was crossing the desert. He didn't want to be seen taking the boodle from the express company at Tucson. He would rather have the impression get out that this was just a casual visit. It occurred to him to bring along some unsuspected party to help him out. The robbers would never expect to find the money on a woman. That's why the major brought his daughter with him. Doesn't it make you some uneasy to be carrying a hundred thousand in small bills sewed in your clothes and hung around your neck?"

She broke into musical laughter, natural and easy.

"I should think, ma'am, you'd crinkle more than a silk-lined lady sailing down a church aisle on Sunday."

A picture in the magazine she was toying with seemed to interest her.

"I expect that's the signal for 'exit Collins.' I'll say good bye till next time, Miss Meredith."

"Oh, is there going to be a next time?" she asked with elaborate carelessness.

"Several of them."

"Indeed!"

He took a notebook from his pocket and wrote. "I ain't the son of a prophet, but I'm venturing a prediction," he explained. She had nothing to say, and she said it eloquently.

"Concerning an investment in futurities I'm making," he continued.

Her magazine article seemed to be beginning well.

"It's a little guess about how this train robbery is coming out. If you don't mind, I'll leave it with you." He tore the page out, put it in an empty envelope, sealed the flap, and handed it to her.

"Open it in two weeks, and see whether my guess is a good one."

The dusky lashes swept around indolently. "Suppose I were to open it tonight?"

"I'll risk it." Blue eyes smiled.

"On honor, am I?"

"That's it." He held out a big, brown hand.

"You're going to try to capture the robbers, are you?"

"I've been thinking that way."

"And I suppose you've promised yourself success."

"It's on the knees of chance, ma'am. I may get them. They may get me."

"But this prediction of yours?" She held up the sealed envelope.

"That's about another matter."

"But I don't understand. You said. . . ." She gave him a chance to explain.

"It ain't meant you should. You'll understand plenty at the proper time." He offered her his hand again. "Good bye . . . till next time."

The suede glove came forward, and was buried in his handshake.

He understood it to be an unvoiced apology of its owner for her suspicions, and his instinct was correct. For how could her doubts hold their ground when he had showed himself a sharer in her secret and a guardian of it? And how could anything sinister lie behind those frank, unwavering eyes or consist with that long, clean stride that was carrying him so splendidly to the smoking compartment?

IV

The experience of Collins had led him to expect that the saloons of southern Arizona would be a more likely field in which to search for the men he wanted than would the far, silent places of the deserts. He gave them a week to hide the treasure and to recover from the first fright of the inevitable fruitless pursuit along imagined trails.

At the expiration of that time he had the pleasure of ripping open a telegram marked *Epitaph,* which read:

Eastern man says you don't want what is salable here.

Collins's keen eye cut out every other word, and garnered the wheat of the message:

Man you want is here.

This was what his correspondent had written, and the sheriff boarded the first train for Epitaph.

Into the Gold Nugget Saloon that evening dropped Val Collins, big, blond, and jaunty. He looked far less the vigilant sheriff than the gregarious cowpuncher on a search for amusement. Del Hawkes, an old-time friend of his staging days, pounced on him and dragged him to the bar, whence his glance fell genially on the roulette wheel and its devotees, wandered casually across the impassive poker and Mexican monte players, took in the enthroned musicians, who were industriously murdering "La Paloma," and came to rest for barely an instant at a distant faro table. In the curly-haired gambler facing the dealer he saw the man he had come seeking. Nor did he need to look for the hand with the missing finger to be sure it was York Neil.

But the man beside Neil, the black-haired, swarthy fellow from whose presence something at once formidable and gallant and sinister seemed to breathe—the very sight of him set Collins's heart to beating fast with a wild guess. Surely here was a worthy figure on whom to fit the name and reputation of the notorious Dolf Leroy.

Yet the sheriff's eyes rested scarcely an instant before they went traveling again, for he wanted to show as yet no special interest in the object of his suspicions. The gathering was a motley one, picturesque in its diversity. For here had drifted not only the stranded derelicts of a frontier civilization, but selected types of all the turbid elements that go to make up its success. Mexican, millionaire, and miner brushed shoulders at the roulette wheel. Chinaman and cowpuncher. Papago and plainsman, tourist and tailor bucked the tiger side-by-side with a democracy found nowhere else in the world. The click of the wheel, the monotonous call of the croupier, the murmur of many voices in alien tongues, and the high-pitched jarring note of boisterous laughter were all merged in a medley of confusion as picturesque as the scene itself.

"Business not anyways slack at the Nugget," ventured Collins to the bartender.

"No, I don't know as 'tis. Nearly always something doing in little old Epitaph," answered the public quencher of thirsts, polishing the glass top of the bar with a cloth.

"Playing with the lid off back there, ain't they?" The sheriff's nod indicated the distant faro table.

"That's right, I guess. Only blue chips go."

"It's Dolf Leroy . . . that Mexican-looking fellow there," Hawkes explained. "A bad man with the gun, they say, too. Well, him and York Neil and Scotty Dailey blew in last night from their mine up at Saguache. Gave it out he was going to break the bank, Leroy did. Backing that opinion usually comes high, but Leroy is about two thousand to the good, they say."

"Scotty Dailey? Don't think I know him."

"That shorthorn in chaps and a red bandanna is the gentleman . . . him that's playing the wheel so constant. You don't miss no world-beater when you don't know Scotty. He's Leroy's Man Friday. Understand they've struck it rich. Anyway, they're hitting high places while the mazuma lasts."

"I can't seem to locate their mine. What's its brand?"

"The Dalriada. Some other guy is in with them . . . Cork Reilly, I believe it is."

"Queer thing, luck . . . strikes about as unexpected as lightning. Have another, Del?"

"Don't care if I do, Val. It always makes me thirsty to see people I like. Anything new up Tucson way?"

The band had fallen on "Manzanilla", and was rending it with variations when Collins circled around to the wheel and began playing the red. He took a place beside the bow-legged *vaquero* with the red bandanna knotted loosely around his throat. For five minutes the cowpuncher attended strictly to his bets. Then he cursed softly, and asked Collins to exchange places with him.

"This place is my hoodoo. I can't win. . . ." The sentence died in the man's throat, became an inarticulate gurgle of dismay. He had looked up and met the steady eyes of the sheriff, and the surprise of it had driven the blood from his heart. A revolver thrust into his face could not have shaken him more than that serene smile.

Collins took him by the arm with a jovial laugh meant to cover their retreat, and led him into one of the curtained alcove rooms. As they entered, he noticed out of the corner of his eye that Leroy and Neil were still intent on their game. Not for a moment, not even while the barkeeper was answering their call for liquor, did the sheriff release Scotty from the rigor of his eyes, and, when the attendant drew the curtain behind him, the officer let his smile take on a new meaning.

"What did I tell you, Scotty?"

"Prove it," defied Scotty. "Prove it . . . you can't prove it."

"What can't I prove?"

"Why, that I was in tha-. . . ." Scotty stopped abruptly, and watched the smile broaden on the strong face opposite him. His dull brain had come to his rescue none too soon.

"Now, ain't it funny how people's thoughts get to running on the same thing? Last time I met up with you, there you was collecting a hundred dollars and keep-the-change cents from me, and now here you are spending it. It's certainly curious how both of us are remembering that little séance in the Pullman car."

Scotty took refuge in a dogged silence. He was sweating fear.

"Yes, sir. It comes up right vivid before me. There was you a-training your guns on me. . . ."

"I wasn't," broke in Scotty, falling into the trap.

"That's right. How come I to make such a mistake? Of course you carried the sack and Cork Reilly held the guns."

The man cursed quietly, and relapsed into silence.

"Always buy your clothes in pairs?"

The sheriff's voice showed only a pleasant interest, but the outlaw's frightened eyes were puzzled at this sudden turn.

"Wearing a bandanna the same color and pattern as you did the night of our jamboree on the Limited, I see. That's mightily careless of you, ain't it?"

Instinctively a shaking hand clutched at the kerchief. "It don't cut any ice because a hold-up wears a mask made out of stuff like this. . . ."

"Did I say it was a mask he wore?" the gentle voice quizzed.

Scotty, beads of perspiration on his forehead, collapsed as to his defense. He fell back sullenly to his first position: "You can't prove anything."

"Can't I?" The sheriff's smile went out like a snuffed candle. Eyes and mouth were cold and hard as chiseled marble. He leaned forward far across the table, a confident, dominating assurance painted on his face. "Can't I? Don't you bank on that. I can prove all I need to, and your friends will prove the rest. They'll be falling all over themselves to tell what they know . . . and Mister Dailey will be holding the sack again, while Leroy and the rest are slipping out."

The outlaw sprang to his feet, white to the lips. "It's a damned lie. Leroy would never. . . ." He stopped again just in time to bite back the confession hovering on his lips. But he had told what Collins wanted to know.

The curtain parted, and a figure darkened the doorway—a slender little figure that moved on springs. Out of its sardonic, devil-may-care face gleamed malevolent eyes that rested for a moment on Dailey, before they came home to the sheriff.

"And what is it Leroy would never do?" a gibing voice demanded silkily.

V

Collins did not lift a finger or move an eyelash, but with the first word a wary alertness ran through him and starched his figure to rigidity. He gathered himself together for what might come.

"Well, I am waiting. What is it Leroy would never do?" The voice carried a scoff with it, the implication that his very presence had stricken conspirators dumb.

Collins offered the explanation. "Mister Dailey was beginning a testimonial of your virtues just as you right happily arrived in time to hear it. Perhaps he will now proceed."

But Dailey had not a word left. His blunders had been crying ones, and his chief's menacing look had warned him what to expect. The courage oozed out of his heart, for he counted himself already a dead man.

"And who are you, my friend, that makes so free with Dolf Leroy's name?" It was odd how every word of the drawling sentence contrived to carry a taunt and a threat with it, strange what a deadly menace the glittering eyes shot forth.

"My name is Collins."

"Sheriff of Pima County?"

"Yes."

The eyes of the men met like rapiers, as steady and as searching as cold steel. Each of them was appraising the rare quality of his opponent in this duel to the death that was before him.

"What are you doing here? Ain't Pima County your range?"

"I've been discussing with your friend the hold-up on the Pacific Transcontinental."

"Ah." Leroy knew that the sheriff was serving notice on them of his purpose to run down the bandits. Swiftly his mind swept up the factors of the situation. Should he draw now and chance the result, or wait for a more certain ending? He decided to wait, moved by the consideration that, even if he were victorious, the lawyers were sure to draw out of the fat-brained Scotty the cause of the quarrel.

"Well, that don't interest me any, though I suppose you have to explain a heap how come they to hold you up and take your gun. I'll leave you and your jellyfish Scotty to your gabfest. Then you better run back home to Tucson. We don't go much on visiting sheriffs here." He turned on his heel with an insolent laugh, and left the sheriff alone with Dailey.

The superb contempt of the man, his readiness to give the sheriff a chance to pump out of Dailey all he knew, served to warn Collins that his life was in imminent danger. On no hypothesis save one—that Leroy had already condemned them both to death in his mind—could he account for such rashness. And that the blow would fall soon, before he had time to confer with other officers, was a corollary to the first proposition.

"He'll surely kill me on sight," Scotty burst out.

"Yes, he'll kill you," agreed the sheriff, "unless you move first."

"Move, how?"

"Against him. Protect yourself by lining up with me. It's your only show on earth."

Dailey's eyes flashed. "Then, by thunder, I ain't taking it. I'm no coyote, to round on my pardners."

"I give it to you straight. He means murder."

Perspiration poured from the man's face. "I'll light out of the country."

The sheriff shook his head. "You'd never get away alive. Besides, I want you for holding up the Limited. The safest place for you is in jail, and that's where I'm going to put you. Drop that gun! Quick! That's right. Now, you and I are going out of this saloon by the back door. I'm going to walk beside you, and we're going to laugh and talk as if we were the best of friends, but my hand ain't straying any from the end of my gun. Get that, *amigo?* All right. Then we'll take a little *pasear.*"

As Collins and his prisoner reappeared in the main lobby of the Gold Nugget, a Mexican slipped out of the back door of the gambling house. The sheriff called Hawkes aside.

"I want you to call a hack for me, Del. Bring it around to the back door, and arrange with the driver to whip up for the depot as soon as we get in. We ought to catch that twelve-twenty up-train. When the hack gets here, just show up in the door. If you see Leroy or Neil hanging around the door, put your hand up to your tie. If the coast is clear, just move off to the bar and order something."

"Sure," said Hawkes, and was off at once, though just a bit unsteady from his frequent libations.

Both hands of the big clock on the wall pointed to 12:00 when Hawkes appeared again in the doorway at the rear of the Gold Nugget. With a wink at Collins, he made straight for the cocktail he thought he needed.

"Now," said the sheriff, and immediately he and Dailey passed through the back door.

Instantly two shots rang out. Collins lurched forward to the ground, drawing his revolver as he fell. Scotty, twisting from his grasp, ran in a crouch toward the alley along the shadow of the buildings. Shots spattered against the wall as his pursuers gave chase. When the Gold Nugget vomited from its rear door a rush of humanity eager to see the trouble, the noise of their footsteps was already dying in the distance.

Hawkes found his friend leaning against the back of the hack, his revolver smoking in his hand.

"For God's sake, Val!" screamed Hawkes. "Did they get you?"

"Punctured my leg. That's all. But I expect they'll get Dailey."

"How come you to go out when I signaled you to stay?"

"Signaled me to stay, why . . . ?" Collins stopped, unwilling to blame his friend. He knew now that Hawkes, having mixed his drinks earlier in the evening, had mixed his signals later.

"Get me a horse, Del, and round up two or three of the boys. I've got to get after those fellows. They are the ones that held up the Limited last week. Find out for me what hotel they put up at here. I want their rooms searched. Send somebody around to the corrals, and let me know where they stabled their horses. If they left any papers or saddlebags, get them for me."

Fifteen minutes later Collins was in the saddle, ready for the chase, and only waiting for his volunteer posse to join him. They were just starting when a frightened Chinaman ran into the plaza with the news that there had been shooting just back of his laundry on the edge of town, and that a man had been killed.

When the sheriff reached the spot, he lowered himself from the saddle and limped over to the black mass huddled against the wall in the bright moonlight. He turned the riddled body over and looked down into the face of the dead man. It was that of the outlaw, Scotty Dailey. That the body had been thoroughly searched was evident, for all around him were scattered his belongings. Here an old letter and a sack of tobacco, its contents emptied on the ground. There his coat and vest, the linings of each of them ripped out and the pockets emptied. Even the boots and socks of the man had been removed, so thorough had been the search. Whatever the murderers had been looking for it was not money, since his purse, still fairly well lined with greenbacks, was found behind a cactus bush a few yards away.

"What in time were they after?" Collins frowned. "If it wasn't his money . . . and it sure wasn't . . . what was it? Guess I'll not follow Mister Leroy just now till my leg is in better shape. Maybe I had better investigate a little bit around town first."

The body was taken back to the Gold Nugget and placed on a table, pending the arrival of the undertaker. It chanced that Collins, looking absently over the crowd, glimpsed a gray felt hat that looked familiar by reason of a frayed silver band around it. Underneath the hat was a Mexican, and him the sheriff ordered to step forward.

"Where did you get that hat, Manuel?"

"My name is José . . . José Archuleta," corrected the olive-hued one.

"I ain't worrying about your name, son. What I want to know is where you found that hat."

"In the alley off the plaza, *señor*."

"All right. Chuck it up here."

212

"Muy bien, señor." And the dusty hat was passed from hand to hand till it reached the sheriff.

Collins ripped off the silver band and tore out the sweat pad. It was an off chance—one in a thousand—but worth trying nonetheless. And a moment later he knew it was the chance that won. For sewed to the inside of the discolored sweat pad was a little strip of silk. With his knife he carefully removed the strip, and found between it and the leather a folded fragment of paper closely covered with writing. He carried this to the light, and made it out to be a memorandum of direction of some sort. Slowly he spelled out the poorly written words:

From Y.N. took Unowhat. Went twenty yards strate for big rock. Eight feet direkly west. Fifty yards in direksion of suthern Antelope Peke. Then eighteen to nerest cotonwood. J.W. begins hear.

Collins read the scrawl twice before an inkling of its meaning came home to him. Then in a flash his brain was lighted. It was a memorandum of the place where Dailey's share of the plunder was buried.

His confederates had known that he had it, and had risked capture to make a thorough search for the paper. That they had not found it was due only to the fact that the murdered man had lost his hat as he scurried down the streets before them.

VI

While the doctor was probing for the bullet lodged in Collins's leg, Collins studied the memorandum found in Dailey's hat. He found it blind, disappointing work, for there was no clearly indicated starting point. Bit by bit he took it:

From Y.N. took Unowhat.

This was clear enough, so far as it went. It could only mean that from York Neil the writer had taken the plunder to hide. But *where* did he take it? From what point? A starting point must be found somewhere, or the memorandum was of no use. Probably only Neil could supply the needed information, now that Dailey was dead.

Went twenty yards strate for big rock. Eight feet direkly west. Fifty yards in direksion of suthern Antelope Peke. Then eighteen to nerest cotonwood.

All this was plain enough, but the last sentence was the puzzler.

J. W. begins hear.

Was J.W. a person? If so, what did he begin? If Dailey had buried his plunder, what had J.W. left to do?

But had he buried it? Collins smiled. It was not likely he had handed it over to anybody else to hide for him. And yet. . . .

He clapped his hand down on his knee. *By the jumping California frog, I've got it!* he told himself. *They hid the bulk of what they got from the Limited all together. Went out in a bunch to hide it. Blindfolded each other, and took turns about blinding up the trail. No one of them can go get the loot without the rest. When they want it, every one of these memoranda must be Johnny on the spot before they can dig up the mazuma. No wonder Dolf Leroy searched so thorough for this bit of paper. I'll bet a stack of blue chips against Dolf's chance of heaven that he's the sorest train robber right this moment that ever punctured a car window.*

Collins laughed softly, nor had the smile died but out of his eyes when Hawkes came into the room with information to the point. He had made a round of the corrals, and discovered that the outlaws' horses had been put up at Tim Webster's place, a tumble-down feed station on the edge of town.

"Jim didn't take kindly to my questions," Hawkes explained, "but, after a little rock-me-to-sleep-mother talk, I soothed him down some, and cut the trail of Dolf Leroy and his partners. The old man give me several specimens of language, unwashed and uncombed, when I told him Dolf and York was outlaws and train robbers. Didn't believe a word of it, he said. 'Twas just like the fool officers to jump an innocent party. I told Jim to keep his shirt on . . . he could turn his wolf loose when they framed up that he was in it. Well, sir! I plumb thought for a moment he was going to draw on me when I said that."

Collins's eyes narrowed to slits, as they always did when he was thinking intensely. Did Jim Webster's interest in Leroy have its source merely in their being birds of a feather, or was there a more direct community of lawlessness between them? He had known of the old man for years as a border smuggler and a suspected horse thief. Was he also a member of Dolf Leroy's murderous gang? Three men had joined in the chase of Dailey, but the tracks had told him that only two horses had galloped from the scene of the murder into the night. The inference left to draw was that a local accomplice had joined them in the chase of Scotty, and had slipped back home after the deed had been finished.

What more likely than that Webster had been this accomplice? He had been for years at outs with the law. He was—*J. W. begins hear.* Like a flash the ill-written scrawl jumped to his sight. J.W. was Jim Webster. What luck!

The doctor finished his work, and Collins tested his leg gingerly. "Del, I'm going over to have a little talk with the old man. Want to go along?"

"You bet I do, Val," said Del Hawkes.

"You mustn't walk on that leg for a week or two yet, Mister Collins," the doctor explained, shaking his head.

"That so, Doctor? And it's nothing but a nice clean flesh

wound. Sho. I've a deal more confidence in you than that.
Ready, Del?"

"It's at your risk, then, Mister Collins."

"Sure." The sheriff smiled. "I'm *living* at my own risk, Doctor. But I'd a heap rather be alive than daid, and take all the
risk that's coming, too. But since you make a point of it, I'll do
my walking on a bronco's back."

They found Mr. Webster just emerging from the stable with a
saddle pony when they rode into the corral. At a word from
Collins, Hawkes took the precaution to close the corral gate.

The old man held a wary position on the farther side of his
horse, the while he ripped out a raucous string of invectives.

"Real fluent, ain't he?" murmured Hawkes as he began to
circle around to flank the enemy.

"Stay right there, Del Hawkes. Move, you red-haided son of
a brand blotter, and I'll pump holes in you!" A rifle leveled
across the saddle emphasized his sentiments.

"Hospitable, ain't he?" Hawkes grinned, coming promptly to
a halt.

Collins rode slowly forward, his hand on the butt of the
revolver that still lay in its scabbard. The Winchester covered
every step of his progress, but he neither hastened nor faltered,
though he knew his life hung in the balance. If his steely blue
eyes had released for one moment the wolfish ones of the old
villain, if he had hesitated or hurried, he would have been shot
through the head.

But the eyes of a brave man are the king of weapons. Webster's fingers itched at the trigger he had not the courage to
pull. For such an unflawed nerve he knew himself no match.

"Keep back!" he screamed. "Damn it, another step and I'll
fire!"

But he did not fire, although Collins rode up to him,
dismounted, and threw the end of the rifle carelessly from him.

"Don't be rash, old man. I've come here to put you under arrest for robbing the Limited, and I'm going to do it."

The indolent, contemptuous drawl, so free of even a suggestion of the strain the sheriff must have been under, completed his victory. The fellow lowered his rifle with a peevish oath.

"You're barkin' up the wrong tree, Val Collins."

"I guess not," retorted the sheriff easily. "Del, you better relieve Mister Webster of his ballast. He ain't really fit to be trusted with a weapon, and him so excitable. That Winchester came awful near going off, my son. You don't want to be so careless when you're playing with firearms. It's a habit that's liable to get you into trouble."

Collins had not shaved death so closely without feeling a reaction of boyish gaiety at his adventure. It bubbled up in his talk like effervescing soda.

"Now we'll go into a committee of the whole, gentlemen, adjourn to the stable, and have a little game of 'Button, button, who's got the button?' You first, Mister Webster. If you'll kindly shuck your coat and vest, we'll begin button hunting."

They diligently searched the old miscreant without finding anything pertaining to *J. W. begins hear.*

"He's bound to have it somewhere," asseverated Collins. "It don't stand to reason he was making his getaway without that paper. We got to be more thorough, Del."

Hawkes, under the direction of his friend, ripped out linings and tore away pockets from clothing. The saddle on the bronco and the saddle blankets were also torn to pieces in vain.

Finally Hawkes scratched his head and looked down on the wreckage. "I hate to admit it, Val, but the old fox has got us beat . . . it ain't on his person."

"Not unless he's got it under his skin," agreed Collins with a grin.

"Maybe he ate it. Think we better operate and find out?"

An idea hit the sheriff. He walked up to Webster and ordered him to open his mouth.

The jaws set like a vise.

Collins poked his revolver against the closed mouth. "Swear for us, old bird. Get a move on you.

The mouth opened, and Collins inserted two fingers. When he withdrew them, they brought a set of false teeth. Under the plate was a tiny rubber bag that stuck to it. Inside the bag was a paper.

VII

Velvet night had fallen over Arizona and blotted out all but the softer tones of color. A million stars looked down upon a land magically flooded with moonlight.

Even through her growing fear, the girl who wandered helplessly across washes and over rises was touched by the wonder-working spell; she felt its beauty as an added horror to the oppression of the heart that was beginning to rise to her throat in sobs. For she was lost, and had been almost from the moment, many hours before, when she had seen her pony disappear over the brow of the nearest hillock while she panted vainly in chase.

Worn-out, she sank down on a sandy hillside, still fighting with her fears and the sense of desolation gripping at her. She had left the Circle Thirty-Three Ranch blithely that morning, all the glory of the wonderful primeval day singing through her like champagne. Sunlight in a flood, miraculous, tempered, had been over the young earth, and the girl had ridden far, rejoicing in the youth that made life such a wild delight. She had dismounted to pick some poppies to take back to the ranch, and her pony, startled at a rattlesnake, had flung up its heels and fled. Since then she had tramped with aching, blistered feet, broiled by the fierce sun, her parched throat a lime kiln. She had thought it would be better after nightfall, but with the evening had come a haunting fear of all this endless moonlit desert space.

Why didn't they look for her? Didn't they know she needed help? Would they leave her to die unfound? She broke down utterly, sobbing like a child and finding relief in self-pity at her situation.

And then, out of that moonlit sea of desert rose a voice, a clear, sweet tenor, swelling bravely with the very ecstasy of pathos. It was the prison song from *Il Trovatore,* and the desolation of its lifted appeal went to the heart like water to the roots of flowers.

> *Ah! I have sigh'd to rest me*
> *Deep in the quiet grave.*

The girl's sob caught in her breast, stilled with the awe of that heavenly music. So for an instant she waited before it was borne in on her that the voice was a human one, and that the heaven from which it descended was the hilltop above her.

A wild laugh, followed by an oath, cut the dying echoes of the song. She could hear the swish of a quirt falling again and again, and the sound of trampling hoofs thudding on the hard, sun-cracked ground. Startled, she sprang to her feet, and saw silhouetted against the skyline a horse and his rider fighting for mastery.

The battle was superb while it lasted. The horse had been a famous outlaw, broken to the saddle by its owner out of the sheer passion for victory, but there were times when its savage strength rebelled at abject submission, and this was one of them. It swung itself skyward, and came down like a pile driver, camelbacked, and without joints in the legs. Swiftly it rose again, lunging forward and whirling in the air, then jarred down at an angle. The brute did its malevolent best, a fury incarnate. But the rider was a match, and more than a match for it. He sat the

saddle like a Centaur, with the perfect, unconscious grace of a
born master, swaying in his seat as need was, and spurring the
horse to a blinder fury.

Sudden as had been the start, no less sudden was the finish
of the battle. The bronco, pounded to a stiff-legged standstill,
trembled for a long minute like an aspen, and sank to a tame
surrender, despite the sharp spurs roweling its bloody sides.

"Ah, my beauty. You've had enough, have you?" demanded
the cruel, triumphant voice of the rider. "You would try that
game, would you? I'll teach you."

"Stop spurring that horse, you bully."

The man stopped in sheer amazement at this apparition that
had leaped out of the ground almost at his feet. His wary glance
circled the hills to make sure she was alone.

"Certainly, ma'am. We're sure delighted to meet up with you.
Ain't we, Two-Step?"

For himself, he spoke the simple truth. He lived in his sensations, spurring himself to fresh ones as he had but just now
been spurring his horse to sate the greed of conquest in him.
And this high-spirited, gallant Diana—for her costume told him
she had been riding—offered a rare fillip to his jaded appetite.
The dusky, long-lashed eyes that always give a woman an effect
of beauty, the splendid fling of head, and the piquant, finely cut
features, with their unconscious tale of Brahmin caste, the long
lines of the supple body, willowy and yet plump as a partridge—
they went to his head like strong wine. Here was an adventure
from the gods—a stubborn will to bend, the pride of a haughty
young beauty to trail in the dust, her untamed heart to break if
need be. The lust of the battle was on him already. She was a
woman to dream about. *Sweeter than the lids of Juno's eyes, Or
Cytherea's breath,* he told himself exultantly as he slid from his
horse and stood bowing before her.

And he, for his part, was a taking enough picture of devil-may-care gallantry gone to seed. The touch of jaunty impudence in his humility, not less than the daring admiration of his handsome eyes and the easy, sinuous grace of his flexed muscles, labeled him what he was—a man bold and capable to do what he willed, and a villain every inch of him.

She said, after that first clash of stormy eyes with bold, admiring ones: "I am lost . . . from the Circle Thirty-Three Ranch."

"Why, no, you're found," he corrected, white teeth flashing in a smile.

"My horse got away from me this morning. I've been"—there was a catch in her voice—"wandering ever since."

He whirled to his saddle, and had the canteen thongs unloosed in a moment. While she drank, he rummaged from his saddlebags some sandwiches of jerky and a flask of whiskey. She ate the sandwiches, he the while watching her with amused sympathy in his swarthy countenance.

"You ain't half bad at the chuck wagon, Miss Meredith," he told her.

She stopped, the sandwich part way to her mouth. "I don't remember your face. I've met so many people since I came to the Circle Thirty-Three. Still, I think I should remember you."

He immediately relieved the duty of her quasi-apology. "You haven't seen my *face* before," he laughed, and, although she puzzled over the double meaning that seemed to lurk behind his words and amuse him, she could not find the key to it. "But you're famous now, Miss Meredith, since the story got out of how you fooled Dolf Leroy's gang out of a hundred thousand dollars."

She frowned. It had annoyed her a good deal that the superintendent of construction on the Elkhorn branch had talked so much of her exploit that it had become common talk in cattle land. No matter into what unfrequented cañon she rode, some silent cowpuncher would look at her with admiring eyes behind which she read a knowledge of the story. It was a lonely, desolate country full of the wide, deep silences of utter emptiness, yet there could not a foot fall but the word was bruited on the wings of the wind.

"D you know where the Circle Thirty-Three is?" she demanded.

He nodded.

"Can you take me home?"

"I surely can. But not tonight. You're done up for fair. We'll camp out, and in the morning we'll hit the trail."

"Is it far?"

"Twenty-seven miles as the crow flies. You sit down on this blanket and watch me start a fire so quick your head will swim."

"I can't stay out alone all night . . . and my father will be anxious. Besides, I couldn't sleep outdoors."

"Now if I'd only thought to bring a load of lumber and some carpenters along . . . and a chaperon," he burlesqued, gathering broken mesquite and cottonwood branches.

She watched him uneasily. "Isn't there a ranch house near?"

"You wouldn't call it near by the time we had reached it. What's to hinder your sleeping here? Isn't this room airy enough? And don't you like the system of lighting? 'Twas patented I disremember how many million years ago."

He soon had a cup of steaming coffee ready for her, and the heat of it made a new woman of her. She sat in the warm fire glow, and began to feel stealing over her a delightful reaction of languor.

"Since you know my name, isn't it fair that I should know yours?" she asked, a more amiable light in her untender eyes than he had yet seen.

"You may call me a shepherd of the desert, since I find the lamb that was lost."

"Then, Mister Shepherd, I'm very glad to meet you," she

said. "I don't remember when I was ever more glad to meet a stranger." And she added with a little laugh: "It's a pity I'm too sleepy to do my duty by you in a social way."

"We'll let that wait till tomorrow. You'll entertain me plenty then. I'll make your bunk up right away."

She was presently lying with her feet to the fire, rolled in his blankets and with his saddle for a pillow. But, though her eyes were heavy, her brain was still too active to permit her to get to sleep immediately. The experience was too near a one, the emotions of the day too vividly poignant, to lose their hold on her at once.

And this fascinating scamp, one moment flooding the moonlit desert with inspired snatches from the opera sung in the voice of an angel, and the next lashing out at his horse like a devil incarnate, was not to be dismissed with a thought. Who and what was he? How reconcile the man he seemed with the man he might have been? For every inflection of his voice, every motion of his person, proclaimed the strain of good blood gone wrong and trampled underfoot of set, sardonic purpose, interpreted him as the fallen gentleman in a hell of his own choosing. Lounging on an elbow in the flickering shadows, so carelessly insouciant in every picturesque inch of him, he seemed to radiate the romance of the untamed frontier.

She fell asleep thinking of him, and when she awakened, his gay whistle was the first sound that fell on her ears. The morning was still very young, but the abundant desert light dismissed sleep summarily. She shook and brushed the wrinkles out of her skirt, and with her handkerchief attempted a dry wash. Already he had the coffee simmering on the fire when she came up noiselessly behind him.

But, although she thought her approach had been silent, his trained senses were apprised.

"Good morning! How did you find your bedroom?" he asked,

without turning from the bacon he was broiling on the end of a stick.

"Quite up to the specifications. I never slept better. But have you eyes in the back of your head?"

He laughed grimly. "I have to be all eyes and ears in my business."

"Is your business of a nature so sensitive?"

"As much so as stocks on Wall Street. And we haven't any ticker to warn us to get under cover. Do you take cream in your coffee, Miss Meredith?"

She looked around in surprise. "Cream?"

"We're in tin-can land, you know, and live on airtights. I milk my cow with a can opener. Let me recommend this quail on toast." He handed her a battered tin plate, and prepared to help her with the frying pan.

"I suppose that is another name for pork?"

"No, really. I happened to bag a couple of hooters last night."

"You're a missionary of the good-foods movement. I shall name your mission Saint Sherry's-in-the-Wilderness."

"Ah, Sherry's! That's since my time. I don't suppose I should know my way about in little old New York now."

She found him eager to pick up again the broken strands that had connected him with the big world from which she had just come. It had been long since she had enjoyed a talk more, for he expressed himself with wit and dexterity. But through her enjoyment ran a note of apprehension. He was for the moment a resurrected gentleman. But what would he be next? She had an insistent memory of a heavenly flood of music broken by a horrible discord of raucous oaths.

It was he that lingered over their breakfast, loath to make the first move to bring him back into realities, and it was she that had to suggest the need of setting out. But once on his feet, he saddled and packed swiftly, with a deftness born of experience.

"We'll have to ask Two-Step to carry double today," he said as he helped her to a place behind him.

Leroy let his horse take it easy, except when some impulse of mischief stirred him to break into a canter so as to make the girl put her arm around his waist for support. They stopped about noon by a stream in a cañon defile to lunch and rest the pony.

"I don't remember this place at all. Are we near home?" she asked.

"About five miles. I reckon you're right tired. It's an unhandy way to ride."

Every mile took them deeper into the mountains, through winding cañons and over unsuspected trails, and the girl's uneasiness increased with the wildness of the country.

"Are you *sure* we're going the right way? I don't think we can be," she suggested more than once.

"Dead sure," he answered the last time, letting Two-Step turn into a blind draw opening from sheer cañon walls.

A hundred feet from the entrance they rode around a great slide of rock into a tiny valley containing a group of buildings.

He swung from the horse and offered a hand to help her dismount. A reckless, unholy light burned in his daring eyes. "Home at last, Miss Meredith. Let me offer you a thousand welcomes."

An icy hand seemed to clutch at her heart. "Home! What do you mean? This isn't the Circle Thirty-Three."

"Not at all. The Circle Thirty-Three is fifty miles from here. This is where I hang out . . . and you, for the present."

"But . . . I don't understand. How dare you bring me here?"

"The desire for your company, Miss Meredith, made of me a Lochinvar."

She saw, with a shiver, that the ribald eyes were mocking her. "Take me back this instant . . . this instant," she commanded, but her imperious voice was not very sure of itself. "Take me home at once, you liar."

"I expect you don't quite understand," he explained with gentle derision. "You're a prisoner of war, Miss Meredith."

"And who are you?" she faltered.

He bowed elaborately. "Dolf Leroy, train robber, outlaw, and general bad man . . . very much at your service."

She sat rigid, her face ashen. "You coward, do you war on women?"

The change in him was instantaneous. It was as if two thousand years of civilization had been sponged out in an eye beat. He stood before her a savage primeval, his tight-lipped smile cruel in its triumph. "Did I begin this fight? Didn't you undertake to make a fool of me by cheating me out of a hundred thousand dollars under my very nose? That was your hour. This, madam, is mine. If your friends want to see you again, they've got to raise that hundred thousand you stole from me. I'll teach you it isn't safe to laugh at Dolf Leroy."

The girl was afraid to the very marrow of her. But she would not show him her fear. She slipped from the horse and stood before him superbly defiant. "You coward!" she cried with a contempt that stung.

"That's twice you've called me that." His eyes glittered savagely. "You'll crawl on your knees to me and ask pardon before I'm through with you. Don't forget that for a moment, you beautiful shrew. You're mine . . . to do with as I please. I'll break your spirit or I'll break your heart."

He turned on his heel and struck the palms of his hands together twice. A Mexican woman came running from one of the cabins. He flung a sentence or two in Spanish at her, and pointed to Miss Meredith. She asked a question, and he jabbed out a threat. The woman nodded her head, and motioned to the girl to follow her.

When Helen Meredith was alone in the room that was to

serve as her prison, she sank into a chair and covered her face with her hands in a despair that was utter.

VIII

Helen Meredith had reason to be grateful at least for one thing. It was the fourth morning of her captivity, and she had been left quite to herself, except when the Mexican woman came to bring her meals and to let her out for her daily half-hour's sun bath. She had spent much of her time reading, for, though the boxful of books she found in her room was a promiscuous one, it had a representative sprinkling of things worthwhile. Stevenson's *Letters,* Tennyson's *Poems,* an old copy of Montaigne's *Essays,* a tattered Villon in the original, and Dumas's *The Three Musketeers* she had unearthed from a pile of yellow-covered trash.

On the occasions of her daily promenade, she had noticed each afternoon a curly-haired young man in chaps lounging on the top of a big rock, apparently enjoying his after-dinner *siesta.* But when she had ventured once to the point where the rock slide hemmed in the valley, he had come running after her so promptly that she could no longer doubt she was being closely watched.

"Better stay in the valley, ma'am . . . you might get lost right easily out there," he had suggested, indicating the outer world with a hand that was minus a forefinger.

But of the outlaw chief himself she had seen or heard nothing until the evening of the third night, when he had apparently arrived from a long journey full of the devil and bad whiskey. She had heard him cursing the Mexican woman, and had been fearful lest he might come in to see her while he was in this mood. But the evening had passed in safety without a visit, and courage had come flowing back to her heart with the daylight.

She was aware that her reprieve was probably near its end, and was not surprised when it proved so. The Mexican attendant brought with her breakfast a note from him signed *Shepherd of the Desert,* asking permission to pay his respects. Miss Meredith divined that he was in his better mood, and penciled on his note, though not without fear, the permission she could hardly refuse.

But she was scarce prepared for the impudent air of jocund spring that he brought into her prison, the gay assumption of camaraderie so inconsistent with the facts. Yet, since safety lay in an avoidance of the tragic, she set herself to watch his mood.

At sight of the open Tennyson, he laughed and quoted:

> *She only said, "The day is dreary,*
> *He cometh not," she said.*

"But, you see, he comes," he added. "What say, Mariana of the Robber's Roost, to making a picnic day of it? We'll climb the Crags and lunch on the summit."

"The Crags?"

"That Matterhorn-shaped peak that begins at our back door. Are you for it?"

While this mood was uppermost in him, she felt reasonably safe. It was a phase of him she certainly did not mean to discourage. Besides, she had a youthful confidence in her powers that she was loath to give up without an effort to find the accessible side of his ruthless heart.

"I'll try it . . . but you must help me when we come to the bad places," she said.

"Sure thing. It's a deal. You're a right game little gentleman, pardner."

"Thank, you, but you had better save your compliments till I make good," she told him with the most piquant air of gaiety in the world.

They started on horseback, following a mountain trail that zigzagged across the foothills toward the Crags. He had unearthed somewhere a boy's saddle that suited her very well, and the pony she rode was one of the easiest she had ever mounted. At the end of an hour's ride they left the horses and began the ascent on foot. It was a stiff climb, growing steeper as they ascended, but Helen Meredith had not tramped over golf links for nothing. She might grow leg weary, but she would not cry "enough." And he, on his part, showed the tactful consideration for the resources of her strength he had already taught her to expect from that other day's experience on the plains. It was a very rare hand of assistance that he offered her, but often he stopped to admire the beautiful view that stretched for many miles below them, in order that she might get a minute's breathing space.

Once he pointed out, far away on the horizon, a bright gleam that caught the sunlight like a heliograph. "That's the roof of the Circle Thirty-Three," he explained.

She drew a long breath, and flashed a stealthy look at him.

"I expect I'll see your father day after tomorrow. Got any message for him?" In answer to her surprised exclamation, he added, with a laugh: "You're wondering why I'm going to see him. You see, I happen to hold a hostage he would be right glad to ransom, I reckon."

The girl pumped out a hesitating question: "Can you come to any agreement?"

He laughed. "Well, I guess yes. The old gentleman will be hitting the trail for Tucson to raise that hundred thousand after we've had our little talk."

"I'm not sure he can raise that much money," she said quietly.

"I'll be right sorry to see the day he does," was his debonair answer as he stroked his black mustache and smiled gallantly at her.

"I'm afraid I'll have to burden your hospitality forever and a day. You seem to value Mariana of the Robber's Roost so highly that you set a prohibitive ransom."

He looked with half-shut, smoldering eyes at her slender exquisiteness, instinct with a vital charm at once well bred and Gypsyish, and the veiled passion in his gaze told her that a ransom was not in his thoughts. He had made an offer, perhaps because his men had insisted on it, but he had of purpose made it an impossible one. Again she felt the chill of fear passing over her.

Deftly she guided the conversation back to less dangerous channels. In this the increasing difficulty of the climb assisted her, for, after they had begun the last ascent, sustained talk became impossible.

"See that trough above us near the summit. You'll have to hang on by your eyelashes, pardner." He always burlesqued the word of comradeship a little to soften its familiarity.

"Dear me! Is it that bad?"

"It is so bad that at the top you have to jump for a grip and draw yourself up by your arms."

"And if one should miss?"

He shrugged. "Ah . . . that's a theological question. If the sky pilots guess right, for you heaven, for me hell."

They negotiated the trough successfully to its uptilted end. She had a bad moment when he leaped for the rock rim above from the narrow ledge on which they stood. But he caught it, drew himself up without the least trouble, and turned to assist her. He sat down on the rock edge, facing the abyss beneath them, and told her to lock her hands together above his left foot. Then slowly, inch by inch, he drew her up till with one of his hands he could catch her wrist. A moment later she was standing on his rigid toes, from which position she warily edged to safety above.

"Well done, little pardner. You're the first woman ever

climbed the Crags." He offered a hand to celebrate the achievement.

"If I am, it is all due to you, big pardner. I could never have made that last bit alone."

They ate lunch merrily in the pleasant Arizona sunlight, and both of them seemed as free from care as a schoolboy on a holiday.

"It's good to be alive, isn't it?" he asked her after they had eaten, as he lay on the warm ground at her feet. "And what a life it is here! To be riding free, with your knees pressing a saddle, in the wind and the sun. There's something in a man to which the wide spaces call. I'd rather lie here in the beating sun with you beside me than be a king. You remember that 'Last Ride' fellow Browning tells about. I reckon he's dead right. If a man could only capture his best moments and hold them forever, it would be heaven to the nth degree."

She studied her sublimated villain with that fascination his vagaries always excited in her. Was ever a more impossible combination put together than this sentimental scamp with the long record of evil?

"Say it," he laughed. "Whang it out! Ask anything you like, pardner."

Pluckily daring, she took him at his word. "I was only wondering at the different men I find in you. Before I have known you a dozen hours, I discover in you the poet and the man of action, the schoolboy and the philosopher, the sentimentalist and the cynic, and . . . may I say it? . . . the gentleman and the blackguard. One feels a sense of loss. You should have specialized. You would have made such a good soldier, for instance. Pity you didn't go to West Point, instead of Harvard."

"I didn't go to Harvard," he said quickly.

"Oh, was it Yale? Well, no matter. The point is that you missed your calling. You were born for a soldier . . . cavalry I should say. What an ornament to society you would have been if your energies had found the right vent. But they didn't find it . . . and you craved excitement, I suppose."

"Wherefore I am what I am. Please particularize."

"I can't, because I don't understand you. But I think this much is true, that you have set yourself against all laws of God and man. Yet you are not consistent, since you are better than your creed. You tell yourself there shall be no law for you but your own will, and you find there is something in you stronger than desire that makes you shrink at many things. You can kill in fair fight, but you can't knife a man in the back, can you?"

"I never have."

"You have a dreadfully perverted set of rules, but you play by them. That's why I know I'm safe with you, even when you are at your worst."

"Oh, you know you're safe, do you?"

"Of course I do. You were once a gentleman, and you can't forget it entirely. That's the weakness in your philosophy of total depravity."

"You speak with an assurance you don't always feel, I reckon. And I expect I wouldn't bank too much on those divinations of yours, if I were you." He rolled over so that he could face her more directly. "You've been mighty frank, Miss Meredith, and I take off my hat to your sand. Now I'm going to be frank a while. You interest me. I never met a woman that interested me so much. But you do a heap more than interest me. No, you sit right there and listen. Your cheeky pluck and that insolent, indifferent beauty of yours made a hit with me the first minute I saw you that night. I swore I'd tame you, and that's why I brought you to Robber's Roost. Your eye flashed a heap too haughty for me to give you the go-by. Mind you, I meant to be master. I meant to make you mine as much as a dog that licks my hand. That's as far as it went with me then, but, before we reached here next day, I knew the thing cut deeper with me. I ain't saying that I love you because I'm a sweep, and it's just likely I don't know passion from love. But I'll tell you this . . . there hasn't been a waking moment since then I haven't been on fire to be with you. That's why I stayed away until I knew I wasn't so likely to slop over. But here, I'm doing it right this minute. I care more for you than I do for anything else on this earth. But that makes it worse for you. I never cared for anybody without bringing ruin on them. I broke my mother's heart and spoiled the life of the girl I was going to marry. That's the kind of scoundrel I am. Even if I could make you care enough to marry me . . . and I'm not such a fool as to dream it for a moment . . . I would drag you through hell after me."

The despair in his beautiful eyes spoke more impressively than his self-scorning words. She was touched in spite of herself. For there is an appeal about the engaging sinner that drums in a woman's head and calls to her heart. All good women are missionaries in the last analysis, and Miss Meredith was not an exception to her sex.

She leaned forward impetuously, a sweet, shy dignity in her manner. "Is it too late? Why not begin now? There is still a tomorrow, and it need not be the slave of yesterday. Life for all of us is full of milestones."

"And how shall I begin my new career of saintliness?" he asked with bitter irony.

"The nearest duty. Take me back to my father. Begin a life of rigid honesty."

"Give you up now that I have found you! That is just the last thing I would do," he cried roughly. "No . . . no. The clock can't be turned back. I have sowed and I must reap." He leaped to his feet. "Come! We must be going."

She rose sadly, for she knew the mood of regret for his wasted life had passed, and she had failed.

They descended the trough and reached the boulder field that had marked the terminal of the glacier. At the farther edge of it the outlaw turned to point out to the girl a great splash of yellow on a mountainside fifteen miles away.

"You wouldn't think poppy flowers would do that, would you? But they do. There are millions and millions of them, and the whole mountain is golden from their glow."

The words were hardly out of his mouth when a rock slipped under his foot, and he came down hard. He was up again in an instant, but Miss Meredith caught the sharp intake of his breath when he set foot to the ground.

"You've sprained your ankle!" she cried.

"Afraid so. It's my own rotten carelessness." He limped forward a dozen steps, but he had to set his teeth to do it.

"Lean on me."

"I reckon I'll have to," he said grimly.

They covered a quarter of a mile, with many stops to rest the swollen ankle. Only by the irregularity of his breathing and the damp moisture on his forehead could she tell the agony he was enduring.

"It must be dreadful," she told him once.

"I've got to endure the grief, little pardner."

Again she said, when they had reached a wooded grove where live oaks disputed with the cholla for the mastery: "Only two hundred yards more. I think I can bring your pony as far as the big cottonwood."

She noticed that he leaned heavier and heavier on her. However, when they reached the cottonwood, he leaned no more, but pitched forward in a faint. The water bottle was empty, but she ran down to where the ponies had been left, and presently came back with his canteen. She had been away perhaps twenty minutes, and when she came back, he waved a hand airily at her.

"First time in my life that ever happened," he apologized gaily. "But why didn't you get on Tim and cut loose for the Circle Thirty-Three while you had the chance?"

"I didn't think of it. Perhaps I shall next time."

"I shouldn't. You see, I'd follow you and bring you back. And if I didn't find you, there would be a lamb lost again in these hills."

"The sporting thing would be to take a chance."

"And leave me here alone? Well, I'm going to give you a show to take it." He handed her his revolver. "You may need this if you're going traveling."

"Are you telling me to go?" she asked, amazed.

"I'm telling you to do as you think best. You may take a hike or you may bring back Two-Step to me. Suit yourself."

"I tell you plainly I sha'n't come back."

"And I'm sure you will."

"But I won't. The thing's absurd. Would you?"

"No, I shouldn't. But you will."

"I won't. Good bye." She held out her hand.

He shook his head, looking steadily at her. "What's the use? You'll be back in half an hour."

"Not I. Did you say I must keep the Antelope Peaks in a line to reach the Circle Thirty-Three?"

"Yes, a little to the left. Don't be long, little pardner."

"I hate to leave you here. Perhaps I'll send a sheriff to take care of you."

"Better bring Two-Step up to the south of that bunch of cottonwoods. It's not so steep that way."

"I'll mention it to the sheriff. I'm not coming myself."

She left him apparently obstinate in the conviction that she would return. In reality he was taking a gambler's chance, but it was of a part with the reckless spirit of the man that the risk appealed to him. It was plain he could not drag himself farther.

Since he must let her go for the horse alone, he chose that she should go with her eyes open to his knowledge of the opportunity of escape.

But Helen Meredith had not the slightest intention of returning. She had found her chance, and she meant to make the most of it. As rapidly as her unaccustomed fingers would permit, she saddled and cinched her pony. She had not ridden a hundred yards before Two-Step came crashing through the young cottonwood grove after her. Objecting to being left alone, he had broken the rein that tied him. The girl tried to recapture the horse in order that the outlaw might not be left entirely without means of reaching camp, but her efforts were unsuccessful. She had to give it up and resume her journey. Of course the men at Robber's Roost would miss their chief and search for him. There could be no doubt but that they would find him. She bolstered up her assurance of this as she rode toward the Antelope Peaks, but her hope lacked buoyancy, because she doubted if they had any idea of where he had been going to spend the day.

She rode slower and slower, and finally came to a long halt for consideration. Vividly there rose before her a picture of the gallant rascal waiting grimly for death or rescue. She knew he would not blame her. He was too game for that. But she could not leave a crippled man to die alone, even though he were her enemy. That was the goal to which her circling thoughts came always home, and with a sob she turned her horse's head. It was a piece of soft-headed folly, she confessed, but she could not help it.

And when an hour later she came on the bandit lying where she had left him, the sudden warmth that lit his dark face at sight of her and softened it amazingly was assurance enough to this impulsive girl that she had done right.

He reached for her hand, and gave it a firm pressure. "You're white clear through, pardner. I'll not forget it as long as I live."

"I tried to leave you. I rode two or three miles. But I found I couldn't do it," she confessed.

His eyes lit. "That settles it right now. You're going back to your father as fast as I can take you."

"Will your . . . friends let me go?"

"They won't know it, and when they find it out, what kicking they do will be done mostly in private."

He clambered to her pony, and she walked beside. She was tired, but she would not confess it, and she was nearer happy than she had been since her capture. For there is more joy over one sinner that repenteth than over the ninety and nine just that need no repentance.

Evening had fallen before they reached Robber's Roost. It was beautifully still, except for the calling of the quails. The hazy violet outline of the mountains came to silhouette against the skyline with a fine edge.

The man drew a deep breath when they came in sight of the pony corral back of the cabins. "I'll never forget today. I'm going to fence it in from all the yesterdays and tomorrows of life. You see, little pardner, it's the day I discovered the one woman I ever met that I could love for keeps. I'm not building on this. It's a cinch I lose, but I want you to remember that something's happened to me that makes me different somehow. It won't change my life. I've gone too far for that. But I'll know the difference, and you're not to forget that you've made even Dolf Leroy whiter for knowing you."

"I'll not forget," she said, brushing tears from her eyes.

York Neil answered his chief's call, and relieved him of his horse.

"You got a visitor in there," Neil said with a grin and a jerk of his thumb toward the house. "Came blundering into the draw sorter accidental-like, but some curious. So I asked him if he wouldn't light and stay a while. He thought it over, and figured he would."

"Who is it?" asked Leroy.

"You go and see. I ain't giving away what your Christmas presents are. I aim to let Santa surprise you a few."

Miss Meredith followed the outlaw chief into the house, and over his shoulder glimpsed two men. One of them was the Irishman, Cork Reilly, and he sat with a Winchester across his knees. The other had his back toward them, but he turned as they entered, and nodded casually to the outlaw. Helen's heart jumped to her throat when she saw it was Val Collins.

The two men looked at each other steadily in a long silence. Dolf Leroy was the first to speak.

"You damn' fool." The swarthy face creased to an evil smile of contempt.

"I certainly do seem to butt in considerable, Mister Leroy," admitted Collins with an answering smile.

Leroy's square jaw set like a vise. "It won't happen again, Mister Sheriff."

"I'd hate to gamble on that heavy," returned Collins easily. Then he caught sight of the girl's white face, and rose to his feet with outstretched hand.

"Sit down," snapped out Reilly.

"Oh, that's all right. I'm shaking hands with the lady. Did you think I was inviting you to drill a hole in me, Mister Reilly?"

IX

"I thought we bumped you off down at Epitaph."

"Along with Scotty? Well, no. You see, I'm a regular cat to kill, Mister Leroy, and I couldn't conscientiously join the angels with so lame a story as a game laig to explain my coming," said Collins cheerfully.

"In that case. . . ."

"Yes, I understand. You'd be willing to accommodate with a hole in the haid instead of one in the laig. But I'll not trouble you."

"What are you doing here? Didn't I warn you to attend to your own business and leave me alone?"

"Seems to me you did load me up with some good advice, but I plumb forgot to follow it."

Leroy cursed under his breath. "You came here at your own risk, then?"

"Well, I did and I didn't," corrected the sheriff easily. "I've got a five-thousand policy in the Southeastern Life Insurance Company, so I reckon it's some risk to them. And, by the way, it's a company I can recommend."

"Does it insure against suicide?" asked Leroy, his masked, smiling face veiling thinly a ruthless purpose.

"And against hanging. Let me strongly urge you to take out a policy at once," came the prompt retort.

"You think it necessary?"

"Quite. When you and York Neil and old man Webster made an end of Scotty, you threw ropes around your own necks. Any locoed tenderfoot would know that."

The sheriff's unflinching look met the outlaw's black frown, serene and clear-eyed.

"And would he know that you had committed suicide when you ran this place down and came here?" asked Leroy with silken cruelty.

"Well, he ought to know it. The fact is, Mister Leroy, that it hadn't penetrated my think tank that this was your *hacienda* when I came mavericking in."

"Just out riding for your health?"

Not exactly. I was looking for Miss Meredith. I cut her trail about six miles from the Circle Thirty-Three, and followed it where she wandered around. Four miles from the ranch she met somebody who camped there with her that night. I'm suspicioning now that somebody was Mister Leroy."

"Four miles from the Circle Thirty-Three?" burst from the girl's lips.

"About four miles, Miss Meredith. Did he tell you it was twenty-four? Next morning you rode pillion behind him, and the trail led directly away from the ranch toward the Galiuros. That didn't make me any easy in my mind. So I just jogged along and invited myself to the party. I arrived some late, but here I am, right-side up . . . and so hearty a welcome that my friend, Cork, won't hear of my leaving at all. He don't do a thing but entertain me . . . never lets his attention wander. Oh, I'm the welcome guest, all right. No doubt about that."

Dolf Leroy turned to Helen Meredith. "I think you had better go to your room," he said gently.

"Oh, no, no, let me stay," she implored. "You would never . . . you would never. . . ." The words died on her white lips, but the horror in her eyes finished the question.

He met her gaze fully, and answered her doggedly. "You're not in this, Miss Meredith. It's between him and me. I sha'n't allow even you to interfere."

"But . . . oh, it is horrible! Let me see you alone for two minutes."

He shook his head.

"You must! Please."

"What use?"

Her troubled gaze shifted to the strong, brown, sun-baked face of the man who had put himself in this deadly peril to save her. His keen, blue-gray eyes, very searching and steady, met hers with a courage she thought splendid, and her heart cried out passionately against the sacrifice.

"You shall not do it. Oh, pardner, let me talk it over with you. Have you forgotten already? . . . and you said you would always remember." She almost whispered it.

She had stung his consent at last. "Very well," he said, and opened the door to let her pass into the inner room.

But she noticed that his eyes were hard as jade. "Don't you see that he came here to save me?" she cried, when they were alone. "Don't you see it was for me? He didn't come to spy out your place of hiding."

"I see that he has found it. If I let him go, he will bring back a posse to take us."

"You could ride across the line into Mexico."

"I could, but I won't."

"But why?"

"Because, Miss Meredith, the money we took from the express car of the Limited is hidden here, and I don't know where it is . . . because the sun won't ever rise on a day when Val Collins will drive me out of Arizona."

"I don't know what you mean about the money, but you must let him go. You spoke of a service I had done you. This is my pay."

"To turn him loose to hunt us down?"

"He'll not trouble you if you let him go."

A sardonic smile touched his face. "A lot you know of him. He thinks it his duty to rid the earth of vermin like us. He'd never let up till he got us or we got him. Well, we've got him now, good and plenty. He took his chances, didn't he? It isn't as if he didn't know what he was up against. He'll tell you himself it's a square deal. He's game, and he won't squeal because we win, and he has to pay forfeit."

The girl wrung her hands despairingly.

"It's his life or mine . . . and not only mine, but my men's," continued the outlaw. "Would you turn a wolf loose from your sheep pen to lead the pack to the kill?"

"But if he were to promise. . . ."

"We're not talking about the ordinary man . . . he'd promise anything and lie tomorrow. But Sheriff Collins won't do it. If you think you can twist a promise out of him not to take advantage of what he has found out, you're guessing wrong. When you think he's a quitter, just look at that cork hand of his, and remember how come he to get it. He'll take his medicine proper, but he'll never crawl."

"There must be some way!" she cried desperately.

"Since you make a point of it, I'll give him his chance."

"You'll let him go?" The joy in her voice was tremulously plain.

He laughed, leaning carelessly against the mantel shelf. But his narrowed eyes watched her vigilantly. "I didn't say I would let him go. What I said was that I'd give him a chance."

"How?"

"They say he's a dead shot. I'm a few with a gun myself. We'll ride down to the plains together, and find a good lonely spot suitable for a graveyard. Then one of us will ride away, and the other will stay, or perhaps both of us will stay."

She shuddered. "No . . . no . . . no. I won't have it."

"Afraid something might happen to me, pardner?" he asked with a queer laugh.

"I won't have it."

"Afraid perhaps he might be the one left for the coyotes and the buzzards?"

She was white to the lips, but at his next words the blood came flaming back to her cheeks.

"Why don't you tell the truth? Why don't you say you love him, and be done with it? Say it, and I'll take him back to Tucson with you safe as if he were a baby."

She covered her face with her hands, but with two steps he had reached her and captured her hands.

"The truth," he demanded, and his eyes compelled.

"It is to save his life."

He laughed harshly. "What a romantic coil! Yes . . . to save your lover's life."

She lifted her eyes to his bravely. "What you say is true. I love him."

Leroy bowed ironically. "I congratulate Mister Collins, who is now quite safe so far as I am concerned. Meanwhile, lest he be jealous of your absence, shall we return now?"

Some word of sympathy for the reckless scamp trembled on her lips, but her instinct told her he would hold it insult added to injury, and she left her pity unvoiced.

"If you please."

But as he heeled away, she laid a timid hand on his arm. He turned and looked grimly down at the working face, at the sweet, shy, pitiful eyes brimming with tears. She was pure woman now, all the caste pride dissolved in yearning pity.

"Oh, you lamb . . . you precious lamb," he groaned, and clicked his teeth shut on the poignant pain of his loss.

"I think you're splendid," she told him. "Oh, I know what you've done . . . that you are not good. I know you've wasted your life and lived with your hand against every man's. But I can't help all that. I look for the good in you, and I find it. Even in your sins you are not petty. You know how to rise to an opportunity."

This man of contradictions, forever the creature of his impulses, gave the lie to her last words by signally failing to rise to this one. He snatched her to him, and looked down, hungry-eyed, at her sweet beauty, as fresh and fragrant as the wild rose in the copse.

"Please," she cried, straining from him with shy, frightened eyes.

For answer he kissed her fiercely on the cheeks and eyes and mouth. "The rest are his, but these are mine," he laughed mirthlessly. Then, flinging her from him, he limped the way into the next room.

X

"If you're through explaining the mechanism of that Winchester to Sheriff Collins, we'll reluctantly dispense with your presence, Mister Reilly. We have arranged a temporary treaty of peace."

Reilly, a huge lout of a fellow with a lowering countenance, ventured to expostulate. "Ye want to be careful of him. He's quicker'n chain lightning."

His chief exploded with low-voiced fury. "When I ask your advice, give it, you fat-brained son of a brand blotter. Until then padlock that mouth of yours. Vamos."

Reilly vanished, his face a picture of impotent malice, and Leroy continued: "We're going to Tucson in the morning, Mister Collins . . . at least, you and Miss Meredith are going there. I'm going part way. We've arranged a little deal all by our own, subject to your approval. You get away without that hole in your head. Miss Meredith goes with you, and I get in return the papers I know you took off Scotty and Webster."

"You mean I am to give up the hunt?" asked Collins.

"Not at all. I'll be glad to death to see you blundering in again when Miss Meredith isn't here to beg you off. The point is that in exchange for your freedom and Miss Meredith's I get those papers you left in a safety deposit vault in Tucson. It'll save me the trouble of sticking up the First National and winging a few indiscreet citizens of that burg. Savvy?"

"That's all you ask?" demanded the surprised sheriff. "You don't want Webster freed?"

"No, I'm not worrying about Jim. You can't prove anything. It won't do him a bit of harm to lie by the heels for a few weeks. All I ask is to get those papers in my hand and a four-hour start before you begin the hunt. Is it a deal?"

"It's a deal, but I give it to you straight that I'll be after you as soon as the four hours are up," returned Collins promptly. "I don't know what magic Miss Meredith used. Still, I must compliment her on getting us out mighty easy."

But though the sheriff looked smilingly at Miss Meredith, that young woman, usually mistress of herself in all emergencies, did not lift her eyes to meet his. Indeed, he thought her strangely embarrassed. She was as flushed and tongue-tied as a country girl in unaccustomed company. She seemed another woman than the self-possessed young beauty he had met two weeks before on the Limited, but he found her shy abashment charming.

"I guess you thought you had come to the end of the passage, Mister Collins," suggested the outlaw with listless curiosity.

"I didn't know whether to order the flowers or not, but 'way down in my heart I was backing my luck," Collins told him.

"Of course it's understood that you are on parole until we separate," said Leroy curtly.

"Of course."

"Then we'll have supper at once, for we'll have to be on the road early." He clapped his hands together, and the Mexican woman appeared. Her master flung out a command or two in her own language.

"*Poco tiempo,*" she answered, and disappeared.

Leroy followed her to bathe his ankle in arnica and bind it up.

In a surprisingly short time the meal was ready, set out on a table, white with Irish linen and winking with cut glass and silver.

"Mister Leroy does not believe at all in doing when in Rome as the Romans do," Helen explained to Collins in answer to his start of amazement. "He's a regular Aladdin. I shouldn't be a bit surprised to see electric lights come on next."

"One has to attempt sometimes to blot out the forsaken desert," said Leroy. "Try this cut of slow elk, Miss Meredith. I think you'll like it."

"Slow elk. What is that?" asked the girl, to make talk.

"Mister Collins will tell you." Leroy smiled.

She turned to the sheriff, who first apologized, with a smile, to his host. "Slow elk, Miss Meredith, is veal that has been rustled. I expect Mister Leroy has pressed a stray calf into our service."

"I see," she flashed. "Pressed veal."

The outlaw smiled at her ready wit, and took on himself the burden of further explanation. "And this particular slow elk comes from a ranch on the Aravaipa owned by Mister Collins. York shot it up in the hills a day or two ago."

"Shouldn't have been straying so far from its range," suggested Collins with a laugh. "But it's good veal, even if I say it and shouldn't."

"Thank you," burlesqued the bandit gravely with such an ironic touch of convention that Helen smiled.

After dinner Leroy produced cigars, and with the permission of Miss Meredith the two men smoked while the conversation ran on a topic as impersonal as literature. A criticism of novels and plays written to illustrate the frontier was the line into which the discussion fell, and the girl from New York, listening with a vivid interest, was pleased to find that these two real men talked with point and a sense of dexterous turns. She felt a sort of proud proprietorship in their power, and wished that some of the tailors' models she had met in society, who held so good a conceit of themselves, might come under the spell of their strong, tolerant virility. Whatever the difference between them, it might be truly said of both that they had lived at first hand and come in touch closely with all the elemental realities. One of them was a romantic villain and the other an unromantic hero, but her pulsing emotions immorally condemned one no more than the other. This was the sheer delight to her esthetic sense of fitness, that strong men engaged in a finish fight could rise to so perfect a courtesy that an outsider could not have guessed the antagonism that ran between them enduring as life.

Leroy gave the signal for breaking up by looking at his watch. "Afraid I must say lights out. It's past eleven. We'll have to be up and on our way with the hooters. Sleep well, Miss Meredith. You don't need to worry about waking. I'll have you called in good time. *Buenas noches.*"

He held the door for her as she passed out, and, in passing, her eyes rose to meet his.

"*Buenas noches, señor* . . . don't forget to attend to that bad ankle," she said.

But both of them were thinking that the hurt from which he would suffer most was not his ankle.

It had been the day of Helen Meredith's life. Emotions and sensations, surging through her, had trodden on each other's heels. Woman-like, she welcomed the darkness to analyze and classify the turbid chaos of her mind. She had been swept into sympathy with an outlaw, to give him no worse name. She had offered him her friendship. Oh, she had pretended to herself it had been to cajole him into freeing her. She had partly believed it until the hour of her unwilling return to him, but she flung aside the pretext now with scorn. The man had fascinated her. That was the plain, unwelcome truth.

Surely that had been bad enough, but worse was to follow. This discerning scamp had torn aside her veils of maiden reserve and exposed the secret fancy of her heart, unknown before even to herself. She had confessed love for this big-hearted sheriff and frontiersman. Here again she could plead an ulterior motive. To save his life any deception was permissible. Yes, but where lay the truth? With that insistent demand of the outlaw had rushed over her a sudden wave of joy. What could it mean unless it meant what she would not admit that it could mean? Why, the man was impossible. He was not of her class. She had scarcely seen him three times. Her first meeting with him had been only two weeks ago. Two weeks ago. . . .

A remembrance flashed through her that brought her from the bed in a barefoot search for matches. When the candle was relit, she slipped a chamois-skin pouch from her neck and from it took a sealed envelope. It was the note in which the sheriff on the night of the train robbery had written his prediction of how the matter would come out. She was to open the envelope in two weeks, and the two weeks were up tonight.

As she tore open the flap, it came to her with one of her little flashing smiles that she could never have guessed under what circumstances she would read it. By the dim flame of a glittering candle, in a cotton nightgown borrowed from a Mexican menial, a prisoner of the very man who had robbed her and the recipient of a confession of love from him not six hours earlier! Surely here was a situation to beggar romance. But before she had finished reading, the reality was still more unbelievable.

I have just met for the first time the woman I am going to marry if God is good to me. I am writing this because I want her to know it as soon as I decently can. Of course, I am not worthy of her, but then I don't know any man that is.

So the fact goes—I'm bound to marry her if there's nobody else in the way. This isn't conceit. It is a deep-seated certainty I can't get away from, and don't want to. When she reads this, she will think it a piece of foolish presumption. My hope is she will not always think so.

Her lover,
Val Collins

Her swift-pulsing heart was behaving very queerly. It seemed to hang delightfully still, and then jump forward with odd little beats of joy. She caught a glimpse of her happy face, and blew out the light for shame, groping her way back to bed with the letter carefully guarded against crumpling by her hand.

Foolish presumption, indeed. Why, he had only seen her once, and he said he would marry her with never a by-your-leave! Wasn't that what he had said? She had to strike another match to learn the lines that had not stuck word for word in her mind, and after that another match to get a picture of the scrawl to visualize in the dark.

How dared he take her for granted? But what a masterly way of wooing for the right man! What idiotic folly if he had been the wrong one. Was he, then, the right one? She questioned herself closely, but came to no more definite answer than this— that her heart went glad with a sweet joy to know he wanted to marry her.

She resolved to put him from her mind, and in this resolve she fell at last into smiling sleep.

XI

When, in after years, Helen Meredith looked back upon the incidents connected with that ride to Tucson, it was always with a kind of glorified pride in her villain-hero. He had his moments, had this 20th-Century Villon, when he represented not unworthily the divinity in man, and this day held more than one of them. Since he was what he was, it also held as many of his black moods.

The start was delayed, owing to a cause Leroy had not foreseen. When York went, sleepy-eyed, to the corral to saddle the ponies, he found the bars into the pasture let down, and the whole *remuda* kicking up its heels in a paddock as large as a good-size city. The result was that it took two hours to run up the bunch of ponies and another half hour to cut out, rope, and saddle the three that were wanted. Throughout the process Reilly sat on the fence and scowled.

Leroy, making an end of slapping on and cinching the last saddle, wheeled suddenly on the Irishman. "What's the matter, Reilly?"

"Was I saying anything was the matter?"

"You've been looking it right hard. Ain't you man enough to say it, instead of playing dirty little three-for-a-cent tricks . . . like letting down the corral bars?"

Reilly flung a look at Neil that plainly demanded support, and then descended with truculent defiance from the fence.

"Who says I let down the bars? You bet I am man enough to say what I think . . . and if ye think I ain't got the nerve. . . ."

His master encouraged him with ironic derision. "That's right, Reilly. Who's afraid? Cough it up and show York you're game."

"By thunder, I *am* game. I've got a kick coming."

"Yes?" Leroy rolled and lit a cigarette, his black eyes fixed intently on the malcontent. "Well, register it on the jump. I've got to be off."

"That's the point." The curly-headed Neil had lounged up to his comrade's support. "*Why* have you got to be off? We don't savvy your game, cap."

"Perhaps you would like to be majordomo of this outfit, Neil?" scoffed his chief, eying him scornfully.

"No, sir. I ain't aiming for no such thing. But we don't like the way things are shaping. What does all this here funny business mean, anyhow?" His thumb jerked toward Collins, already mounted and waiting for Leroy to join him. "Two days ago this world wasn't big enough to hold him and you. Well, I git the drop on him, and then you begin to cotton up to him right away. Big dinner last night . . . champagne corks popping, I hear. What I want to know is what it means. And here's this Miss Meredith. She's good for a big ransom, but I don't see it ambling our way. It looks darned funny."

"That's the ticket, York," derided Leroy. "Come again. Turn your wolf loose."

"Oh, I ain't afraid to say what I think."

"I see you're not. You should try stump speaking, my friend. There's a field for you there."

"I'm asking you a question, Mister Leroy."

"That's whatever," chipped in Reilly.

"Put a name to it."

"Well, I want to know what's the game, and where we come in."

"Think you're getting the double-cross?" asked Leroy pleasantly, his vigilant eyes covering them like a weapon.

"Now you're shouting. That's what I'd like right well to know. There *he* sits"—with another thumb jerk at Collins—"and I'm a Chinese if he ain't carrying them same two guns I took offen him, one on the train and one here the other day. I ain't saying it ain't all right, cap. But what I do say is . . . how about it?"

Leroy did some thinking out loud. "Of course I might tell you boys to go to the devil. That's my right, because you chose me to run this outfit without any advice from the rest of you. But you're such infants, I reckon I had better explain. You're always worrying those fat brains of yours with suspicions. After we stuck up the Limited, you couldn't trust me to take care of the swag. Reilly here had to cook up a fool scheme for us all to hide it together, blindfolded. I told you straight what would happen, and it did. When Scotty crossed the divide, we were in a jim-dandy of a hole. We had to have that paper of his to find the boodle. Then Webster gets caught, and coughs up his little recipe for helping to find hidden treasure. Who gets them both? Mister Sheriff Collins, of course. Then he comes visiting us.

Not being a fool, he leaves the documents behind in a safety deposit vault. Unless I can fix up a deal with him, Mister Reilly's wise play buncoes us and himself out of a hundred thousand dollars."

"Why don't you let him send for the papers first."

"Because he won't do it. Threaten nothing! Collins ain't that kind of a hairpin. He'd tell us to shoot and be damned."

"So you've got it fixed with him?" demanded Neil.

"You've a head like a sheep, York," admired Leroy. "*You* don't need any brick wall hints to hit you. As your think tank has guessed, I have come to an understanding with Collins."

"But the gurl . . . I allow the old major would come down with a right smart ransom."

"Wrong guess, York. I allow he would come down with a right smart posse and wipe us off the face of the earth. Collins tells me the major has sent for a couple of Apache trailers from the reservation. That means it's up to us to hike for Sonora. The only point is whether we take that buried money with us or leave it here. If I make a deal with Collins, we get it. If I don't, it's somebody else's gold mine. Anything more the committee of investigation would like to know?" concluded Leroy, as his cold eyes raked them scornfully and came to rest on Reilly.

"Not for mine," said Neil with an apologetic laugh. "I'm satisfied. I just wanted to know. And I guess Cork corroborates."

Reilly growled something under his breath, and turned to hulk away.

"One moment," LeRoy snapped. "You'll listen to me, now. You have taken the liberty to assume I was going to sell you out. I'll not stand that from any man alive. Tomorrow night I'll get back from Tucson. We'll dig up the loot and divide it. And right then we quit company. You go your way and I go mine."

And with that as a parting shot, Leroy turned on his heel and went directly to his horse.

Helen Meredith might have searched the West with a fine-tooth comb and not found elsewhere two such riders for an escort as fenced her that day. Physically they were a pair of superb animals, each perfect after his fashion. If the fair-haired giant, with his lean, broad shoulders and rippling flow of muscles, bulked more strikingly in a display of sheer strength, the sinewy, tigerish grace of the dark Apollo left nothing to be desired to the eye. Both of them had been brought up in the saddle, and each was fit to the minute for any emergency likely to appear.

But on this pleasant morning no test of their power seemed likely to arise, and she could study them at her ease without hindrance. She had never seen Leroy look more the vagabond enthroned. For dress, he wore the common equipment of cattle land—jingling spurs, fringed chaps, leather cuffs, gray shirt, with kerchief knotted loosely at the neck, and revolver ready to his hand. But he carried them with an air, an inimitable grace that marked him for a prince among his fellows. Something of the kind she hinted to him in jesting paradoxical fashion, making an attempt to win from his sardonic gloom one of his quick, flashing smiles.

He countered by telling her what he had heard York say to Reilly of her. "She's a princess, Cork," York had said. "Makes my Epitaph gurl look like a chromo beside her."

All of them laughed at that, but both Leroy and the sheriff tried to banter her by insisting that they knew exactly what York meant.

"You can be very splendid when you want to," reproached the train robber.

She laughed in the slow, indolent way she had, taking the straw hat from her bronze head to catch better the faint breath of wind that was soughing across the plains.

"I didn't know I was so terrible. I don't think *you* ever had any awe of anybody, Mister Leroy." Her soft cheek flushed in unexpected memory of that moment when he had brushed aside all her maiden reserves and ravished mad kisses from her. "And Mister Collins is big enough to take care of himself," she added hastily, to banish the unwelcome recollection.

Collins, with his eyes on the light-shot waves of copper that crowned her vivid face, wondered whether he was or not. If she had been a woman to desire in the queenly, half-insolent indifference of manner with which she had first met him, how much more of charm lay in this piquant gaiety, in the warm sweetness of her softer and more pliant mood. It seemed to him she had the gift of comradeship to perfection.

They unsaddled and ate lunch in the shade of the live oaks at El Dorado Springs, which used to be a much-frequented watering hole in the days when Camp Grant thrived and muleskinners freighted supplies in to feed Uncle Sam's pets. Six hours later they stopped again at a truck farm on the edge of the Santa Cruz wash, six miles from Tucson.

It was while they were re-saddling that Collins caught sight of a cloud of dust a mile or two away. He unslung his field glasses, and looked long at the approaching dust swirl. Presently he handed the binoculars to Leroy.

"Five of them, and that round-bellied Papago pony in front belongs to Sheriff Forbes, or I'm away wrong."

Leroy lowered the glasses, after a long, unhurried inspection. "Looks that way to me. Expect I'd better be burning the wind."

In a few sentences he and Collins arranged a meeting for next day up in the hills. He trailed his spurs through the dust toward Helen Meredith, and offered her his brown hand and wistful smile irresistible. "Good bye, little pardner. This is where you get quit of me for good."

"Oh, I hope not," she told him impulsively. "We must always be friends."

He laughed ruefully. "Your father wouldn't endorse those unwise sentiments, I reckon . . . and I'd hate to bet your husband would," he added audaciously, with a glance at Collins. "But I love to hear you say it, even though we never could be. You're a right game, staunch little pardner. I'll back that opinion with the lid off."

"You should be a good judge of those qualities. I'm only sorry you don't always use them in a good cause."

He swung himself to his saddle. "Good bye."

"Good bye . . . till we meet again."

"And that will be never. So long, Sheriff. Tell Forbes I've got a particular engagement in the hills, but I'll be right glad to meet him when he comes."

He rode up the draw and disappeared over the brow of the hillock.

She caught another glimpse of him a minute later on the summit of the hill beyond. He waved a hand at her, half turning in his saddle as he rode. Presently she lost him, but faintly the wind swept back to her that haunting snatch of the prison song she had heard from his lips once before.

> *Ah, I have sigh'd to rest me*
> *Deep in the quiet grave.*

XII

To Sheriff Forbes, drifting into the draw a few minutes later with his posse, Collins was a well of misinformation literally true. Yes, he had followed Miss Meredith's trail into the hills and found her at a mountain ranch house. She had been there a couple of days, and was about to set out for the Circle Thirty-Three with the owner of the place, when he arrived and volunteered to see her as far as Tucson.

"I reckon there ain't any use asking you if you seen anything of Dolf Leroy's outfit," said Forbes, a weather-beaten Westerner with a shrewd, wrinkled face.

"No, I reckon there's no use asking me that," returned Collins with a laugh that deceptively seemed to include the older man in the joke.

"Old man Webster's pirootin' around the country somewhere. He broke jail last night and is making his getaway to the hills, I reckon."

"Jim Webster?"

"That's whoever. Well, I'll be moving. Glad you found the lady, Val. She don't look none played out from her little trek across the desert. Funny, ain't it, how she could have wandered that far and her afoot?"

The Arizona sun was setting in its accustomed blaze of splendor, when Val Collins and Helen Meredith put their horses again toward Tucson and the rainbow-hued west. In his contented eyes were reflected the sunshine and a serenity born of life in the wide open spaces. They rode in silence for long, the gentle evening breeze blowing in soughs.

"Did you ever meet a man of such promise gone wrong so utterly? He might have been anything . . . and it has come to this, that he is hunted like a wild beast. I never saw anything so pitiful. I would give anything to save him."

He had no need to ask to whom she was referring. "Can't be done. Good qualities bulge out all over him, but they don't count for anything. 'Unstable as water.' That's what's the matter with him. He is the slave of his own whims. Hence he is only the splendid wreck of a man, full of all kinds of rich outcropping pay ore that pinch out when you try to work them. They don't raise men gamer, but that only makes him a more dangerous foe to society. Same with his loyalty and his brilliancy. He's got a haid on him that works like they say old J.E.B. Stuart's did. He would run into a hundred traps, but somehow he always worked his men out of them. That's Leroy, too. If he had been an ordinary criminal, he would have been rounded up years ago. It's his audacity, his iron nerve, his good horse-sense judgment that saves his skin. But he's certainly up against it at last."

"You think Sheriff Forbes will capture him?"

He laughed. "I think it more likely he'll capture Forbes. But we know now where he hangs out, and who he is. He has always been a mystery till now. The mystery is solved, and, unless he strikes out for Sonora, Leroy is as good as a dead man."

"A dead man?"

"Does he strike you as a man likely to be taken alive? I look to see a dramatic exit to the sound of cracking Winchesters."

"Yes, that would be like him," she confessed with a shudder. "I think he was made to lead a forlorn hope. Pity it won't be one worthy of the best in him."

"I guess he did have more moments set to music than most of us, and I'll bet, too, he had hidden away in him a list of 'Thou shalt nots.' I read a book once by a man named Stevenson that was sure virgin gold. He showed how every man, no matter how low he falls, has somewhere in him a light that burns, some rag of honor for which he is still fighting. I'd hate to have to judge Leroy. Some men, I reckon, have to buck against so much in themselves that even failure is a kind of success for them."

"Yet you will go out to hunt him down?" she said, marveling at the broad sympathy of the man.

"Sure I will. My official duty is to look out for society. If something in the machine breaks loose and goes to ripping things to pieces, the engineer has to stop the damage, even if he has to smash the rod that's causing the trouble."

The ponies dropped down again into the bed of the wash,

and plowed across through the heavy sand. After they had reached the solid road, Collins resumed conversation at a new point.

"It's two weeks and a day since I first met you, Miss Meredith," he said, apparently apropos of nothing.

She felt her blood begin to choke. "Indeed!"

"I gave you a letter to read when I was on the train."

"A letter!" she exclaimed in well-affected surprise.

"Did you think it was a book of poems? No, ma'am, it was a letter. You were to read it in two weeks. Time was up last night. I reckon you read it."

"Could I read a letter I left at Tucson, when I was fifty miles away?" She smiled with sweet patronage.

"Not if you left it at Tucson," he assented with an answering smile.

"Maybe I did lose it." She frowned, trying to remember.

"Then I'll have to tell you what was in it."

"Any time will do. I dare say it wasn't important."

"Then we'll say this time."

"Don't be stupid, Mister Collins. I want to talk about our desert Villon."

"I said in that letter. . . ."

She put her pony to a canter, and they galloped side-by-side in silence for half a mile. After she had slowed down to a walk, he continued placidly, as if oblivious of an interruption: "I said in that letter that I had just met the young lady I was expecting to marry."

"Dear me, how interesting. Was she in the smoker?"

"No, she was in Section Three of the Pullman."

"I wish I had happened to go into the other Pullman, but, of course, I couldn't know the young lady you were interested in was riding there."

"She wasn't."

"But you've just told me. . . ."

"That I said in the letter you took so much trouble to lose that I expected to marry the young woman passing under the name of Miss Wainwright."

"Sir!"

"That I expected . . ."

"Really, I am not deaf, Mister Collins."

". . . expected to marry her, just as soon as she was willing."

"Oh, she is to be given a voice in the matter, is she?"

"Certainly, ma'am."

"And when?"

"Well, I had been thinking now was a right good time."

"It can't be too soon for me," she flashed back, sweeping him with proud, indignant eyes.

"But I ain't so sure. I rather think I'd better wait."

"No, no! Let us have it done with once and for all."

He relapsed into a serene, abstracted silence.

"Aren't you going to speak?" she flamed.

"I've decided to wait."

"Well, I haven't. Ask me this minute, sir, to marry you."

"Certainly, if you can't wait. Miss Meredith, will you. . . ."

"No, sir, I won't . . . not if you were the last man on earth," she interrupted hotly, whipping herself into a genuine rage. "I never was so insulted in my life. It would be ridiculous if it weren't so . . . so outrageous. You *expect*, do you? And it isn't conceit, but a deep-seated certainty you can't get away from."

He had her fairly. "Then you *did* read the letter."

"Yes, sir, I read it . . . and for sheer, unmatched impudence I have never seen its like."

"Now, I wish you would tell me what you really think," he drawled.

Not being able, for reasons equestrian, to stamp her foot, she gave her bronco the spur.

When Collins again found conversation practicable, Tucson, a white adobe huddle in the moonlight, lay peacefully beneath them in the valley.

"It's a right quaint old town, and it's seen a heap of rough-and-tumble life in its day. If those old adobe bricks could tell stories, I expect they would put some of these romances out of business."

Miss Meredith's covert glance questioned suspiciously what this diversion might mean.

"It's an all right business town, too . . . the best in the territory," he continued patriotically. "She ain't so great as Douglas on ore or as Phoenix on lungers, but, when it comes to the git-up-and-git hustle, she's there rounding up the trade from early morn till dusk."

He was still expatiating in a monologue with grave enthusiasm on the town of his choice, when they came to the narrow adobe-lined streets that opened into the plaza. They drew rein at the porch of the San Augustine Hotel, remodeled from an old Spanish convent to serve the needs of the great American drummer.

"Some folks don't like it . . . call it adobe town, and say it's full of greasers. Well, everybody to his taste, I say. Little old Tucson's good enough for me."

He helped her dismount, and then held out his big hand in farewell.

"I'll be saying good night, Miss Meredith. I reckon I'll see you again one of these days, maybe," he said genially, and trailed, with clanking spurs, back to his horse.

Miss Meredith, safely in her room, gave herself over to laughter sardonic till the tears ran.

"I forgot to ask him whether he loves me or Tucson more, and, as one of the subjects seems to be closed, I'll probably never find out," she mourned.

Nevertheless, there was a queer little tug of pain at her heart.

XIII

"Good evening, gentlemen. Hope I don't intrude on the festivities."

Leroy smiled down ironically on the three flushed, startled faces that looked up at him. Suspicion was alive in every rustle of the men's clothes. It breathed from the lowering countenances. It itched at the fingers longing for the trigger. The unending terror of a bandit's life is that no man trusts his fellow. Hence one betrays another for fear of betrayal, or stabs him in the back to avoid it.

The outlaw chief had slipped into the room so silently that the first inkling they had of his presence was that gentle, insulting voice. Now, as he lounged easily before them, leg thrown over the back of a chair and thumbs sagging from his trouser pockets, they looked the picture of schoolboys caught by their master in a conspiracy. How long had he been there? How much had he heard? Full of suspicion and bad whiskey as they were, his confident contempt still cowed the very men who were planning his destruction. A minute before they had been full of loud threats and boastings; now they could only search each other's faces sullenly for a cue.

"Celebrating Webster's return from captivity, I reckon. That's the proper ticket. I wonder if we couldn't afford to kill another of Collins's fatted calves."

Mr. Webster, not enjoying the derisive raillery, took a hand in the game. "I expect the boys hadn't better touch the sheriff's calves, now you and him are so thick."

"We're thick, are we?" Leroy's indolent eyes narrowed slightly as they rested on him.

"Ain't you? It sure seemed that way to me when I looked out

of that mesquite wash just above Eldorado Springs and seen you and him eating together like brothers and laughing to beat the band. You was so close to him I couldn't draw a bead on him without risking its hitting you.

"Laughing, were we? That must have been when he told me how funny you looked in the altogether, shedding false teeth and information about hidden treasure."

"Told you that, did he?" Mr. Webster incontinently dropped repartee as a weapon too subtle, and fell back on profanity.

"That's right pat to the minute, cap, what you say about the information he leaks," put in Neil. "How about that information? I'll be plumb tickled to death to know you're carrying it in your vest pocket."

"And if I'm not?"

"Then ye are a bigger fool than I had expected to come back here at all," said the Irishman truculently.

"I begin to think so myself, Mister Reilly. Why keep faith with a set of swine like you?"

"Are you giving it to us that you haven't got those papers?"

Leroy nodded, watching them with steady, alert eyes. He knew he stood on the edge of a volcano that might explode at any moment.

"What did I tell you?" Webster turned savagely to the other disaffected members of the gang. "Didn't I tell you he was selling us out?"

Somehow Dolf Leroy's revolver seemed to jump to his hand without a motion on his part. It lay loosely in his limp fingers, unaimed and undirected.

"Say that again, please."

Beneath the velvet of Leroy's voice ran a note more deadly than any threat could have been. It rang a bell for a silence in which the clock of death seemed to tick. But as the seconds fled, Webster's courage oozed away. He dared not accept the invitation to reach for his weapon and try conclusions with this debonair young daredevil. He mumbled a retraction, and flung, with a curse, out of the room.

Leroy slipped the revolver back in his holster, and quoted, with a laugh: " 'To every coward safety, and afterward his evil hour.' "

"What's that?" demanded Neil. "I ain't no coward, even if Jim is. I don't knuckle under to any man. You got a right to ante up with some information. I want to know why you ain't got them papers you promised to bring back with you."

"That's the way to chirp, York. I haven't got them because Forbes blundered on us, and I had to take a *pasear* awful sudden. But I made an appointment to meet Collins tomorrow."

"And you think he'll keep it?" scoffed Neil.

"I know he will."

"You seem to know a heap about him," was the significant retort.

"Take care, York."

"I'm not Jim Webster, cap. I say what I think."

"And you think?" suggested Leroy gently.

"I don't know what to think yet. You're either a fool or a traitor, I don't know which. When I find out, you'll hear from me straight. Come on, Cork." And Neil vanished through the door.

An hour later there came a knock at Leroy's door. Neil answered his permission to enter, followed by the other pair of flushed beauties. To Dolf Leroy it was at once apparent with what Dutch courage they had been fortifying themselves to some resolve. It was characteristic of him, though he knew on how precarious a thread his life was hanging, that disgust at the foul breaths with which they were polluting the atmosphere was his first dominant emotion.

"I wish, Webster, next time you break prison you'd bring another brand of poison out to the boys. I can't go this stuff.

Just remember that, will you?"

The outlaw chief's hard eye ran over the rebels and read them like a primer. They had come to depose him certainly, to kill him perhaps. Though this last he doubted. It wouldn't be like Neil to plan his murder, and it wouldn't be like the others to give him warning and meet him in the open. Warily he stood behind the table, watching their awkward embarrassment with easy assurance. Carefully he placed face downward on the table the Villon he had been reading, but he did it without lifting his eyes from them.

"You have business with me, I presume."

"That's what we have!" cried Reilly valiantly, from the rear.

"Then suppose we come to it and get the room aired as soon as possible," Leroy said tartly.

"You're such a slap-up dude you'd ought to be a hotel clerk, cap. You're sure wasted out here. So we boys got together and held a little election. Consequence is we . . . fact is we. . . ."

Neil stuck, but Reilly came to his rescue. "We elected York captain of this outfit."

"To fill the vacancy created by my resignation. Poor York! You're the sacrifice, are you? On the whole, I think you fellows have made a wise choice. York's game, and he won't squeal on you, which is more than I could say of Reilly or Jim. . . . But you want to watch out for a knife in the dark, York. 'Uneasy lies the head that wears a crown,' you know."

"We didn't come here to listen to a speech, cap, but to notify you we was dissatisfied, and wouldn't have you run the ranch any longer," explained Neil.

"In that event, having heard the report of the committee, if there's no further new business, I declare this meeting adjourned. Kindly remove the perfume tubs, Captain Neil, at your earliest convenience."

The trio retreated ignominiously. They had come prepared to

gloat over Leroy's discomfiture, and he had mocked them with that insolent ease of his that set their teeth in helpless rage.

But the deposed chief knew they had not struck their last blow. Throughout the night he could hear the low-voiced murmur of their plottings, and he knew that, if the liquor held out long enough, there would be sudden death at Robber's Roost before twenty-four hours were up. He looked carefully to his rifle and his revolvers, testing several shells to make sure they had not been tampered with in his absence. After he had made all necessary preparations, he drew the blinds of his window and moved his easy chair from its customary place beside the fire. Also, he was careful not to sit where any shadow would betray his position. Then back he went to his Villon, a revolver lying on the table within reach.

But the night passed without mishap, and with morning he ventured forth to his meeting with the sheriff. He might have slipped out from the back door of his cabin and gained the cañon by circling, unobserved, up the draw and over the hogback, but he would not show by these precautions any fear of the cut-throats with whom he had to deal. As was his scrupulous custom, he shaved and took his morning bath before appearing outdoors. In all Arizona no trimmer, more graceful figure of jaunty recklessness could be seen than this one stepping lightly forth to knock at the bunkhouse door behind which he knew were at least two men determined on his death by treachery.

Neil came to the door in answer to his knock, and within he could see the villainous faces and bloodshot eyes of the other two peering at him.

"Good morning, Captain Neil. I'm on my way to keep that appointment I mentioned last night. I'd certainly be glad to have you go along. Nothing like being on the spot to prevent double-crossing."

"I'm with you in the fling of a cow's tail. Come on, boys."

"I think not. You and I will go alone."

"Just as you say. Webster, I guess you better saddle Two-Step and the Lazy B roan."

"I ain't saddling ponies for Mister Leroy," returned Webster with thick defiance.

Neil was across the room in two strides. "When I tell you to do a thing, jump! Get a move on you, and saddle those bronc's."

"I don't know as. . . ."

"*¡Vamos!*"

Webster sullenly slouched out.

"I see you make them jump," commented the former captain audibly, seating himself comfortably on a rock. "It's the only way you'll get along with them. See that they come to time or pump lead into them. You'll find there's no middle way."

Neil and Leroy had hardly passed beyond the rock slide before the others, suspicion awake in their sodden brains, dodged after them on foot. For three miles they followed the broncos as the latter picked their way up the steep trail that led to the Dalriada Mine.

"If Mister Collins is here, he's lying almighty low!" Neil exclaimed as he swung from his pony at the foot of the bluff from the brow of which the gray dump of the mine straggled down like a Titan's beard.

"Right you are, Mister Neil."

York whirled, revolver in hand, but the man who had risen from behind the big boulder beside the trail was resting both hands on the rock before him.

"You're alone, are you?" demanded York.

"I am."

"I don't like to misdoubt a gentleman's word, but I allow you'll pardon me if I keep my poppers handy."

"I understood I was to meet you alone, Mister Leroy," said the sheriff quickly, his blue-gray eyes on the former chief.

"That was the agreement, Mister Collins, but it seems the boys are on the anxious seat about these little socials of ours. They've embraced the notion that I'm selling them out. I hated to have them harassed with doubts, so I invited the new majordomo of the ranch to come with me. Of course, if you object. . . ."

"I don't object in the least, but I want him to understand the agreement. I've got a posse waiting at Eldorado Springs, and, as soon as I get back there, we take the trail after you."

York grinned. "We'll be in Sonora then, Val. Think I'm going to wait and let you shoot off my other fingers?"

Collins fished from his vest pocket the papers he had taken from Scotty's hat and from Webster. "I think I'll be jogging along back to the springs. I reckon these are what you want."

Leroy took them from him and handed them to Neil. "Don't let us detain you any longer, Mister Collins. I know you're awful busy these days."

The sheriff nodded a good day, cut down the hill on the slant, and disappeared in a mesquite thicket, from the other side of which he presently emerged astride a bay horse.

The two outlaws retraced their way to the foot of the hill and remounted their broncos.

"I want to say, cap, that I'm eating humble pie in big chunks right this minute," said Neil shamefacedly, scratching his curly head and looking apologetically at his former chief. "I might 'a' knowed you was straight as a string, all I've seen of you these last two years. If those coyotes say another word, cap. . . ."

An exploding echo seemed to shake the mountain, and then another. Leroy swayed in the saddle, clutching at his side. He pitched forward, his arms around the horse's neck, and slid slowly to the ground.

Neil was off his horse in an instant, kneeling beside him. He lifted him in his arms and carried him behind a great outcropping boulder. "It's that hound, Collins," he muttered as he propped the wounded man's head on his arm.

Leroy opened his eyes and smiled faintly. "Guess again, York."

"You don't mean. . . ."

He nodded. "Right this time . . . Webster and Reilly. They shot to get us both."

Neil choked. "You ain't bad hurt, old man. Say you ain't bad hurt, Dolf."

"More than I can carry, York . . . shot through and through. I've been doubtful of Reilly for a long time."

"By the Lord, if I don't get the rattlesnakes for this!" swore Neil between his teeth. "Ain't there nothin' I can do for you, old pardner?"

In sharp succession four shots rang out. Neil grasped his rifle, leaning forward and crouching for cover. He turned a puzzled face toward Leroy. "I don't savvy. They ain't shooting at us."

"The sheriff," explained Leroy. "They forgot him, and he doubled back on them."

"I'll bet Val got one of them!" cried Neil, his face lighting.

"He's got one . . . or he's quit living. That's a sure thing. Why don't you circle up on them from behind, York?"

"I hate to leave you, cap and you so bad. Can't I do a thing for you?"

Leroy smiled faintly. "Not a thing. I'll be right here when you get back, York."

The curly-headed young giant took Leroy's hand in his, gulping down a boyish sob. "I ain't been square with you, cap. I reckon after this . . . when you get well . . . I'll not be such a coyote any more."

The dying man's eyes were lit with a beautiful tenderness. "There's one thing you can do for me, York. . . . I'm out of the game, but I want you to make a new start. I got you into this life, boy. Quit it, and live straight. There's nothing to it, York."

The cowboy-bandit choked. "Don't you worry about me, cap. I'm all right. I'd just as lief quit this deviltry, anyhow."

"I want you to promise, boy." A whimsical, half-cynical smile touched Leroy's eyes. "You see, after living like a devil for thirty years, I want to die like a Christian. Now, go, York."

After Neil had left him, Leroy's eyes closed. Faintly he heard two more shots echoing down the valley, but the meaning of them was already lost to his wandering mind.

When Collins and Neil returned from their grim work of justice, he was babbling feebly of childhood days back in the Kentucky homeland. The word oftenest on his lips was *Mother*.

XIV

Helen Meredith hesitated between the hotel parlor and their private one, but conceded enough to the unchaperoned West and her own desire, to decide in favor of the latter.

"You may send the gentleman in," she told the bellboy, and, when he had gone, she deftly rearranged the cushions in the deep window seats built in the recesses of the thick adobe wall.

She had vanished, however, before he appeared on the scene, and she allowed him to get seated before she sailed in from the next room. The young man, looking up at her with clear-eyed discernment, was instantly aware that the relation of intimacy existing between them had slipped back a few cogs. She was on guard, fully armed with the evasions and complexities of her sex.

"This *is* a surprise, Mister Collins." She smiled sweetly.

"And a pleasure?" he laughed.

"Of course. Did you come to see my father? I'm sorry. He's out."

"You needn't be sorry for me. I didn't come to see the major."

"How nice of you to say so. I have a hundred questions to

ask you. About these rumors . . . are they true?"

"I don't know what the rumors are," he said, falling instantly grave. "You see, I reached town less than an hour ago, and I came to you at once . . . as soon as I could."

Her patrician manner disappeared for the moment. "That was good of you, knowing how anxious I must be to hear the facts ungarbled. Is it true that you have captured Mister Leroy?"

She thought he looked at her with a sort of pity. "No, that is not true. You remember what we said of him . . . of how he might die?"

"He is dead . . . you killed him!" she cried quickly, going the color of chalk.

"He is dead, but I did not kill him."

"Tell me," she commanded.

And he told her, beginning at the moment of his meeting with the outlaws at the Dalriada dump and continuing to the last moments of the tragedy. It touched her so nearly that she could not hear him through dry-eyed.

"And he spoke of me, you say?" she asked, after he had finished.

"Yes . . . when his mind cleared just at the last. He told me to tell you it was better so. He called you 'little pardner.' " Presently Collins added: "If you don't mind my saying so, I think he was right. He was quite content to go . . . quite cheerful in his whimsical, gay way. If he had lived, there could have been no retracing of his steps. The tragedy would have been a greater one."

"Yes, I know that, but it hurts one to think it had to be . . . that all his splendid gifts and capabilities should end like this, and that we are forced to see it is best. He might have done so much."

"And instead he became a miscreant. I reckon there was a

lack in him somewhere."

"Yes, there was a great lack in him somewhere."

They were silent a minute or two before she asked whether he had recovered any of the money taken from the Limited.

"I think we got all that was left, and that was four-fifths of it. We found Reilly's memorandum in the heel of his boot, and Neil gave up his as soon as I mentioned it. Neil promised Leroy to try to lead a straight life after this, and I believe he will. He is only a wild cowpuncher gone wrong. Given the right environment, he should be all right."

"Couldn't you give him a place?"

He smiled. "Hardly. He is in Sonora now . . . slipped away while I was arranging to have Leroy buried. Strange how things work around, isn't it? Out of the five train robbers that held up the Limited, only one left alive."

"Father will want to thank you for recovering the money. It means a good deal to him."

"I had rather it meant a good deal to your father's daughter," he told her, and noticed at once the subtle stiffening of resistance in her will.

"Thank you."

Her voice, cool as the plashing of ice water, might have daunted a less daring man. But this man had long since determined the manner of his wooing, and was not to be driven from it.

"Sho! I ain't going to run away and hide because you look like you don't know I'm in Arizona. What kind of a lover would I be, if I broke for cover every time you flashed those dark eyes at me?"

"Mister Collins. . . ."

"My friends call me Val," he suggested, smiling.

"I was going to ask, Mister Collins, if you came here to try to bully me," she retorted.

"You know a heap better than that, Miss Meredith. All your life you haven't done anything but trample on sissy boys. Now, I expect I'm not a sissy boy, but a fair imitation of a man, and I shouldn't wonder but you'd find me some too restless for a doormat." His maimed hand happened to be resting on the back of a chair as he spoke, and the story of the maiming emphasized potently the truth of his claim.

"Don't you assume a good deal, Mister Collins, when you imply that I have any desire to master you?"

"Not a bit," he assured her cheerfully. "Every woman wants to boss the man she's going to marry, but, if she finds she can't, she's glad of it, because then she knows she's got a man."

"You are quite sure I am going to marry you?" she asked gently—too gently, he thought.

"I'm only reasonably sure," he informed her. "You see, I can't tell for certain whether your pride or your good sense is the stronger."

She caught a detached glimpse of the situation, and it made for laughter.

"That's right, I want you should enjoy it," he said placidly.

"I do. It's the most absurd proposal . . . I suppose you call it a proposal . . . that ever I heard."

"I expect you've heard a good many in your time."

"We'll not discuss that, if you please."

"I *am* more interested in this one," he agreed.

"Isn't it about time to begin on Tucson?"

"Not today, ma'am. There are going to be a lot of tomorrows for you and me, and Tucson will have to wait till then."

"Didn't I give you an answer last week?"

"You did, but I didn't take it. Now I'm ready for your sure-enough answer."

She leaned back among the cushions and mocked his confidence. "I've heard about the vanity of girls, but never in my experience have I met any so colossal as this masculine vanity now on exhibit. Do you really think, Mister Collins, that all you have to do to win a woman is to look impressive and tell her that you have decided to marry her?"

"Do I look as if I thought that?" he asked her.

"It is perfectly ridiculous . . . your absurd attitude of taking everything for granted. Well, it may be the Tucson custom, but where I come from it is not in vogue."

"No, I reckon not. Back there a boy persuades a girl he loves her by ruining her digestion with candy and all sorts of ice arrangements from a soda fountain. But I'm uncivilized enough to assume you're a woman of sense, and not a spoiled schoolgirl."

"You *are* uncivilized." She leaned forward audaciously, chin in hand, her eyes sparkling. "Would you beat me when I didn't obey?"

He laughed, admiring her with lazy eyes. "Perhaps, but I'd love you while I did it."

"Oh, you would love me." She looked up under her long lashes, not as boldly as she would have liked, and her eyes fell before his ardent, possessive ones. "I didn't know that was in the compact you proposed. I don't think I have heard you mention it."

He came forward with three clean strides and sat down beside her, looking what he was, a man out of a thousand. "That's my last trump, girl, and my biggest. Would I go throwing it away early in the game? I'm no desert poet, but I love you from that copper crown of yours to those suede shoes that tap the floor, so impatient. I love you all the time, no matter what mood you're in . . . when you flash those angry eyes at me and when you laugh in that slow, understanding way nobody else on earth has the trick of. Makes no difference to me whether you are mad or glad, I enjoy you just the same. That's the reason why

I'm going to make you love me."

"You can't do it," she said, speaking in a low voice, apparently to the tassel she was tearing to pieces.

"Why not? I'll show you."

"But you can't . . . for a good reason."

"Name it."

"Because . . . I love you already." She burlesqued his drawl with a little, joyous laugh. "I reckon if you're so set on it, I'll have to marry you, Val Collins." Then, as he caught her to him, her shy eyes fluttered up to meet his.

ABOUT THE AUTHOR

William MacLeod Raine, hailed in his later years to be the "greatest living practitioner" of the genre and the "dean of Westerns," born in London, England in 1871. Upon the death of his mother, Raine immigrated with his father to Arkansas in the United States where he was raised. He attended Sarcey College in Arkansas and received his Bachelor's degree from Oberlin College in 1894. He was troubled in his early years by a lung ailment that was eventually diagnosed as tuberculosis. He moved to Denver, Colorado in hopes that his health would improve, and worked as a reporter and editorial writer for a number of newspapers. He began writing short stories for the magazine market. His first Western novel, *Wyoming* (Dillingham, 1908), proved so popular with readers that it was serialized in the first issues of Street & Smith's *Western Story Magazine* when that publication was launched in 1919. During World War I, Raine's Western fiction was so popular among British readers that 500,000 copies of his books were distributed among British troops. By his own admission, Raine concentrated on character in his Westerns. "I'm not very strong on plot. Some of my writing friends say you have to have the plot all laid out before you start. I don't see it that way. If you have it all laid out, your characters can't develop naturally as the story unfolds. Sometimes there's someone you start out as a minor character. By the time you're through, he's the major character of the book. I like to preside over it all, but to let the book do its own growing." It would appear that because of this focus on character Raine's stories have stood the test of time better than those of some of his contemporaries. It was his intimate knowledge of the American West that provides verisimilitude to all of his stories, whether in a large sense such as the booming industries of the West or the cruelties of Nature—a flood in *Ironheart* (1923), blizzards in *Ridgway of Montana* (1909) and *The Yukon Trail* (1917), a fire in *Gunsight Pass* (1921). It is perhaps Raine's love of the West of his youth, the place and the people where there existed the "fine free feeling of man as an individual," glimmering in the pages of his books that will warrant the attention of readers always. His next Five Star Western will be *Long Texan*.